Splendor

Also by Elana K. Arnold

Sacred

Burning

$\mathcal{S}$plendor

ELANA K. ARNOLD

DELACORTE PRESS

Text copyright © 2013 by Elana K. Arnold
Jacket photograph copyright © 2013 by
Illina Simeonova/Trevillion Images

All rights reserved. Published in the United States by Delacorte Press, an imprint of Random House Children's Books, a division of Random House LLC, a Penguin Random House Company, New York.

Delacorte Press is a registered trademark and the colophon is a trademark of Random House LLC.

Visit us on the Web! randomhouse.com/teens

Educators and librarians, for a variety of teaching tools, visit us at RHTeachersLibrarians.com

Library of Congress Cataloging-in-Publication Data
Arnold, Elana K.
Splendor / Elana K. Arnold. — First edition.
   pages cm
Sequel to: Sacred.
Summary: "Continues the story of Scarlett and Will, two teenagers madly in love with each other, but now separated by distance and goals that threaten their forever love"— Provided by publisher.
ISBN 978-0-385-74213-9 (hc) —
ISBN 978-0-307-97415-0 (ebook) —
ISBN 978-0-375-99043-4 (glb) [1. Love—Fiction. 2. Family problems—Fiction. 3. Best friends—Fiction. 4. Friendship—Fiction. 5. Horses—Fiction. 6. Santa Catalina Island (Calif.)—Fiction.] I. Title.
PZ7.A73517Spl 2013
[Fic]—dc23
2012046716

The text of this book is set in 12-point Goudy.
Book design by Kenny Holcomb

Printed in the United States of America

10 9 8 7 6 5 4 3 2 1

First Edition

For my siblings—

SASHA, ZAK, AND MISCHA

And for Shayna,

WHEREVER YOU ARE

I like living. I have sometimes been wildly, despairingly, acutely miserable, racked with sorrow, but through it all I still know quite certainly that just to be alive is a grand thing.

—*A*gatha Christie

All around him was darkness, accompanied by a rhythmic pulse: da-dum, da-dum, da-dum. He was safe, and warm, and he knew the beat was forever and always. Sometimes, the beat got faster; and sometimes, for long stretches when the world around him lay still, it softened and subtly slowed. He loved the beat, as he loved the warmth and wetness that cradled him.

But there was something else—an awareness, a knowing of something other—a pull. When this sensation overwhelmed him, the pulse pounded fiercely, each beat tripping over the one before. Something was happening in the world outside his, but after a time the beat settled and slowed, settled and slowed, back to its steady rhythm.

The pulling went away, then; the world around him had fixed the problem. He relaxed in the warmth and the rhythm and rolled contentedly over and over again.

ONE

Conception

I had Delilah secured in the washracks. Alice was in the office, getting ready for the procedure, so I had a moment alone with my mare.

"You're such a pretty girl," I said, stroking her red mane. I fed her lumps of alfalfa and molasses from a bucket just out of her reach. Delilah was relaxed, absolutely unaware that mere steps away, Alice was preparing to change her life.

It happens like that, more often than not. Sure, sometimes you get to make the big decisions that take you in new directions, like whether or not to go to college, or to go all the way with your boyfriend . . . but life doesn't always give you the choice.

Sometimes a more powerful force steps in. God? Fate? Karma? Whatever you call it, it can kick your ass, and unexpectedly. Like when my brother Ronny died just after I turned sixteen—a grade 6 cerebral aneurysm in the middle of a soccer game at UCLA, where he was a freshman. I hadn't seen that coming. I'm pretty sure Ronny didn't, either.

Or last summer, just about a year back from this day, when I'd ridden my mare across the heart of Catalina Island and had come around a bend to find Will Cohen stopped dead in the middle of the trail; he'd been waiting for me.

The only thing that's certain, I thought, is uncertainty. You might as well get used to it. Then maybe, if you're smart, you can enjoy the ride.

Alice swung through the office door, her eyes focused on a large plastic syringe connected to a long thin tube, coiled now, resting in her palm like a snake.

"You're sure she's ready?" I asked. My stomach churned, as if I were doubly anxious since Delilah had no idea what was about to happen. I was starting to second-guess this whole thing now that it seemed too late to back out.

"Absolutely. I palpated her this morning. She's good to go."

Alice was in "business" mode now. That was one of my favorite things about her, something I even tried to emulate—her ability to separate emotion from the task at hand.

All through the long winter after my brother's death, when my mother had disappeared into her bedroom and her depression and her pills, Alice had remained steadfast, giving me a ride each day to the stable from our little town of Avalon, trying to keep an eye on me—noticing when I'd lost too much weight, monitoring the increasing seriousness of my attraction to Will. And though my mother had managed to return to the land of the living, it seemed I still couldn't count on her for much. For all intents and purposes, Alice was the best mother I had.

Which made it all the more strange to watch when, after handing me the tubing and syringe, she pulled a long rubber glove over her hand and up the length of her arm in preparation for getting my mare pregnant.

It was hot on the island. We had entered July, and at midday the sun felt especially intense. Not a drop of rain had fallen since early spring. Each step across the stable grounds sent up a puff of dust, and the flowers that lined the driveway were pale and lackluster, though the gardeners watered them dutifully each morning.

I'd done my best to combat the sticky heat by wearing a tank top and cutoffs with the eight-hole Doc Martens I always wore around the stable and pulling my blond hair into a messy bun at the nape of my neck. My frayed straw hat provided some shade from the sun, which I could feel silently frying my exposed shoulders. Our island's center was its hottest place, and surrounded by the dust and the dirt of the stable, the heat felt almost intolerable.

Alice must have been hot, too, but you'd never have known it from looking at her. Her light brown hair was exactly as long as it always was—chin length—and though she'd tucked it behind her ears, it looked as neat and well maintained as usual, the antithesis of my messy bun. Not a bead of sweat marred her face.

That was just the term for Alice: well maintained. She never seemed to age, and I'd bet she still fit into the same jeans she wore in college. Alice was the only woman I knew who, without fail, wore collared shirts. This one, a crisp pink-and-white striped oxford, was tucked into her jeans. Her dark brown braided leather belt matched her stable boots. Both the belt and the boots looked freshly oiled. I narrowed my eyes and examined her face more closely.

"Is that . . . lipstick?"

Alice was distracted, winding a long elastic wrap around Delilah's tail to keep it out of the way. "You like it? Melon berry. I picked it up in town last weekend."

"Sure," I answered. "It's nice." It was no use explaining to Alice how strange I found it that she'd bother with makeup out here at the stable.

"Okay," said Alice. "Let's do this thing."

Alice had spent the first month of summer visiting stables in the south, with four days dedicated to an equine artificial insemination workshop in Kentucky. There, she'd learned how to impregnate mares with shipped, frozen (and then defrosted of course) stallion semen. After she'd returned to the island, the two of us pored over various stallion websites, debating each stud's strengths and weaknesses as a potential father for Delilah's future foal. We oohed and aahed over the video clips of the stallions in action: one leaping cleanly over a fence; another, his well-muscled neck tucked in the classic dressage pose, flinging out his legs in an extended trot. We eyed their musculature, the gleam of their coats, the thickness of their legs and haunches. Finally we'd settled on a nine-year-old stallion from Georgia named Flame, in part because his red coat, combined with Delilah's, seemed the best bet for producing a like-colored foal. And his stats were terrific: just over sixteen hands high, impressive in both dressage and cross-country competitions, clean, pure bloodlines.

So today I'd be helping Alice insert Flame's semen into my mare. When I had explained how all this would work to my best friend, Lily, she'd wrinkled her nose distastefully. "So, the poor horse has to get all fat and pregnant without any of the fun stuff?"

Leave it to Lily to phrase it like that. "We don't really have a choice," I told her. "Delilah's related to all the stallions on the island, and anyway, I think live cover is way too dangerous for the mare."

"Live cover?"

I blushed a little explaining it. "You know . . . the breeding process. Stallions can be pretty aggressive . . . mares get hurt . . . even the handlers can get seriously injured."

"Whoa. Back up. Handlers?"

"Usually two. One person holds the mare, another controls the stallion."

"I don't get it. Why don't you let them go at it in a field or something?"

"That's just not how it's done."

"I've heard some pretty weird stuff, Scar. But frozen stallion semen? What does Will think?"

She could tell from the set of my mouth that the conversation was over, much to her amusement. Will, too, was one part amused by the situation, one part grossed out—a lot like Lily. But mostly he was distracted. And even though there was still nearly a month before he left the island for Yale, I could feel him beginning to move away already.

We had promised each other that we would focus on what we had—these last days before he left—without dwelling on the future. This included not having "the talk" about whether we expected to remain exclusive while apart.

So though our time together still felt magical, it was tinged with unspoken tension. All the talk in the world about staying in the present couldn't keep my mind from straying, sometimes even while Will held me in his arms, to the day he would sail away.

But this moment in the stable yard had nothing to do with Will, or Lily either, who had left Catalina with her family for their annual vacation, though they'd be returning early this year, in August instead of September. They'd headed to the Netherlands to explore Lily's dad's ancestral roots. Last summer, I'd been too numbed by my brother's death to really miss Lily; this summer, most of my energy was focused on trying not to notice that the days continued to pass, bringing us closer to fall.

Again, with the deliberateness I'd grown so good at, I pushed the thought of Will to the side—not entirely out of my mind, but far enough away that I could focus on the task at hand. Passing Alice the syringe and tubing, I grasped Delilah's tail, pulling it up and away from her rump.

With her gloved hand, Alice dipped a sponge in a bucket of soapy water and lathered Delilah's vagina. The mare shied a little to the side, so I patted her and made soothing noises. Her ears rotated back toward the sound of my voice, trusting me, and she settled.

I watched as Alice took the end of the tubing and gently inserted it inside Delilah. She pushed her arm in farther than I had thought possible, and then, once her arm had disappeared up past the elbow, she depressed the syringe.

The white liquid that would—we hoped—find Delilah's egg and create a foal traveled from the syringe down the clear tubing, disappearing inside my mare.

In biology class my freshman year, we'd seen a video about pregnancy and birth. We all knew that though the movie was shown under the premise of being educational, it was actually meant to terrify us.

I hadn't been terrified; I was fascinated. The voice that narrated the "journey of the sperm"—that was really what they called it—went on and on about how the sperm raced fiercely toward the prize, competing to be the first to reach the egg and burrow into its core, claiming her for its own.

That wasn't how it looked to me. The grainy, black-and-white video seemed to tell a different story than the man who narrated it wanted us to believe. The sperm, like tiny crooked tadpoles, seemed aimless, lost . . . bumping into the walls of the birth canal, some even swimming in the wrong direction entirely. And when they arrived at the egg, as giant as a world to their tiny tailed bodies, it seemed that many begged in unison to be let in, and the egg selected which one she would grant entrance. Still, the narrator's booming masculine voice insisted that the victorious sperm had conquered in a "fiercely contested battle."

Delilah's whole procedure took no more than a few minutes, and then Alice withdrew her arm, turning the glove inside out as she pulled it off.

"That's it?" I asked.

"That's it," Alice answered. "Easy peasy."

"Lemon squeezy," I murmured, releasing Delilah's tail and feeding her another chunk of A&M.

I should have felt excited by the possibility of it all. A foal . . . in eleven months, if everything went according to plan. And tonight I had a date with Will. But as I walked Delilah back to her stall, I felt heavy, weighed down, as if carrying a burden of my own.

Maybe it was the heat.

My dad's old Volvo wagon pulled into the stable yard just as I was fastening Delilah's stall door. I watched him emerge from behind the wheel, straightening slowly and rubbing the small of his back. His eyes scanned the stable yard. When he caught sight of me, his hand shot up in a wave.

"Hey, Dad," I called. "I'll just be a minute."

I jogged back over to the crossties to retrieve the bucket of A&M, which I stowed in the tack room. I hung my straw hat on a hook near my saddle, and pulled my hair out of its elastic as I headed toward the car.

Alice was standing next to him. Their heads were bowed toward each other's, and I slowed my approach, suddenly feeling that they hadn't expected me to show up so fast. They were talking about something serious, I could tell from the incline of their heads. I would have bet money that they were talking about my mom.

But when they heard me coming, of course they stopped and switched the topic to something innocuous. "So," Alice said, "I'll be by tomorrow to help turn over the rooms."

"You don't have to do that, Alice," Dad protested, but I knew him well enough to see that he was grateful for the offer. "Scarlett and I can probably handle it."

"You have a full house this weekend, don't you?"

Dad nodded. "And it's a good thing, too. We need the money."

My family owned a bed-and-breakfast; last year, we'd missed the high season entirely in the aftermath of Ronny's death, so it was particularly important to keep our guests happy this summer.

"I'll come by," Alice insisted. "Just for a few hours, anyway, in the morning. I'm sure you could use the help with breakfast."

Dad looked a little embarrassed. "Yeah, that's the hardest part for me," he admitted. "Changing the beds, vacuuming, no problem. But those little quiches and mini loaves of banana bread . . . can't say I've figured out all those recipes just yet."

"It's simple chemistry," I said as I walked over to them. I was irritated by Dad's helplessness in the kitchen. I wasn't much of a cook, either, but come on. We could handle things at the B&B on our own.

"Easy for you to say." Dad rumpled my hair in that dad way of his. "Coming from the science whiz."

I groaned. Ever since the results of my AP Chemistry test came in, my dad had been calling me "Professor" and "Doc," only half jokingly. The idea of pursuing a medical degree had always been in my mind, but as senior year came around and the college application process became a reality, I grew more serious about considering it.

"Can we go? Will and I are going out later."

"Sure, sure." Dad tossed me the keys to the Volvo. "Why don't you drive?"

"See you, Alice," I called, slipping into the worn driver's seat. "Keep an eye on Delilah, will you?"

"Of course." Alice stood in the stable yard and watched us drive away, waving.

I didn't feel like talking with my dad, so I focused really hard on the road, as if it took all my concentration to safely navigate the turns. Maybe my dad didn't feel like talking, either, because he didn't even make his usual comments about my driving—cracking jokes, pretending to hold on for dear life. He just gazed out the window, the warm breeze lifting and moving his hair.

It was thinning. A couple of years ago, maybe even last year, it hadn't been so noticeable. But now it was clear that my dad was going bald.

One of the things I loved about him was that he wasn't trying to hide it. In spite of the slowly spreading bald spot on the back of his head, Dad went on with the same short hairstyle he'd had my whole life—maybe *his* whole life. He didn't attempt a comb-over, didn't grow his hair longer to try to hide his dome.

And he didn't go the other route, either, that lots of guys went for—he didn't shave it all off and pretend he liked it that way. Maybe he didn't even notice that his hair was disappearing. He probably had bigger things to think about.

It had been nearly two months since my mother had left the island. At first, she said that she *had* to do it—had to return to Los Angeles and resume her former career as a lawyer to supplement the paltry income we earned from the B&B. But it became obvious pretty fast that Mom was not coming back. The first few weekends she claimed to be "too busy" to get away . . . and then she started inviting me to come to the mainland for the weekends.

"My apartment has two bedrooms," she offered, as if to sweeten the deal.

It shouldn't have been a surprise. She'd been mostly gone since Ronny's death, anyway.

"Your mother just needs her space right now" was the best my father could do to explain it.

Her space, my ass.

But Mom did send money. She'd managed to get hired at a firm that handled real estate law, helping homeowners who were facing foreclosure delay the inevitable. Lots of that going around, so our money problems on the island were eased some.

And then there were two, I mused, remembering an old Agatha Christie book I had read. Come to think of it, that story was set on an island . . . a deadly island, where a group of vacationers, strangers to one another, were picked off, one at a time, until just two were left, Philip Lombard and Vera Claythorne, each certain that the other was the murderer.

First my brother Ronny, then my mother . . .

Glancing at my father as I drove, I wondered two things: First, was it *his* fault my mother had left? Had he driven her away somehow, by being too nice, too kind, too weak? Second, as his gaze slipped sideways to meet mine, I wondered if he was like Agatha Christie's Philip Lombard, suspecting me just as I suspected him.

TWO

Lily Comes Home

*L*ily and her family came back from vacation earlier than expected, in the first week of August. I went to their house the day they coptered back to the island. Jack and Laura were in the kitchen furiously chopping vegetables. I don't know why, but the air seemed spiked. There was energy, as always, only not the good kind.

All the elements added up to trouble: the way their backs were turned to each other's, Laura working at the oversized butcher block in the kitchen's center island, Jack over near the sink. Laura's shoulders were pulled up practically to her ears and Jack's whole back seemed laced with tension. Plus, they weren't listening to music.

Lily's parents *always* listened to music. Something quiet and classical, no words, during family game time. Classic rock when they did the dishes. And jazz when they cooked.

"Makes the food better," Jack often said of the music. "Adds flavor."

The kitchen was eerily quiet and the sounds of their dueling knives slicing through the vegetables clanked, over and over again, like tiny guillotines.

It wasn't enough that my own parents were split apart? Now the Adamses, my favorite parental unit, were unhappy, too?

"Welcome home." I stood awkwardly in the doorway, half in, half out, wondering if I should have knocked even though I'd been letting myself into Lily's house unannounced since middle school.

"It's Scarlett!" Laura's face warmed in a smile, and she set aside her knife and came around the butcher block to embrace me.

"Our favorite blonde," Jack boomed, and he joined Laura. "How's summer treating you?"

They stood side by side, smiling at me, and though their faces looked tired, they seemed perfectly happy to be standing close together. So maybe I had been wrong . . . maybe everything in the Adams house was okay after all.

"Good," I answered. "It's nice to have you back."

"Stay for dinner?" Laura offered, returning to her chopping.

"Sure." I grabbed a tomato slice from the pile. "What are we having?"

"Just simple summer veggies over pasta. It's easy to make on short notice."

And then I noticed something. Laura's roots were showing. Her lovely caramel curls looked a bit less perfect than usual, and at the crown of her head, there was an undeniable quarter inch of gray.

16

In all the years I'd known Laura, I'd never—not once—known her to have roots. Something was wrong.

"Um . . . where's Lily?" It was only one of the many questions I wanted to ask, but it seemed the safest.

"Isn't that what we all want to know." Jack's tone was wry.

"She's by the pool." Laura looked like she wanted to say something else. But she just followed up with, "She'll be happy to see you."

Even though Lily's family was one of the island's wealthiest, they didn't really live like it in their everyday life. Comfortable, sure, but not overdone or obnoxious. Still, they liked their luxuries . . . and their pool was nicer than anything the local hotels had to offer.

I found Lily in the Jacuzzi. Her head was lolled back against the side, her eyes hidden behind dark sunglasses. Even like this, at rest, there was something about her face that seemed different.

I knelt next to the Jacuzzi. She didn't move. I scooped a handful of water and splashed it at her.

She sputtered awake. "What the hell . . ." Then she saw it was me, and her trademark Lily smile made everything else fade by comparison. "Thank *god*," she squealed. Jumping up, she hugged me around the neck.

"Whoa, watch it!"

But Lily doesn't do things halfway. She yanked me off-balance, pulling me into the water with her.

I knew it was useless to fight. What Lily wants, Lily gets. And right then she wanted company in the Jacuzzi. At least I'd worn flip-flops. They were easy enough to fish out of the hot water, and then I shimmied out of my shorts. "You'll hand me a towel when I get out, right?"

"Absolutely. We don't want the twins to get an eyeful. Might send them into early puberty."

"Where are the boys, anyway?"

Lily shrugged. "In their room, probably. The whole family is furious with me. They're avoiding me like I'm a pair of acid-washed jeans."

Leave it to Lily to find a fashion metaphor. "What did you do?"

She grinned again and pushed her sunglasses on top of her head. "The question is . . . what *didn't* I do?"

So I settled in to listen.

Honestly, I don't know what Jack and Laura were thinking, taking Lily to Amsterdam. I'd never been there myself—I'd never been much of *anywhere*—but I knew the basics. Legalized drugs, superliberal population, and of course, the red-light district. Basically about a million ways for Lily to find trouble.

And she had. "His name's Adrian," she began. "He's twenty-two."

"Lily," I groaned.

"Oh my god, Scarlett, he's not like anyone you've ever met. He's tall, for one thing. *Really* tall, like basketball player tall. Only he's not a basketball player." She paused, as if for effect. "He's a poet."

I groaned again.

"Shut up! His poetry is beautiful. It makes me cry. Really, it does. I mean, it's in Dutch, of course, but he translated some of it for me. It's even better when he reads it in his own language." She leaned in across the bubbles and said, wide-eyed, "He even wrote some poems about *me*."

"So what did Jack and Laura think?"

She shrugged. "Hated him. Of course. They wouldn't even give him a chance! But, Scarlett, you would have *loved* him!"

Her eyes were pleading. She wanted, desperately, to share. I felt my resistance beginning to crack. At last I said, "I'm sure he must be pretty great, Lil, if you like him. Tell me *everything*."

And then the floodgates opened. Lily must have talked for close to an hour, telling me about how they'd met on a tour boat, because, of course, poets are undervalued, so to earn money, Adrian gave canal tours.

"And the whole time he was talking, Scar, you know, pointing out the Anne Frank House, rattling off statistics about people and employment and all that, he never took his eyes off me. Not once. Of course, Jack was seething, but I think my mom thought it was kind of cute. And when I was getting off the boat at the end of the tour, Adrian gave me his hand to help me out. And he slipped me a note with his phone number on it! That night when my folks took the boys out to dinner and a movie, I told them I had a head-ache and stayed behind at the hotel. I called him. Scarlett, I totally get it now about you and Will. The way you look at each other . . . like you share something magical . . . that's how it felt with Adrian."

Her eyes were shining as she remembered him. "He's got

the most beautiful blond hair, Scar. Almost the same shade as yours except, you know, on a guy. He wears it kind of long, tucked behind his ears. . . ." She reached up to her own head to show me how his hair looked. "And his eyes were icy blue, and his smile was amazing, and the way he kissed . . ." She whistled and gazed off into the distance. "He's no island boy, that's for sure."

"What did you do together?"

"That first night, he took me all over. You know, to places that only locals go. Not the silly tourist bars."

"He took you to bars?"

She snorted. "Don't be such a baby, Scarlett. Of course we went to bars. We drank *jenever*, this Dutch gin. At first it tasted just awful, but after a while I liked it. It was sort of sweet. And it's so cute how you drink it—they serve it in a shot glass, full to the brim, and you take the first sip without using your hands, just bending down to the glass. Adrian could drink the whole shot like that, tipping it up into his mouth without his hands. He has very talented lips," she said, smiling wickedly.

"So of course your parents found out." I tried to hurry the story along a little. "How'd they catch you?"

Lily's expression turned stormy. "It was just a couple of days ago. I guess they were getting suspicious of all my headaches, because about an hour after they left with the twins to see a play, my mom came back. Good thing she was alone. Jack would have gone ballistic. I still don't know if Mom told him what we were doing."

"What *were* you doing?"

Lily raised her terribly expressive eyebrows. "What do you think we were doing?"

I gasped. I couldn't help it. "Lily . . . did you have *sex* with him?"

"Uh . . . of *course* I did!"

I didn't know what to say. My mouth opened and closed like a fish's.

"Don't look so shocked, Scar. I mean, I know you're private and everything, but it's common knowledge that you and Will have been going at it since last spring."

I barked out a laugh. "Common knowledge, huh? You'd think *I'd* know about it, then."

Lily narrowed her eyes. "Do you mean that you and Will . . ."

"No, Lily, we're not having sex. Don't you think I would have told you if we were?"

"Maybe you would have told me *before*, Scar. . . ."

She didn't have to tell me before what. I knew what she meant. Before Ronny Died. Back then, Lily and I had shared everything. She was like the other half of me. But losing someone close to you can cut your ties, even those you thought were the tightest. You can string them back together again. But not everything fits just the same anymore.

Our silence was uncomfortable, and we sat listening to the jets pump out their streams of hot water. Finally I asked, "Well? How was it?"

For a minute Lily looked like maybe she wouldn't tell me. Like she'd punish me by keeping it a secret. But I knew she wouldn't be able to contain herself.

21

"Pretty terrible, actually," she burst out. "I mean, it hurt. More than I thought it would. We only did it twice—once at his place, this little tiny apartment. It was *one room*! It didn't even have a separate kitchen. And I don't know the last time he washed his sheets. The second time was at the hotel, the night Mom caught us. I mean, I think maybe I could have grown to like it . . . if we'd done it a few more times . . . but honestly, Scar, the kissing was better. *Way* better."

She looked glum now, and I wanted to cheer her up. "Well, at least you beat me to it."

"I guess. I can't believe it, though. What's up? Why aren't you and Will . . ."

I shrugged. "I don't know. We just haven't."

"Are you going to? He's leaving in, like, less than a month."

I shrugged again. "We haven't really talked about it."

And it was true—Will and I hadn't talked about it. It was one of several things we'd avoided discussing this summer— that, and Will's departure for Yale. We didn't even talk about his almost unbelievable ability to sense impending violence in the world, accompanied by a pull to intercede and stop it from happening.

When we were together, I didn't much feel like talking. I felt like touching. I wanted to put my body as close as possible to Will's; I wanted to twine fingers, and legs, and tongues. I wanted the press of him against me. I wanted his hands in my hair. I wanted to run my hands up underneath his shirt, across the flat panel of his stomach, across the line of downy hair that began at his belly button and extended down into the mystery beneath his pants.

And he didn't argue. But though we wound our bodies together in the hidden cove near my house, or on the trail while our horses munched grass, neither of us had begun to unfasten the buttons and zippers that kept us safely separated.

"So your mom came in?" I nudged Lily back to her story.

"Boy, did she. I heard the sound the hotel door makes after someone's stuck a key card in the slot and the little electric mechanism is unfastening the lock. And Adrian froze—absolutely *froze*—on top of me. I remember thinking, 'Please, God, anyone but Dad,' so when it was my mom, for a second I felt *relieved*, you know? And then she said, 'I will give you two minutes to disappear, young man.' She actually called him *young man*. At least she waited in the next room while he got dressed."

"What did he say?"

"He was mumbling something in Dutch, and he fell over as he pulled up his jeans." Lily laughed, remembering. "He did wear them pretty tight." Her face grew somber. "But then he left, and that was the last I saw of him. Mom didn't let me out of her sight again until we were back on the island."

"Wow. I can't believe they're even letting me talk to you."

"I think they're hoping you'll be a good influence on me."

We sat together in the Jacuzzi, even though the water had grown too warm for comfort. I reached out and found Lily's hand. "I'm sorry, Lil."

She shrugged and lowered her sunglasses back over her eyes. "At least now I know what it's like." After a moment she said, "So I'm on like permanent restriction. And they don't even know about the tattoo."

"Yeah," I joked. "That would really piss them off."

But Lily didn't laugh.

"You didn't."

She looked at me over the rim of her glasses, then looked both ways to see if anyone was watching. When she seemed confident that we were alone, she stood, turned around, and pulled her bikini bottom halfway down. There, on her left cheek, was a blue-and-green sparrow.

"Tell me that's temporary."

She laughed. "Come on, Scar. You know that wouldn't be my style."

I shook my head. "You are a mystery, Lily."

"*You're* the mystery. A whole summer on the island with Will and you still haven't done it?"

I felt myself bristling. This wasn't something I wanted to discuss in any more detail.

"Yeah, well, we're not all as adventuresome as you." I pulled myself out of the water and grabbed Lily's towel. "I've got to borrow some of your stuff, okay? I can't walk home like this."

"Go for it." Lily leaned her head back again and closed her eyes. "I'm not going anywhere."

I found a pair of Lily's cutoffs and a tank top. Her room looked just as it had before she left on the trip: a lovely bed, layered in luxurious sheets and duvets; gossamer-fine curtains billowing in the late-afternoon breeze; a thick, soft rug across the gleaming wood floor.

But the girl who slept in this room . . . she was different. She looked about the same, save for the tattoo . . . but it was no wonder Jack and Laura were concerned. Lily was a worry.

Across the room, in my backpack, I heard my phone vibrate and then begin to ring.

It was Will.

"Miss me already?"

I did, even though I had seen him just the night before. He'd borrowed his dad's Jeep and come across to Avalon to make dinner with me. That was something we'd been doing a lot this summer. With my mother gone and my father distracted by one project or another, my house was a good place to find privacy, even though the first floor was usually filled with tourists.

"Desperately," he answered. His tone was light, but I got the feeling he wasn't entirely kidding. "You have any plans tonight?"

"I'm over at Lily's right now. We're going to eat in a few minutes."

"And later?"

"I don't know. Just the usual, I guess." For me the usual involved some reading, moving around a few loads of laundry for the B&B, maybe playing a game of gin rummy with my dad.

"Wanna go to a party?"

This was different. Will—like me—was more of the stay-at-home-and-read type than the go-get-hammered-with-a-bunch-of-semi-friends type.

"Um . . . okay?"

"Great. I'll pick you up at eight."

Downstairs, Jack and Laura were serving up the pasta. When I walked into the kitchen they stopped their conversation mid-sentence. Laura's last words hung in the air: ". . . being a jackass."

From Jack's expression, it was pretty clear she was talking about him.

I pretended I hadn't heard. Henry and Jasper were taking turns killing each other on some video game in the living room. They looked taller. Lily waltzed in, wet from the Jacuzzi, and sat down at the table. She dripped a quiet puddle onto the floor.

"Lily, hon, go get dressed for dinner," Laura said, a cheer in her voice.

"I don't see the point," Lily said. "I mean, you're never letting me leave the house. Why bother changing clothes? At least if I stay in my bathing suit I'm ready for the one pleasurable activity available to me in this jail cell."

I looked around. The casual chandelier, made of antique cutlery bent into ridges and curves, glowed prettily. The flatscreen TV on the far wall, muted now, showed CNN. In the family room, endless rows of games and puzzles waited to be played. Some prison.

"Honey, we didn't say you couldn't go out *at all*," Laura began.

26

I don't think she saw the look Jack shot at her, but she must have been able to *feel* it. Positively withering.

"So can I go out tonight?" Lily's eyes widened in characteristic charm, and she leaned forward in her chair. Her bikini top strained under the pressure. "Please? Brandon texted me that he's having a party, and I haven't seen *anyone* all summer!"

I laughed. "Hello?" I said. "Don't I count?"

Lily waved her hand dismissively in my direction. "Except you," she said. *"Please?"*

Laura looked about ready to capitulate, but Jack was a shade of red normally reserved for tomatoes. "Absolutely under no circumstances are you to leave this house, young lady."

I wouldn't have argued with that voice. Most people probably wouldn't have. But most people aren't Lily Adams.

The next twenty minutes were some level of hell. If Dante had been present at that table, he would have found a way to work it into his *Inferno*. Lily begged and cried and cursed; Jack fumed and boiled and cursed louder.

The twins giggled and kicked each other under the table every time someone spat an expletive. They must have had seriously bruised shins by the time dessert was served.

Finally, Lily retreated into stormy silence. Jack reverted into "perfect host" mode, seeming to notice at last that I was still there.

"So, Scarlett, tell us about your summer. How's that mare of yours?"

I swallowed a bite of the fudge brownie Laura had served

me. "She's good. Hopefully she's pregnant. We'll know in a couple of weeks when the vet comes to the island."

The twins seemed to find this as funny as the fight.

"Your mare had sex?" asked Jasper.

"Well, sort of." I figured it might be better not to go into the details.

"Lily had sex," said Henry. "Is she gonna be pregnant like your horse?"

That was when I decided it was time to go. I pushed back from the table, dropping my napkin on the plate. "Laura, Jack, dinner was great," I said lamely. "Sorry I can't help with the dishes. I've got a . . . date."

"Are *you* gonna have sex?"

I couldn't tell if Henry or Jasper asked this question. I was already heading for the door.

"Good night! Call me tomorrow, Lily," I threw over my shoulder. The yelling started again before the door latched behind me.

Outside, I took a deep, cleansing breath. I felt like a coward for ducking out of the conversation, but nothing I could have said would have improved the situation.

At home I found Dad in the great room, deep in conversation with a couple that was honeymooning on the island. They were debating the relative benefits and drawbacks of snorkeling versus scuba diving. It sounded like Dad had them pretty close to convinced that scuba diving was worth the extra money.

"Hey! There's my girl!" Dad threw his arm across my shoulder and planted a kiss on the top of my head. "How's Lily?"

"Trouble."

"So, the same."

"I guess."

Before I headed upstairs, I told him about my plans with Will.

Our little space on the third floor of the B&B used to feel crowded, back when Ronny and Mom were still with us. Fights about who got to use the bathroom first were a daily occurrence. But now, with Ronny dead and Mom on the mainland, even our little flat felt way too large. Sometimes it bothered me how quiet it got at home, but after witnessing the row at Lily's house, I welcomed the peace.

It wouldn't be long before Will came to pick me up. I swapped Lily's shorts for a pair of jeans and buttoned a flannel over the tank top before sitting down at my desk to try to pull some of the tangles out of my hair. I'd trimmed a few inches the other night, but it still reached past my bra line. It also smelled like chlorine from the hot tub. I wouldn't have time to wash it, so I wound it into a braid, watching as my mirror fingers plaited the hair in reverse.

Not that long ago, I couldn't have done this—looked at my reflection, or enjoyed what I saw. Tonight, though, I felt the strands of my hair and imagined how it would look later, when Will took it down—wavy and soft, a private curtain for the two of us.

Dad must have let Will in, because I didn't hear him coming. His steps were quiet on the runner in the hallway; it wasn't until his reflection appeared behind me, framed by the doorway, that I knew he had arrived.

He smiled at me, that dear smile I loved. It made my heart ache in my chest. How many more times would I see it before he left?

I pushed this thought away and smiled back. "Hey."

He crossed the room and ran his hand across my cheek. "Hey," he answered. His voice was husky, complicated. He knelt next to me and fit his lips against mine. His kiss was hot and long, and I found myself drifting deeply into it, pressing myself forward toward his warmth.

I didn't know who stopped the kiss. It seemed impossible that it could have been me.

"You ready to go?"

"Go where?" I leaned forward, trying to recapture his lips.

He laughed a little, steadying me before I fell off my perch on the edge of the chair. "Remember? The party?"

This time it was definitely Will that broke away. He rolled back on the balls of his feet and stood, pulling me up with him. "If we don't get going, we're going to have to check into one of the rooms." He was trying to make a joke, but it hit a little too close to home to be funny.

"We can't," I said. "All the rooms are booked."

"Well, I guess it's the party, then." A last kiss, and then he stepped away.

"Right. The party." I straightened my shirt and pushed a strand of hair behind my ear.

In the great room, Dad was still talking to the honeymooners. They were starting to look a little desperate. Out of charity, I called, "Hey, Dad!"

He excused himself from the couple, who took the opportunity to escape to their room. The Yellow Room.

"Heading out, kids?"

"We'll be at Brandon's house," Will told my dad. "We'll be back before one."

Who told a parent where the party was? Only Will.

"Sounds good," Dad said. "The Beckers, huh? They're a nice family." He looked like he was going to say something more, but then he didn't. "Have fun, kids."

Like almost everything else in Avalon, Brandon's house was within walking distance. Outside, Will took my hand. Our fingers laced together easily, just right. And his thumb danced gently against my palm in that fabulously distracting way Will had.

"So why the party?"

Will shrugged. "I thought we could use some normal teenage socialization."

I laughed.

If by "normal teenage socialization" Will meant binge drinking, cruel cajoling, and overwhelmingly loud music, we got it in spades as the evening wore on.

Still, Will seemed determined to have fun. He had half a glass of beer—"Everything in moderation," he said, in a good imitation of his father.

Beer held no pleasure for me. I drank water.

We danced together. We'd improved over the past few months, though we wouldn't be winning any prizes. Our bodies had learned to anticipate each other's movements, and as we'd grown more comfortable—and as I'd reclaimed my body, learning to love it again—it felt better and better to move together.

I found myself thinking about Lily and the boy she'd slept with in Amsterdam . . . Adrian, was it? How had their bodies moved together? How might it feel to move in so intimate a dance with another?

Not far from us, I spotted my ex-boyfriend, Andy. He was holding Kaitlyn Meyers in his arms. Last I'd heard they had broken up, but by the way they were dancing, Andy pushed up tightly against her, it was pretty clear they were back together.

I tried not to watch as Andy dipped his head to Kaitlyn's neck, biting her throat with mock ferocity. The sound she made was half laugh, half scream, clearly delighted and designed to attract attention.

"Let's get some air," Will suggested. We made our way out the front door, struggling past a clutch of people in the hallway.

Outside, the cold salty air felt wonderful. We wandered through the Beckers' yard, sidestepping the entwined bodies of a couple of sophomores, and made our way to the back of the house.

"You going to your mom's place next weekend?"

I shook my head. "Not yet."

I didn't need to tell him what I was waiting for. Our days together were numbered, so the thought of spending any of the precious time we had left away from each other seemed wasteful. Besides, I was in no hurry to see my mom's new life.

"Try to take it easy on her, huh?"

I couldn't hide my irritation. "Is this why you brought me to the party? To lecture me about how to treat my mother?"

Will's smile was infuriating. "No," he said. "*That's* why I brought you to the party."

He raised his chin in the direction of the back door.

Curious, I walked up the steps to the door. Will followed. Just before I opened the door he said, "I thought she might listen better to you."

Of course. Lily. There she was, sitting at the kitchen table surrounded by boys: Brandon Becker, Connell Reed, and Mike Ryan. Mike had graduated with Will, but he wouldn't be heading off to college. Most likely he'd spend the rest of his life right here on the island, his football bulk slowly converting into fat.

Tonight, though, he was pouring the drinks for some game they were all playing. Lily was just finishing a shot in the Dutch manner she'd described to me: no hands. Connell poured her another.

They didn't look up when we entered the kitchen.

"Lily." My voice sounded harsh, parental. It startled her; her chin hit the rim of her shot glass, toppling it.

"Damn," she said, wiping the spilled liquid from her shirt. I could see the shape of her triangle-top bikini beneath her T-shirt; I don't think anyone in the room wasn't watching closely as she dried her chest. "Scarlett!" She smiled up at me. "What are you doing here?"

I looked at Will. His expression was blank, but his jaw was tensed.

"Actually, we were just heading home, Lil. Want to walk with us?"

"No way," Lily motioned to Connell to refill her glass. "I just got here."

I watched her raise the drink to her mouth. Her hand was unsteady. She'd been drinking for a while.

"I think you've had enough to drink." But when I tried to take Lily's glass, Connell moved to block my way.

"Hey, Big Red," he said, but his grin was cold. "Want a drink?"

"No thanks."

"Oh, come on, Scar, loosen up," said Mike.

"Yeah, Red Vine. Live a little." Connell draped his arm across my shoulder, but he looked past me at Will, clearly taunting him. "You must be getting tired of Jew Boy by now."

I felt the restraint it took Will not to move from his place by the door.

"Lil, we really should get you home."

She had finished off another shot and was peeling Brandon Becker's fingers away from his cup of beer so that she could commandeer it.

"Your parents will be worried."

"My parents can blow me."

This earned appreciative laughter from the boys at the table, and Brandon handed over his cup.

I looked to Will for help. He shrugged. I knew he wasn't afraid to get involved—I'd seen him in action before—but probably he figured that if Lily wouldn't listen to me, she wouldn't listen to anyone.

Time to change tactics. I smiled at Connell and squeezed past him, sliding in next to Lily on her chair. I leaned into her, smelling the bitter-stale scent of beer on her breath. "Lily," I murmured, as calmly as I could, loud enough for

34

just her to hear, "Will and I are going to take you home. If you go quietly, we'll try to sneak you in without your parents hearing. But if you make a fuss . . . I'll tell your parents where you are. I swear I will."

Lily looked at me through the haze of her drunkenness. "You'd do that to me?"

"Absolutely."

She sipped her beer while she considered this. "I can see you've gone to the dark side," she said at last. "I'll go with you, Scar, but I'll remember this."

She drained her beer and then threw the plastic cup in Will's general direction. When she stood up I had to grab her arm to keep her from toppling over. Honestly, I doubted she'd remember anything about tonight . . . but her words hurt.

"Really know how to kill a party, Big Red."

I ignored Connell. Will held open the door for us and moved to take Lily's other arm. "Not a chance," she snapped.

Halfway down the block, Lily stopped and hurled in Mrs. Pearson's flower bushes. After that, she didn't complain when Will tried to help her walk.

But when she headed up the path to her house and slipped inside her front door, she didn't turn to wave goodbye. In all the years we'd been friends—all my life, since preschool— she'd never not waved goodbye.

THREE
If Only

Some things can't be prevented, like the passing of time. And so the final days of our summer slipped away from us, and the day came when Will left for college.

I'd been neglecting my duties at the B&B and around the stable all week. It came to the point where I almost wished Will was already gone, that his leaving was behind me.

But on the morning that he was to board the ferry for the mainland, then an airplane for the five-hour flight to the East Coast, I would have given anything for just one more sunset with the boy I loved.

Dad and I had laid out breakfast for the guests; then we'd retreated to our little kitchen on the third floor. Usually we ate with the guests, but after a summer full of croissants and quiches, a bowl of cereal, alone, was more what I needed.

Dad sensed my mood. He sat across from me, sipping his coffee, watching me eat.

"So today's the day," he said. Not a question.

"Yep."

He looked as though he was struggling for the right words, but when he spoke, they were all wrong. "It may be for the best, sweetheart. You and Will have been inseparable this summer. It might be nice for you to have more time for your girlfriends. Like Lily. I haven't seen her once since she got back."

There was a good reason for this. Since the night Will and I had extracted Lily from Brandon's party, Lily hadn't been exactly receptive to my calls. Not that I had been trying too hard to get ahold of her; there would be time for that after Will was gone. Too much time.

And I was pretty sure that my dad wouldn't be so keen for me to hang out with Lily if I gave him an earful about her steamy nights with Adrian, not to mention her new tattoo. But of course I didn't tell him any of this; my loyalties were clear.

Instead I mumbled a cursory "uh-huh" and carried the empty bowl to the sink. Inside, though, I seethed. Relationship advice from my dad, really? I still wondered how much of my mother's decision to leave the island was fueled by my dad's passivity.

"I guess you're going to spend the morning with Will?"

"Yeah. Can I take the Volvo for a few hours? I told Will I'd drive him to the ferry."

It looked like my dad was going to say no. Even though I had my license, I rarely drove alone.

But he nodded and dug the keys out of his pocket. "Just be careful, okay?"

• • •

To get to Will's little village of Two Harbors I took the winding road that bisected the island so I could stop in at the stable and check on Delilah. The vet would be coming out next month, right around the first day of school. But I felt pretty sure the insemination had been successful.

Delilah didn't *look* any different, but she *seemed* different . . . softer, somehow. When I set her loose in the arena that morning she didn't race so wildly. She trotted half-heartedly across the sand and put her neck through the far fence to go after a crop of grass that was just out of reach.

I climbed up on the railing. It was early still, just after nine, but already the chill was gone from the air. Today would be hot. Again.

After a while I hopped down and slogged through the sand after Delilah. She hadn't gotten any grass, so I fetched a handful and offered it to her. Her breath was warm and damp against my wrist as she started munching.

Driving out to the stable, I'd had to fight back tears several times. But now I felt calmer than I had in days, maybe weeks. Will was leaving. But Delilah was here. Her coat was soft; her breath was warm. Life would go on.

I made it to Will's house just before eleven. From the outside, his cottage looked the same as it always did: brown shingles, a slightly overgrown lawn, a flowering vine that wound through the wooden pickets of the front gate.

Will's dad, Martin, opened the door when I knocked. He looked the same, too: Will's unruly wavy hair, but streaked

38

with gray; a full beard; a belly that showed proof of his love for rich meals and good wine.

"Ah, Scarlett, welcome!" As usual, Martin seemed genuinely glad to see me. Behind him in the hallway sat Will's green canvas duffel bag, stuffed full, and his backpack.

Martin saw me looking at Will's bags. His expression of empathy was painful to bear.

"Is Will in his room?"

"He is. Gathering up the last of his things. Scarlett, I'll be on the island for a little while longer and I'd like to have you out for a meal before I leave, if you're up for it."

I smiled. Martin was a good guy. He'd helped me last year when I'd needed someone to talk to. And he was letting me take Will to the ferry without him.

"That sounds nice," I said. "Especially if you bake some of your famous bread."

"It wouldn't be a meal without bread."

I found Will sitting on the edge of his bed, flipping through a book. I stopped in the doorway and watched him for a minute—the grace of his hands holding the book, the tilt of his head, the lovely line of his throat.

"You going to stand there and stare at me, or are you coming in?"

I didn't trust myself to speak, so I slid next to him on the bed. He closed the book and set it down, entwining his fingers with mine. His chin rested on the top of my head. His warm breath in my hair reminded me of Delilah.

Normally if we were too quiet in Will's room, Martin started whistling or banging pans together to keep us honest, but just then the house was quiet all around us. Will caressed my cheek and tilted my face up to his. I didn't realize I was crying until Will bent his face down and kissed my tears away—first my left cheek, then my right. And then his lips caught mine.

This time when I wound my arms around his neck, I held him so tightly it must have hurt, but Will didn't complain. He answered my fierceness with a matching heat, his hands around my waist, in my hair, pulling me into his chest as the kiss deepened.

I welcomed the crush of his arms. If only he could crush me completely against him until we were enmeshed, until we were one body. If only we could stay like this forever.

Suddenly I heard Martin opening and closing cabinets in the hallway, rustling around inside of them and muttering to himself. I guess Will and I had been silent a little too long. But Will didn't seem to hear his dad; his attention to me didn't slacken, not at all. If anything it was the opposite; his hands held my face just so, and his mouth, soft and hard all at once, devoured mine.

I made a little sound, a whimpering of pleasure, and guided one of Will's hands down from my cheek, encouraging him to reach beneath my shirt. Everywhere my skin was tingling, awake, aware.

He would have pressed me back into the pillows on his bed. He would have pulled my shirt up and away from my body. He would have lost himself in me—but Martin let something heavy fall from the cabinet just past the door, and the thud of it against the wood floor drew Will away, cursing softly.

My heart pounded and my lips felt swollen from Will's kisses, but he looked even more pulled apart than I felt; there was a shift in his eyes, a hunger that I hadn't seen there before.

I had ignited it, that need. A surge of something that felt like triumph flashed through me.

"We'd better go," Will managed to say. "I don't want to miss the ferry."

I rearranged my hair and straightened my shirt while Will pulled a last few things from his bedside table—his wallet, his phone, a pocketknife. The book he'd been reading slipped to the floor, and I picked it up.

It was his playbook from last spring—*The Importance of Being Earnest*. We had performed the leads opposite each other.

"Well, my boy," Martin said, walking us to the door, "you'll be careful, won't you?"

Normally every parent cautions his kid, but Will's psychic ability—which he had once seen as a curse, but had come to accept as a blessing, strange as it was—lent deeper meaning to Martin's worry.

"Yes, Dad. I'll be careful. I always am."

Strictly, this wasn't really true. I remembered the way Will had looked last spring when he'd rushed into a burning building, sure someone was trapped inside, and earlier, last Halloween, when he'd come barreling into Andy's bedroom and yanked Andy off me. Will hadn't looked like he was being careful then.

Martin was right to be concerned. I understood how hard it must be for him to watch his son venture off on his own.

41

Of course, Martin wouldn't be far away for long; he'd be returning to Connecticut, too, though Will would be living in the Yale dorms and not in the family home, which had been shut up since they came to the island a year ago.

Martin had spent the past five years—since Will had his bar mitzvah at thirteen—trying to protect Will from himself. But things were different now. Will had told us both that his abilities were changing. He wasn't driven in quite the same way to intercede and stop violent crimes from being committed. For better or worse, now his awareness of danger and suffering was more diffused, more universal.

Still, he could attune himself to specifics if he wanted. What kind of trouble might have manifested for Lily at Brandon's party if Will hadn't brought me there to take Lily home?

I remembered what Will had told me: many of the crimes he'd stopped were similar to what Andy had almost done to me at last year's Halloween party. I shuddered a little. That wasn't how it should be, sex.

That wasn't how it would be with Will, if he and I ever made love. It would be beautiful.

"Call me when you get to LAX," Martin directed. "And again when you land. Betty is going to meet you at the airport. She'll see you safely to campus."

"Betty?" I heard the edge in my voice, and blushed.

Martin laughed, but gently. "A family friend."

"I'll call," Will promised. "And I'll be safe."

They hugged then, patting each other on the back. Martin held Will tightly for an extra moment, and when he released him he held on to his son's shoulders, looking into his eyes. *"Yasher koach,"* he said.

Will looked back at him, and nodded.

Martin cleared his throat. "Better get going."

I watched Will heft his duffel bag into the back of the station wagon and place his backpack beside it.

"Let me know if you need me to send anything," Martin offered. "And I'll see you in a few weeks."

I said goodbye to Martin and hugged him, then climbed behind the wheel to give them a moment alone.

As I drove us back through the heart of the island and toward Avalon, where Will would board the ferry that would take him away from me, I asked, "What did that mean, Will? The thing your dad said to you?"

"Yasher koach," said Will. "It's a blessing. It means 'strength'—may you have it, or may your strength be increased."

"He wants you to be strong?"

"That's one thing he wants for me, strength. It's a way of wishing a person the strength to continue doing good in the world. It's a way too of showing that he understands the effort it takes. Understands the effort doing good—performing mitzvahs—takes for me. For *anyone*, but I guess me, particularly."

The old Volvo didn't have air-conditioning, so we drove with the windows down. The sound of the wind rushing by didn't leave much room for conversation, but there wasn't much to say. A new driver, I kept both hands on the wheel, and even though he was right across from me, it felt like

Will was already very far away. He looked relaxed, though, as he gazed out the window at our island's chaparral; his green eyes were heavy-lidded against the wind.

"I can catch the three o'clock ferry instead of the one-thirty." He continued to look away rather than at me when he spoke. "My flight doesn't leave until nine tonight."

So rather than driving down the winding road into Avalon, I cut the engine not far from the stable, pulling the car to the side of the road where it widened slightly to leave room for any cars that might need to pass.

Will climbed out and came around to my side, where I sat as if frozen behind the wheel. He opened my door and offered me his hand.

I looked up into his eyes. They were so incredibly green. The color of life. I smiled and took his hand. I knew wherever Will led me, I would follow.

We walked along the road for a little ways; then a trail broke off on our right. I knew this trail well—it was one of my favorite routes to take with Delilah. We turned together toward the more private path without speaking. When the trail narrowed so it was too tight for us to walk side by side, Will stretched his arm behind him to keep his hold on my hand. A moment later the trail widened again, opening onto a small field.

All around us were trees and grass and the bright blue sky. Will turned to me, and I to him, and when we kissed the fire that sprang up between us was undeniable, as certain as the sun and just as hot.

Together we sank into the grass, together we knelt in something that felt as close to a prayer as anything I had ever known—our bodies turned in toward each other's, the long press of Will's chest against mine.

And when he lay me down in the meadow and pushed his body to mine, I welcomed the weight of him. The ground was hard beneath me, not comfortable at all—later I would find a darkening bruise on the small of my back where a rock had been—but I didn't shift my weight.

His hands—at last!—pulled my T-shirt up from the waistband of my jeans, and his fingers splayed against my rib cage, tracing little lines against my skin, threatening to drive me mad.

Every inch of my body felt alive. I would have said yes to anything. Of that I am sure.

But when Will broke the kiss, his face just inches away from mine, he didn't ask me a question. Instead he said, "Scarlett, I want you to know that I love you."

This was the first time he'd said that to me. I smiled at him and tilted my mouth up for another kiss. "I love you too," I murmured, straining toward him.

Will didn't kiss me again, not right away. He shifted up to sitting, pulling me with him.

I didn't want to sit up; I didn't want to untangle our limbs and talk. Not even about love.

But Will's face was serious, and what he said next forced me to listen. "I think you saved me last year, Scarlett."

I laughed. "I don't think so, Will. That's not how I remember things."

"But it's true. Scarlett, you helped me see that I have a choice—there's always a choice. Right now, I want to choose this"—he lowered his head to my neck, tracing kisses along my collarbone in a way that raised goose bumps on my skin—"but I'm not sure you want to choose it, too."

"Will," I said, "stop talking."

He laughed a little, and I pulled him on top of me as I lay back down.

Ahh. The press of him—the luxurious weight of his body stretched against the length of mine. This time the thrust of his hips was unmistakable. I felt a tingle of fear mixed with desire in the pit of my belly, and lower. There was mystery there, in the masculine hardness of him, and perhaps danger, too.

Will sensed me stiffen a little in his arms. "Are you okay?"

"Just nervous," I admitted. "Aren't you?"

He didn't answer right away, and in the gap of his silence I was struck by a realization. "You've done this before?"

I had rarely seen Will at a loss for words. He was now. His mouth opened, then closed. His fingers loosened from my side.

I don't know how to name the mix of emotions I felt. Surprised, I guess, and hurt . . . and embarrassed, too. I pushed hard on his chest and he shifted enough for me to slide out from underneath him.

"Tell me," I said.

He nodded. "It was last summer, before we came to the island."

The jealousy I felt was all-consuming. Rageful. Fire-bright

and hot. But even in the midst of it a tiny voice asked me what right I had to be angry. Will was talking about a time before he even knew I existed.

"Who was she?"

He sighed and sat up, running his fingers through his hair. "Are you sure you want to talk about this?"

I wasn't sure about anything—not anymore. The island was so quiet, the air stifling and still. "If we hurry," I said as I got up, "we can still get you to the one-thirty ferry."

Will tried twice to engage me in conversation—once on the trail, again in the car. Both times I shook him off and retreated into silence. After that he stopped trying. I could feel him getting angry next to me as we neared town. Good.

The dock was a madhouse as it always was: streams of tourists with kids disembarked from the ferry, and a long winding line of more tourists hauled their bags, waiting to board.

Will's duffel bag was heavy, but he yanked it out of the back of the Volvo easily, probably fueled by his irritation with me. And though I was mad, swallowing back the bilious feeling of betrayal, I couldn't bring myself to watch from the car as Will joined the line of people. So I followed miserably as he walked to the ticket booth and then followed the crowd waiting for the ferry to depart.

Will's jaw was tensed and he looked miserable too. Our last day together. Could it have gone more wrong?

Already it was after one o'clock. Soon he'd board the

ferry. I could have kicked myself for wasting our last hours together consumed with jealousy.

"Will."

He looked at me. His gaze softened. "I'm sorry. I should have told you. I'll tell you now, if you want."

I shook my head. That wasn't how I wanted to remember our last minutes together, with Will telling me all about the other girl he'd slept with. "Maybe another time. Now let's just be here together."

The crowded dock was worlds away from the private trail, but I tried to content myself by holding Will's hand, feeling his warmth beside me.

"I'll call you every day," he promised.

"Write me letters," I said. "Long romantic ones."

Will laughed. "Okay. We'll write letters. But I'll call, too."

Too soon the boat's horn sounded, announcing that it was time to board. The sun high above our heads stared down unblinking as I lost myself one last time in Will's embrace. And then he walked down the gangplank and onto the ship.

When he disappeared into the boat's cabin I felt a moment of panic. Would I see him again? Was he gone from me already? But then he appeared on the stern, pushing through the flood of passengers to get to the very back of the boat, closest to the dock. He raised his hand to wave to me and then stretched his arm out, as if he could span the distance between us. And as the boat pulled away, as Will grew smaller and smaller and finally disappeared, I felt the presence of him still, both coming like a wave from the ocean and radiating, too, from somewhere within me. As if wherever Will went—no matter how far—he was forever present, braided with some part of my soul, parts of us tangled up together, intractably.

Was this how love felt?

The time came when the world constricted around him, grasping him tightly, then too tightly, and he didn't want to leave. He wanted to stay even though the world had grown too small, or he too big for it—but some choices are not ours, his first lesson, and he was squeezed and pushed. The weight of the world seemed to be collapsing upon him, the pressure almost too much to bear. The beat, his constant friend and companion, faded farther and farther away. Then a new sensation—a touch on the top of his head. As he slipped away from his universe, his arms unbound, the freedom was overwhelming and terribly frightening.

The cold emptiness of the air was painful against his skin, and he flailed in it. The sound of his own cry startled him, redoubling his fear. Then hands passed him into arms and a warmed blanket tented over him. At last, he heard it again, though this time muffled, as if hidden behind a wall—his companion, the beat he loved. And he felt the warmth of bare skin against his body; it was different than the wetness and the warmth of before—but it was good. And he opened his eyes and looked up into other eyes, green and so full of love, and he knew he was seeing the world that he'd come from, and he stretched up his hand as best he could to touch her cheek.

FOUR

Fly Away

At last, Lily forgave me. It took her until the end of the first week of school. She'd done a really good job of punishing me, especially for someone whose family I doubt had ever subjected her to a bout of the silent treatment.

School started on the Tuesday after Labor Day. The first three days Lily went out of her way to show me exactly how she felt. She even went so far as to request a locker change so that we wouldn't be right next to each other anymore. The vice principal, Mr. Steiner, told her to stop being so dramatic.

I don't know many people who can flounce and prance as well as Lily. The way she was acting reminded me of a song my mom used to sing to me when I was acting bratty as a child:

> *There was a little girl*
> *Who had a little curl*

Right in the middle of her forehead.
When she was good,
She was very, very good,
But when she was bad, she was horrid.

"My hair is straight," I'd always answer.

But Lily's wasn't. Her lovely dark hair fell in ringlets, so she fit the verse perfectly. The day of her temper tantrum over the locker, I found myself humming the song all afternoon.

Part of Lily's charm was her willingness to take fashion risks. The first two days of school she wore wooden clogs—actual *wooden clogs* that she must have picked up in Amsterdam. And even though she wouldn't let me get close enough to compliment her, I had to admire her panache. On Wednesday she paired her clogs with white knee-highs—thick woolen ones—and a little dress with a flared skirt and a white bodice that proudly displayed two of Lily's best features.

But Friday, Lily showed up to school late, after first period had already ended. I was just coming out of English class when I saw her arguing with Mr. Steiner in the hallway outside of the main office.

She was wearing jeans and a T-shirt. On anyone else this might not have been noteworthy; on Lily, it meant that something was majorly wrong. Her curls were extra wild, not even glossed with their usual pomade.

"I know school started an hour ago, Mr. Steiner," she said, "and I would have been here on time, but I had terrible cramps. It's my menses, you know. Some months are just really hard."

Mr. Steiner began stuttering something I couldn't make out from my position outside of the classroom, but the tone of his voice and the sudden tenseness in his shoulders made it pretty obvious that he was uncomfortable discussing the intimacies of Lily Adams's female cycle.

"Just be sure you have a note next time," he blustered before walking into the office, shutting the door firmly behind him.

Lily caught my eye and winked. Ah, a patented Lily wink. How I'd missed them.

At lunch, Lily slid next to me with her tray as if nothing had happened between us. I handed her half my sandwich and she pushed across two of her four Oreos.

"So Adrian is officially a toad," she said, biting into the sandwich half. "Mmm, pastrami!"

"Glad you like it. What happened with Adrian?"

"More like what *didn't* happen. Did you know that the turd ignored my friend request on Facebook?"

Of course I didn't know this—Lily hadn't spoken two words to me since the night of the party. But I felt it might be better to let that particular comment go unsaid.

"That's terrible. Has he called you or anything?"

She shook her head, curls bouncing vehemently. "Not once. Not *once!*" She tore into the sandwich, chewing and swallowing. "I burned the stupid shoes," she added. "Poof!"

"Probably for the best. You were bound to twist an ankle in those things eventually."

"Maybe *you* would," she scoffed. "I've never yet met a pair of shoes I can't master. But it was, you know, symbolic."

I kept my face straight and nodded. "Very powerful symbolism."

And just like that, Lily Adams was my best friend again.

"So what about Will?" Lily asked later, as we headed out of school after the last bell.

"Well, he writes, and he calls, and he texts." I felt like I was walking a delicate line. I wanted to open up to Lily, but at the same time talking about Will—about our relationship— felt too tender. He'd been gone from the island for over a week now. A week and three days.

I thought about him more times every day than I cared to admit. Upon waking, always. And sometimes in the early morning, in the quiet of my room, soft light filtering through the gauzy curtains, I would be overwhelmed by an almost palpable sensation that Will was with me—right there, just out of my reach.

"So what do you think? Are you guys going to stay together?"

This was exactly the question I'd avoided asking myself— probably because I didn't want to acknowledge any doubts.

When Will had chosen Yale, he and I had decided not to have "the talk." The one about the future. It seemed silly. I just turned seventeen in April, and Will was only a year older.

The way I felt about him—and the way I hoped he felt about me—those seemed like forever feelings. But then, I'd *never* have thought my parents would ever split up . . . and now they were separated by an ocean.

Maybe that was a little dramatic. I mean, Catalina is only

twenty-two miles from the mainland, so the body of water isn't vast. But it seemed true that an ocean of emotions divided my parents now.

After my riding accident last year, it seemed for a while that everything would be better. Lots had broken in each of us with Ronny's death, but much had healed, too, in the year since that terrible phone call. And I'd gained strength I hadn't known I'd had.

I figured my parents' marriage would be like that, too. Different, maybe, but still solid. And though my mom made a good show of things after I was thrown from Traveler—finally leaving her self-imposed isolation in her bedroom, tossing out the sleeping pills and working through the shakes—ultimately I guess she just wasn't as mended as I had thought.

And so she flew away. Away from the island, from her pain, from her marriage . . . and from me.

If she could leave her kid behind, who's to say that Will couldn't leave me, too?

"I hope so, Lil," I said. "I sure do miss him."

She nodded, thoughtful. "Well, at least the dating pool around here improved while I was away. It looks like Brandon Becker's been eating his Wheaties." She gave him one of her smiles as he crossed in front of us on the school's front lawn.

He smiled back, but Katie Ellis, who had a death grip on his right hand, shot daggers at us.

"So you wanna come over?"

Tempting. Lily's place had always been my second home.

But I shook my head. "Can't. The vet's coming out today to check on Delilah."

"I still think it's creepy—artificial horse insemination? Gross."

I shrugged. "Sometimes life is gross, Lil."

She laughed. "You're telling me."

If Lily had seen the procedure that the vet, Dr. Rhonda, used to determine if Delilah was pregnant, she would have had something to say, for sure. Dr. Rhonda—a young vet, one of those girls who was probably tormented in high school for her lack of fashion sense (she actually wore a *bolero*) and her single-minded focus on her goal of becoming a large-animal vet—was practically jumping up and down as she explained the ultrasound equipment to me.

"This is the perfect time to do the ultrasound, if your mare is in foal. When did you do the insemination? Early July?"

I nodded.

"Perfect. Today's the ninth of September, which makes her approximately sixty-five days along. That is, if she's pregnant."

"I think she is," I said. "She seems a little different."

"Different how?"

"Oh, I don't know . . . softer, I guess. Not quite as high-strung, maybe."

"That could all be in your head. You want her to be in foal, so you could be seeing things that aren't really there."

This set my teeth on edge. I knew my own mare. I wasn't stupid.

Dr. Rhonda must have seen my jaw tense, because she laughed. "Sorry, Scarlett, it's just that I see it all the time. People often see what they *want* to see instead of what's really there. But we'll know in a minute."

She had set up the ultrasound machine near the crossties where I'd brought Delilah. It looked like a small TV monitor, or an older-model computer, with about a ten-inch screen. Attached to it was a long thin cord, and at the end of the cord was a probe.

"We insert that into your mare's rectum," said Dr. Rhonda. "It will allow us to see a heartbeat and the placenta, and if we're lucky we'll be able to determine the gender."

Aside from the part about shoving the probe into my mare's rectum, this was exciting news. "Really? This soon?"

Dr. Rhonda grinned at me. "Isn't technology amazing?"

I was admittedly a little weirded out when she squirted some clear jelly on the tip of the probe and made her way around to the rear of my mare, but Delilah didn't seem to mind as long as her nose was dipped into the bucket of A&M I'd set in front of her.

"Well, you were right," Dr. Rhonda said. "There's the fetus."

And on the screen, there it was—a little lump of something that magically looked like a tiny, tiny horse, with a frantically fluttering dot right near the center of it.

Life. Right there, on the screen—and in my mare.

"That's it?" I asked. "That's the baby? And that flutter there"—I poked my finger at the screen—"that's the heartbeat?"

"Sure is." She pressed some keys and took several still images for measurements. "He looks healthy. Everything is just the way it should be."

"He?"

"Yep." Dr. Rhonda zoomed in on the foal and an arrow appeared on the screen. "See there? That's his penis."

"Wow."

"Pretty incredible. It—he—is about two, two and a half inches long. About the size of a hamster. But he's hairless still. And look—he has tiny little hooves."

We stood side by side and gazed at the images of the tiny foal on the black-and-white monitor. Then Delilah cleaned out the bucket, stomped loudly, and shook her head.

Dr. Rhonda laughed. "She's done with us, I guess. I'll print you out a copy of these pictures."

She removed the probe and cleaned it, then snapped off her gloves inside out. I watched her movements carefully. I liked how respectful she was with my mare; she wasn't rough at all, like the farrier could be. She loved her job. That was obvious. She spoke to the horses like I did, as if she expected them to answer.

"So have you given any thought to what you might want to study when you go off to college?"

I shrugged. "I used to think I'd study literature," I said, "or acting. But lately . . . maybe medicine?"

"You'd be great!" Dr. Rhonda had that encouraging, eager tone that adults get when someone mentions an interest in their career. "Veterinary medicine?"

"I don't know. Maybe. Or maybe I'd like to study the brain."

Dr. Rhonda nodded. "Your brother died from an aneurysm, didn't he?"

I felt the sting of tears but managed to blink them back. "Grade six cerebral aneurysm." My voice sounded surprisingly even.

She shook her head. "Such a loss."

Dr. Rhonda attached a little printer to the ultrasound machine, and a long roll of images emerged from it. She handed them to me. "Take good care of them."

She may have meant the pictures, or she may have meant Delilah and her foal. It was strange that the plural pronoun now applied.

"I will. Is there anything I need to do differently? You know, like special feed or exercise restrictions?"

"Not for now. Just keep feeding her what she's been getting and make sure she always has access to fresh water. Later—in the last four months or so, her last trimester—you'll need to start thinking about adding in some extra calories and calcium."

"And I can keep riding her, right?"

"You'd better. She's perfectly healthy, just pregnant. She'll slow down a bit as she gets heavier."

Dr. Rhonda packed the ultrasound machine and the printer carefully into a foam-lined case, then stroked Delilah's muzzle before she headed out.

"This is a really nice mare you've got here," she said. "What will you do with her and the foal when you go to college next fall?"

"They'll stay here. But I'll have to go somewhere I can take them with me my sophomore year."

Dr. Rhonda whistled. "That's a pretty tall order. Limits your choices a bit, huh?"

I shrugged.

"Well, I'm sure you'll figure it out. That's a lot of money, though, to transport two horses off the island and to who knows where."

Suddenly I was tempted to grab the good doctor's bolero and cinch it tightly around her neck. "I'll figure it out."

"Sure you will." Dr. Rhonda gave me what felt like an evaluating look. "You seem like a girl with her head on pretty straight, Scarlett. I'm sure you'll find a way."

Later, after she was gone and Delilah was pulling up chunks of fresh grass in the back field, I sat on the fence and looked again at the ultrasound pictures.

The photos didn't look that different from the ones I'd seen of a human fetus: the spine and head were curved in the same C shape, there were four limbs and the beginnings of a face.

Looking at the pictures, I started to get the strangest tingle of déjà vu . . . as if I'd been here before, as if I'd seen inside a pregnancy.

Then like a wave, the dreams I'd been having crashed into me. The strength of them was so visceral that I almost toppled from my perch on the fence. I grabbed the rail to balance myself, the streamer of pictures floating to the grass.

I remembered someone floating, turning, breathing water in and out. I remembered the rhythmic, soothing sound of a heartbeat.

Had I dreamt it? It seemed too much like a memory to be

just a dream. Another wave of sensations flooded my mind. A pressure, a squeezing, as if my own body was being compressed.

As if I was being birthed.

And then I was myself again, sitting on a splintery wooden rail, and my pictures were blowing away. I hopped down and retrieved the photos of Delilah's baby.

When I got back home, where I'd left my cell phone, I found two messages waiting for me. One from my mother, the other from Will.

My mother's was first.

"Hi, Scarlett. Just wanted you to know that I made it to the mall this morning and I picked up the cutest bedding for your room here! I sure hope you can come visit soon. I know you're busy, of course . . . but I'd love to show you around, and maybe pick up some back-to-school clothes for you. Anyway, call your old mom when you get a chance, okay? Love you."

I hit 7 to erase the message.

Then Will.

"I bet you're at the stable. Today's the day, huh? The visit from the vet? Give me a call, let me know about the . . . what do you call it? Yearling? No, that can't be right; it would have to be a year old. Colt? Foal? Whatever. Anyway, I hope everything is good. I sure do miss you, Scarlett."

There was a long silence before he hung up, as if he didn't have anything else to say but was unwilling to disconnect, anyway.

I hit 9 to save.

• • •

I found my father out by the koi pond. He was staring down into the water, scratching his head.

"Hi, Dad."

He blinked up at me, smiling vaguely. "Hey there, hon."

"How are the fish?"

"You know, it's the darnedest thing." He shook his head. "I don't know. . . . We seem to be missing a few of them."

"Well, they couldn't have walked away." I peered into the shadow-deep water. I counted three fish, their long, slippery orange-and-white bodies lazing through the pond. "Didn't we have five?"

"I thought we had six. So we're down two, then, not three."

"What happened to them, do you think?"

He shrugged. "Who knows? A hawk, maybe, or an over-zealous neighborhood cat. I would have thought they were too big to be picked off so easily, but I guess I was wrong."

It took me a minute to define the emotion I was feeling. Not frustration or annoyance, but something stronger. Anger. I felt it welling up in my chest. I wasn't angry at the hawks or the opportunistic house cats, I was angry at my *father*, of all people. He just looked so damned *complacent*! "Jeez, Dad, aren't you even *upset* about this? I mean those were *your fish*!"

He laughed and rumpled my hair. "Easy, Scarlett! They're just fish. No use fighting Mother Nature. Say, how about a pizza for dinner?"

I swallowed back the words I wanted to say. I wanted to

shake him. Didn't he have any *fight* in him? Any desire to hold tight to what he had, even if it was only a few stupid fish?

I couldn't help wondering whether Mom would have stayed if Dad had been willing to fight for her. Had he watched her with that same bewildered smile on his face as she boarded the ferry and moved on to a different life, one in which she was buying me new, color-coordinated sheets and pillows?

Would he put up a fight if I decided to follow her to the mainland? Or would he just scratch his head and wave goodbye?

Was anything worth fighting for? Or would Mother Nature win out every time?

I sighed.

"Yeah, Dad, pizza. That sounds good."

FIVE
An Open Door

Without Will, his house should have felt like an empty shell. That was what I'd prepared myself for, in the days leading up to my dinner with Martin. When I pulled the Volvo up in front of the little brown-shingled cottage, I sat for a few minutes before I walked up to the front door, dreading going inside.

I wasn't expecting it to feel *good* in there. I knocked, and Martin called, "Come in, Scarlett!"

I pushed open the door slowly, uncertainly, waiting for the wave of Will's absence to slam into me. But it didn't come. Instead I felt a release, a relaxing of muscles I hadn't meant to tense. The leather couch and chair, softened by years of use, beckoned me to sit. Stacks of books, many folded open, covered almost every available surface. A low fire burned in the hearth, even though the late-September air held barely a chill.

I crossed through the living room and headed into the kitchen. Martin was standing by the back door, watching the sky fill with orange and pink light as the day ended.

We were quiet together, but it wasn't awkward to see Martin without Will present. I could tell he'd been neglecting himself a little; his beard and hair were longer than usual, more unkempt. His eyes looked tired, like he'd been working a lot.

As the sky's colors dimmed into dark, Martin turned to me. "Scarlett," he said, "so good to see you."

We hugged briefly. *"L'shanah tovah,"* he said.

I must have looked confused, because he laughed.

"Tonight's sunset marks the end of Yom Kippur," he explained. "I'll tell you more over dinner. So let's get cooking."

It wasn't like Martin not to have dinner already bubbling on the stove, but I didn't say anything as he pulled a red iron pot from the refrigerator and set it on a burner, lighting the flame beneath it.

"There's a loaf of bread in the basket," Martin said, gesturing to the counter. "Why don't you slice it while I warm the stew."

I found a cutting board and a knife and unwrapped the bread. It was seasoned with rosemary and smelled wonderful as I cut into it.

As the stew heated and I sliced the bread, Martin asked me about school and my mare. What class was I most enjoying? Anatomy. How was Delilah? Right as rain. Neither of us seemed anxious to mention Will, and I suspected it was because we both missed him painfully.

When we were seated at the table, a bowl of steaming stew in front of each of us, and the bread between us, Martin spoke the words of blessing over the food, words I had come to know over the past year as I visited the Cohen household. "So what did those words you said earlier mean?"

"Ah," said Martin, "Yom Kippur."

I nodded. I knew Yom Kippur was the name of a Jewish holiday, but I didn't know any more than that. Embarrassed by my ignorance, I ate a spoonful of the stew. Hot, peppery, delicious.

"Yom Kippur," Martin said, slipping into his "teacher" voice (after all, he had been a professor of religious studies at Yale before he moved with Will to the island), "is arguably the most serious of Jewish holidays. It occurs in the fall right after Rosh Hashanah—the Jewish New Year. It's not a celebratory day. It's also called the Day of Atonement. Yom Kippur gives us an opportunity to repent and speak our guilt. To seek forgiveness for wrongs we may have done—against God, against our fellow men."

"I can't imagine *you* have much to apologize for," I said.

"Certainly not for this stew," Martin said, slurping a little as he ate. "It's definitely tasty. Pass the bread, will you, Scarlett?"

I did, smiling a little. Neither of the Cohen men was above complimenting his own cooking.

"During Yom Kippur," Martin continued, "we fast for a day and a night, and we pray. We abstain from work, from food and drink, from bathing, from wearing shoes made of leather"—he winked at me and waved his feet, clad only in dark brown socks—"and from sex. After sundown the following day—today—we eat a simple meal prepared ahead of time."

"Ah," I said. "Thus the stew."

"Thus the stew. And our tradition tells us that through prayer, through our requests for absolution, we will be absolved of our sins. We can start the New Year with a clean slate, so to speak."

"And those words you said before?"

"*L'shanah tovah*. When we wish someone a happy new year, we are wishing that he or she be inscribed in the Book of Life and sealed for a new year."

"The Book of Life?"

"It's a list kept by God, of all the people whom he considers righteous." Martin smiled. "Not unlike Santa's nice list."

"Is there a naughty list, too?" I asked, joking.

"Most certainly there is," said Martin. "The Book of the Dead."

"*Really?*"

"Really." He sipped from his wineglass.

"Huh." I took a drink too, a long sip of water. Then I posed a question, one I had asked before at this same table: "Do you really believe in all that?"

Martin laughed, remembering, I'm sure, our first theological discussion. "Metaphorically, most definitely. Literally . . . I don't know what I believe," he said. "Moreover,

I'm not even sure it *matters* what I believe. What matters, I think, is what I *do*. And what I *know*."

"So what do you know?"

He pushed his bowl, now empty, slightly away. "I know Will has been back in New Haven for three weeks now. I know that—so far—he has been safe. But I also know that this will not last forever."

I didn't say anything. Of course I had been thinking these same thoughts—how much time could go by in a big city like New Haven before Will felt the pull of a violent act about to be perpetrated? A few weeks? Or months? Inevitably, something would happen, and Will wasn't the kind of person—wasn't capable of *being* the kind of person—who just ignored it. When he felt the pull, he would answer it. And wasn't it only a matter of time before it pulled him into a dangerous situation he couldn't handle, just as it had his mother?

"You don't *know* that he won't be safe," I said. "You just *assume* it's true. You fear it. But you can't *know* that it will happen that way."

Martin didn't argue with me, most likely because he knew that really I was arguing with my own fears. Instead he said, "Let's have more stew. What do you say?"

Later, while Martin prepared tea, I stoked the fire and added another log. It took a minute to catch, but then it did, and the flames warmed my face and hands. I had grown cold without noticing.

We sat on either side of the fireplace and Martin added cream and sugar to both the cups before handing one to me. Sipping our tea, we gazed into the fire, each lost in our own thoughts.

After a bit, Martin said, "I leave for New Haven this coming week, Scarlett. I want to ask you for a favor."

"Anything," I said.

He reached up to the mantel and retrieved a key. "This is for the house. If you can arrange it, perhaps you could check in on the place every week or two?"

I took the key. "Sure," I said. "Anything in particular you need me to do?"

"No," said Martin, "but we—Will and I—would be glad if you found this place to be something of a retreat. A place to come when you need a space of your own."

"Really?"

He nodded.

"You mean I could come inside, maybe make myself a pot of tea . . . and hang out?"

"Absolutely," said Martin. "And avail yourself of any books that strike your fancy. We have quite a collection, as you've noticed, more than I can possibly drag all the way back east with me each fall."

"So you'll be back in the summer? Both of you?"

Martin smiled. "I don't think Will would have it any other way."

I felt warmer now, with the key tucked in my pocket. The thought of coming here, whenever I wanted to, of being in Will's space, was certainly better than nothing.

"Thanks, Martin. I'll take good care of things."

"I'm sure of it."

We sat in companionable silence. There was a plate of

cookies nearby and Martin thoughtfully munched on one, and then another, and then a third.

"You know," he said, "fasting always reminds me what a pleasure it is to eat. It's a sacred act, I think—the taking in of sustenance, the transformation of food into energy."

I'd had my own struggles with food; eating hadn't always felt like such a great thing last year. Not after Ronny died. In fact, refusing to eat had been a way of punishing myself. A way that I withheld pleasure from my body. But I knew what Martin meant. Paying attention to how the food I ate was nourishing and strengthening my body gave meaning to the ritual of eating.

"Often people think of the body as something 'other than' themselves," Martin continued. "As if it's not essential to the person."

"Right," I said. "Isn't the real person the soul? And the body just the vessel?"

"That's a nice thing to think, especially when the bodies of those we love are no longer living. But it's not something we *know*. It is something all of us *hope,* to greater or lesser degrees. What we *know* is that we each have a body. What we may or may not believe is whether or not we *are* those bodies."

I sipped my tea, mindful of its sweetness and warmth, the way it seemed to spread through my chest and down to my stomach as I swallowed.

"Judaism says much about the body, contradicting itself in many ways," Martin said. "The body is a temple. It is a prison. It is sacred. It is profane. It is God's form. It is dust."

"So which is it?"

"Maybe all of them. Maybe none." He took another cookie and bit into it. Then he handed one to me.

It was crispy, lacy. Cinnamon and something else.

"Did you make these?"

Martin nodded.

"What's in them? I can't place it. Is it . . . ginger?"

"Cardamom."

I finished the cookie. Then I remembered the book I'd brought and stood up. "I almost forgot to return this," I said, digging into my bag by the door to retrieve it. "Here," I said, passing it to Martin. "Thank you for lending it to me."

He gazed at the golden words on the book's blue cover. *A Guide to the Sefirot*. Martin had loaned me the book the year before, when I had asked him for guidance in dealing with my grief over Ronny and my inability to properly care for myself.

"Ah," Martin said, "one of my favorites. Did you read it all the way through?"

I had. Each of its chapters dealt with one of the ten Sefirot, or manifestations of God. "I read it all," I said, "but I probably understood only about a third of it."

He chuckled. "Then you probably got more out of it than most first-time readers. I'll tell you what—I'll leave it here, at the house. That way you can revisit it if the urge strikes you."

"Thank you," I said. "I do want to learn more."

"Do you? What about?"

"All of it—the Sefirot, Kabbalah, Will's abilities—everything."

Martin nodded. "Then there's someone you should meet."

"Where—here?" It seemed impossible that anyone on the island could have anything more to teach me than Martin.

"No. But nearby. In Los Angeles. Her name is Sabine Rabinovich. I think you could learn a lot from her."

"Like what?"

"My own knowledge is limited by my skepticism. Though I wish to believe things—even when I see with my own eyes how my son embodies the truly miraculous—I am full of doubt. Doubt and incredulity. Not so Sabine. Her energy is different than mine. She doesn't allow herself to be held back—not in any way. You'll see for yourself when you visit her. She and her family are not exactly traditional Jews. They have their own way of doing things."

Martin didn't seem to question whether I would go to the mainland to see this friend of his. And, with annoyance, I realized that once on the mainland I'd have no good reason not to visit my mother, as well.

"Sabine studies Kabbalah?"

"She breathes it," said Martin. "For me, study is a matter of books and charts and mental exercises. My route to understanding is what is called theosophical Kabbalah. Though I've delved into the more esoteric Kabbalah in my attempt to better understand Will, I have found the most personal satisfaction in the language of the Sefirot, most particularly in the Zohar."

"The Zohar?" It sounded like one of those old fortune-telling machines, the kind where you put in a coin and it spits out a little slip of paper with some predetermined snippet of wisdom, like a fortune cookie.

"It's a Hebrew word. Translated, it means 'splendor.' The Zohar is actually a series of texts, and I've spent the bulk of my career—from my PhD dissertation onward—studying them. Among other things, the Zohar focuses on the oldest questions: what is God? What is Man? What is our connection? But studying the Book of Splendor—as the Zohar is called—is no easy undertaking. The hope is that within its pages one can find answers about the meaning of our time here and our connections to a higher power, however one might define it."

"So the book you loaned me was theo . . . theosophical Kabbalah?" I tripped a little over the new word.

"Yes, definitely. Being my particular area of interest, it seemed a good direction to point you in. But now that I'm leaving, I think perhaps you may be interested in exploring a new path, one for which Sabine is the ideal guide—ecstatic Kabbalah."

"Ecstatic Kabbalah. What is that?"

"Better to let Sabine explain," Martin said. "Suffice it to say that while theosophical Kabbalah is about book learning, ecstatic Kabbalah is experiential. You have to feel it to believe it."

"Sounds cool." Honestly, it sounded kind of ridiculous, but I didn't want to insult Martin by saying so.

His look told me that he heard the hesitancy in my tone, but he didn't call me on it. "It is definitely cool," he said, "if you can manage to let go of yourself enough to really experience it. I never could get the hang of it. Meryl, though, thought it was transformative."

I didn't know what to say. Meryl—Martin's wife, Will's mother—had died in a car accident that turned out not to be an accident at all. It was just before Will's thirteenth birthday.

Silent, I sat with Martin as his thoughts turned, no doubt, to his wife. I'd seen his expression on each of my parents' faces—I'd even seen it on my own face. But Meryl had been dead for more than five years now. Maybe wounds like that never really healed completely. They just scabbed over, and then reopened with the slightest touch.

"Visit Sabine," Martin finally said. "You'll like her."

I nodded. My teacup was empty, but still I didn't want to leave. At the end of the road waited my house, full of strangers. "Tell me something about Will," I said.

"What sort of something?"

"Anything. What was he like as a little boy?"

Martin chuckled. "You know, if you asked most fathers about their children, each would tell you how his was the exception, the prodigy, the something special."

"But not you, right? Will was perfectly ordinary?"

"No," said Martin, "I'm no better than the rest of them. Of course I thought my son was special, even before I knew the ways he really was set apart from the rest of us. It's funny, but now that I know about his gift, it's the ways he was ordinary—rather than extraordinary—that give me comfort."

"Like what?"

"He was—at best—a mediocre baseball player. It was my favorite sport growing up, so naturally when I was blessed with a son I envisioned teaching him how to pitch, the two of us playing catch. But it seems not all of a man's dreams are meant to be manifested."

"Let me guess . . . he hated it?"

"Not exactly. He kept asking me—over and over—why we were throwing a ball back and forth. What was the point? Who said that this activity should be fun? Who made the rules for baseball? And why? As long as I kept answering his questions, Will was perfectly willing to humor me, but it was clear that that was exactly what he was doing. He'd throw a few balls, catch a few pitches, then he'd drift off, staring at a bird or kicking at the leaves at his feet. He wasn't terrible. He wasn't great. Just average."

I found this hard to believe. I couldn't think of anything about Will that was "just average." Certainly not his kissing. But then I remembered the way he danced—not terribly, but not great, either.

It felt strange to think about Will in a way that didn't idealize him. And it was weird too to hear Martin focusing on his son's weaknesses rather than his strengths.

This must have shown on my face, because Martin said, "You know, Scarlett, none of us is perfect."

"Not me, that's for sure," I said.

"None of us. Perfect heroes—they're the stuff of myths and legends. Of biblical stories."

Even though I knew Martin wasn't necessarily the most

devout of men, it was still strange to hear a *rabbi* lump people from the Bible in with myths and legends.

"The Torah," Martin went on, "what Christians call the Old Testament, is full of superheroes and supervillains. Everyone in it is there for a purpose—everyone has a metaphorical job to fill. Take Abraham. Do you know about Abraham?"

I shook my head.

"The father of the Jews. According to our story, it's Abraham we have to thank for our covenant with God. You see, Abraham's father—like most of the people of his time—worshipped a series of idols, praying to this one for rain and that one for sun, and so on. But Abraham felt this was wrong. It seemed clear to him that there could only be one true God, one creator. *Ein Sof.* And so he formed a covenant with God—he would leave his family, his people, his home . . . and God would build him a great nation and bless him. Abraham was unshakable in his faith, even going so far as to be circumcised at the age of ninety-nine to seal the covenant."

Gruesome. "He sounds devoted," I managed to say.

"Exactly," said Martin, pleased. "He was a superman of his day. Unwavering faith. Absolute devotion. Unquestioning obedience."

"Is that a good thing?"

"That, my dear, is a very modern question."

"Well, I don't think it's so great," I said. "What about Socrates? Questioning authority?"

"A good point," Martin said. "What do you think?"

"I think unquestioning obedience is dangerous."

He nodded. "So does Will. Will has many qualities that mark him as un-Abraham-like."

"Such as?"

"God was fond of testing Abraham's loyalty. He told Abraham that he wanted him to sacrifice his son, Isaac. Abraham prepared the altar."

"He *killed* his *son?*"

"No, no. At the last moment an angel appeared and stopped him. A ram was sacrificed in Isaac's place."

"Yeah, I can't see Will sacrificing anyone he loves, not for any reason."

As I spoke, I remembered last spring, when Will had stopped calling me. It was after he'd learned that his mother had purposefully positioned her car to save the life of a pregnant woman who was about to be struck by another vehicle. A noble sacrifice . . . except her husband and son had been in the car with her. Neither of them had been badly hurt, but they could have been. Will didn't ever want to be in that situation—forced to choose between my safety and answering the pull he felt to help someone.

Martin was watching me work through all of this. "It's a lot to ask of anyone," he said softly. "To weigh the worth of one life against another."

I nodded. Suddenly it seemed that maybe Will had been glad to get into Yale for more reasons than just because it was an Ivy League school. Maybe he was glad to leave me behind—on the island, where it was safe.

The fire felt hot now, stifling. I rose to leave. Martin stood, too. "Thanks for dinner, Martin," I said.

"Thank *you*, Scarlett, for the company. Drive safely, will you?"

I nodded. We embraced. Martin's sweater was scratchy against my cheek and smelled like smoke.

Outside, the world blurred—cars and cars and more cars, red and black and white and red again. In front of him were the backs of two heads—in the driver's seat, a woman's, dark brown waves falling to her shoulders, and directly in front of him a man's, hair curly and uncombed, woven with the occasional gray.

A CD played, one of his parents' favorites, James Taylor. This song was a sort of lullaby—"Sweet Baby James," about a cowboy and his horse and his cows, all alone together out on the range. The tune was quiet and dreamlike. As their car pulled off the freeway, James Taylor crooned, "With ten miles behind me and ten thousand more to go," and their car slowed as they made their way through town, the trees in blossom, the sky bright and blue and open. Heading home. All was right with the world.

There was a moment of silence as the song's last notes faded. He saw that his mother's right hand had reached for his father's left. Their fingers interlaced in a way that both embarrassed and pleased him as he watched from the backseat.

And then there was the next moment. In that instant all the air in the car was gone. Something electric replaced it, something charged and sinister and on the cusp of pain.

His father didn't notice the change. His sloped shoulders didn't raise, his thumb, gently rubbing the hand it held, did not stop.

But his mother felt the shift, too. Will saw her flinch,

and the force it took her to settle, and then she squeezed his father's hand and pulled hers away.

"You missed your turn," his father said, but his mother didn't seem to hear. She grasped the wheel tightly with both hands and her foot pressed down hard on the gas pedal, and the engine roared, and Will felt his heart beating faster and faster, as if it was that pedal, as if his mother was stepping on his heart, harder and harder until it would surely burst.

She turned the car sharply, tires squealing as they skipped across the asphalt. They raced down the street, his father shouting at his mother, but Will's heart was pounding too loudly for him to make out the words, and then there was a woman—pregnant or fat, he couldn't tell which—and another vehicle, a pickup truck, traveling too fast as well, into the intersection up ahead, and just before the impact, before his mother placed their car between the woman and the truck, he saw in the rearview mirror green, desperate eyes—his mother's or a reflection of his own, he couldn't tell which, not then or in the years to follow.

His father rode in the back of the ambulance alongside his mother. It screamed off without him, leaving Will standing in the rainbow of shattered glass and oil. It was almost pretty.

Finally a policeman offered him a ride in the cruiser; numbly he accepted and lowered himself into the backseat, behind the metal cage that protected the officers from their passengers. The policeman flipped on the siren. Its scream seemed to give voice to the feeling in Will's chest. As they pulled away from the crash—his mother's car and the pickup truck left behind, entangled like lovers—it seemed to Will that he was sitting exactly where he belonged.

And he wondered what the eyes in the mirror had wanted to tell him.

SIX

Liminal Spaces

I hadn't been many places. The island had always been my home, and since our family business revolved around the tourist season, we were pretty trapped during spring break and summer. The farthest I'd ever gone was on a weeklong road trip with Ronny and my dad to visit colleges during the spring of Ronny's senior year. Mom had to stay home at the B&B. The three of us had taken the ferry to the mainland and rented a car, heading up the coast to check out the schools Ronny had gotten into—UCLA, UC Santa Cruz, and UC Berkeley—and the one school he *really* wanted but was wait-listed at, Stanford.

I was a freshman. The weather was beautiful the whole trip. Ronny sat up front with Dad, taking turns doing the driving. I had the backseat to myself, and I'd brought a stack of books to read. Mostly, though, I held the books open on my lap, listening to my dad and my brother talk.

"Can't we just line the pond with rocks?" Dad asked.

"No way!" Ronny sounded emphatic. "If you want the pond to last, and if you really want koi, we've got to use a rubber liner. And we need a bottom drain, and a good filter, and—"

"Do we really need koi? Why not just get some goldfish?"

"Jesus, Dad, come on. If we're going to go to all the trouble of making a pond, we might as well make it the coolest pond on the island. Otherwise, what's the point? I'm not interested in digging a freakin' mud pit."

That was Ronny's philosophy—go big or go home. No wonder he was hoping Stanford would upgrade him from wait-listed to accepted.

Ronny turned around to look at me in the backseat. "What do *you* think, kiddo?"

I shrugged. "Aren't koi really friendly?"

He nodded. "Like cats. They'll eat from your hand."

"Cool. Then let's have those."

Dad sighed. "Two to one," he said. "Koi it is."

They built the koi pond that summer, before Ronny left for UCLA. It was the last project they did together. I didn't do much of the digging, but I provided moral support, hanging out in the gazebo with my books and watching them work. They laughed a lot.

Stanford didn't end up accepting Ronny. Looking back, I'm glad; if they had, I probably would have seen even less of him that last year of his life.

But the fact that he ended up at UCLA meant that every time I traveled to the city now, I was reminded of Ronny's death and felt myself calculating the distance to the soccer field on UCLA's campus where Ronny collapsed and died.

On this day—the seventh of October—as I walked up a street named Linnie Canal in Venice Beach, I guessed I was no more than ten miles away from that soccer field.

My mom's new apartment, in Westwood, was even closer. Two, three miles, tops. But I hadn't been there yet. After the ferry had delivered me to Marina del Rey, I'd shouldered my backpack and started walking. It was only a couple of miles from where the boat docked to the house I was searching for—the home of Sabine Rabinovich.

She'd responded to the email I'd sent, writing that she'd be home all weekend and that I was welcome to stop by. So I was surprised when, after finding the house—number 234— and knocking on its door, no one answered.

The house wasn't much to look at. From the street it mostly looked like a two-car garage, green-painted wood with one of those white slide-up doors, and a second story atop it. A long thin path along the side of the house led to the front door, and next to the door was a side gate.

Maybe I'd gotten the wrong house. I rechecked the map and directions I'd printed out. No, this was the right place: 234. But apparently, no one was home. I rang the doorbell and knocked again, loudly. Still nothing. On the right side of the doorframe, close to eye level, I noticed something familiar—a little rectangular metal object, hung on an angle, with a brass symbol on the front. It looked like a fancy W. I'd seen something like this before on the doorframe to

Will's house. The thought of Will sent a shot of longing through me and I turned away.

It was cold. I zipped up my hoodie, shoved my hands in my pockets, and contemplated my options. I'd told my mom that I'd call her when I was ready for her to pick me up, but it was barely past five o'clock and I was in no rush to see her so soon. Honestly, I wanted to put off our visit as long as possible.

I could walk to a restaurant and get something to eat. I was hungry. But I didn't want to do that, either. I wanted to meet Sabine Rabinovich.

And then I heard the music. At first it was quiet, but it grew louder and I began to pick out the instruments—a flute, maybe, and drums. Cymbals. It wasn't professional; it sounded cobbled together, and the musicians seemed to miss as many notes as they hit. The music came from the back of the house.

As I unlatched the gate and walked slowly along the side yard, people joined in clapping to the music's quick beat. Someone laughed and a voice said, "That's the way, Ziva!"

I came around the corner of the house and stopped short, not sure what I was seeing.

It was like a paradise. I realized now that what I had thought was the front of the house was actually its rear, and this was the home's true face, with a wide covered porch and a small lawn spilling down toward a sidewalk, and on the other side of the sidewalk, a canal.

Of course. LA's Venice was named—and modeled—after the famous canal city in Italy. All the houses here faced canals, many with a short private dock out onto the water and a rowboat tied to it.

The front of the house was shaded by a wide awning, and the porch was lined with tables, each draped in colorful cloth, with bowls of fruit and dip, and trays of crackers with cheeses atop them. In the center of the lawn was a tent, its walls made from panels of thick burlap painted in wild brilliant swirls of every color, its thatched roof formed of palm fronds. On the lawn sat a cluster of wooden chairs, two of which were occupied, by a woman and a man.

Next to the tent were the musicians, none of them more than twelve years old, a group of three of the most beautiful children I had ever seen. The oldest was a girl, her long dark hair in twin plaits down her back, each ending in a curl. She held a flute to her lips and tapped her foot as she played. She wore a dark green skirt that brushed the ground and a yellow-and-red scarf tied around her waist, a long triangle of it layering over her skirt in obvious mimicry of the woman who had to be her mother; they shared the same long curls, though the woman's hair was loose instead of braided.

The other children were boys—the elder, about nine years old, sitting behind a drum set wearing a jaunty linen newsboy cap, a white shirt, and a brown linen vest, his eyes on his sister's foot as she beat out the rhythm of their song.

The youngest was wild, spinning in circles and banging a tambourine to a tune evidently he alone could hear, totally offbeat, barefoot and half-naked in a pair of knee-length cutoffs and nothing else.

Their parents watched and rose, clapping, from their seats

on the lawn. It wasn't that the mother was so beautiful or the father was so handsome; they weren't, particularly. He was an average-looking middle-aged man, well dressed in pressed slacks and a buttoned shirt, she a moderately heavy, large-breasted woman, almost exactly the same height as her husband. Their beauty was in their gaze, the way they looked at their children, full of delight and pride.

The song ended and they all clapped louder, even the children, for themselves. They still hadn't seen me standing there, sort of awkward, off to the side.

"I probably should have called first," I said, both as a way to call attention to myself and as an apology for obviously crashing their party.

All five heads swiveled in my direction.

"A guest!" screamed the younger boy, and he ran, flapping his arms, straight at me. I dropped my backpack and held my hands out in front of me in preparation for the impact, but he stopped just inches short of running into me, grinned widely, and stuck out his hand.

"Um . . . hi," I said, extending my hand for him to shake. His grip was strong, nothing childlike about it. "I'm Scarlett."

"I'm Ari," he said, and then yelled over his shoulder, still gripping my hand, "Mama! We have a guest!"

"I can see that, Ari," the woman said, crossing the yard toward us. "Scarlett, welcome! I am Sabine. We are so pleased that you're here."

"If it's a bad time . . . ," I began.

"A bad time?" She laughed.

"I didn't mean to intrude on your party."

"Intrude? This party is for you!"

Confused, I said, "But you didn't even know I was coming tonight."

"It's Sukkot!" Ari said, as if that should clear everything up.

"Um . . . I don't know what that is." I felt my cheeks reddening.

"You don't know about Sukkot?"

"Ari, shush," his sister said, coming to stand beside her mother.

"We'll tell you all about it, Scarlett," said Sabine. "Please, join us for dinner."

It took them a few tries to convince me that I really wasn't in the way. Finally they pulled me into their tent— "Our sukkah," Ari enunciated carefully, as if speaking to a small child—and insisted I take the most comfortable seat, an upholstered straight-backed dining chair pulled to the head of the table.

The other children introduced themselves—the girl, Ziva, offered me a drink and went into the house to fetch it. Daniel, after shaking my hand, returned to his drums, where he sat quietly beating out a rhythm. Ari danced on the lawn, occasionally picking up his tambourine, then tossing it aside to turn a cartwheel or grab a handful of crackers from the table.

After introducing himself, Sabine's husband, David, set to work roasting meat on the barbecue, long strips of sirloin with vegetables that smelled fabulous. Sabine and I sat in the sukkah. A breeze filled the structure with cool movement, the walls of fabric undulating gently around us. The palm fronds above smelled dusty and tropical, though there was no reason I should know what "tropical" smelled like.

We faced the walking path and, beyond it, the canal. A blue rowboat paddled by, two shirtless men inside it. They waved and Sabine raised her hand in response.

It was quiet in the sukkah. It reminded me of Catalina Island and I felt at home, peaceful. I was still a little worried, though, about being in the way.

Before I could voice my concerns, Sabine said, "Ari is right, you know. This celebration *is* for you—or any guest we are fortunate enough to receive this week."

"What are you celebrating, exactly?"

"Sukkot is an ancient Jewish holiday. It's a celebration of the harvest—therefore celebrated in the fall—and it joyously anticipates the promise of rains to come. And, most pointedly, we build a sukkah." She spread her hands to indicate the structure we sat in. "Literally, a sukkah is a hut. We build it and live in it for seven days. The children, of course, love it. Their favorite holiday! It's like camping right in our own yard. And it commemorates all the years our predecessors spent as wanderers, without a permanent home, without a permanent land, until they were permitted access to the Holy Land—Israel."

"Neat," I said, thinking the word wasn't nearly big enough to encompass all Sabine was telling me.

"Indeed," she said. "But I think too the sukkah reminds us of how temporary all of life is, and how there is beauty to be found in that temporality."

"What about the guests?"

Sabine smiled. "Ah, guests. We consider the receiving of guests to be a tikkun—an act of healing. So your arrival was serendipitous. But it is not only corporeal guests we welcome."

"There's another kind?"

"There is. At Sukkot we invite our ancestors to visit and sit with us at our meal."

"Like . . . ghosts?" I tried to keep the dubiousness from my voice, and I guess it's a credit to my acting skills that I think I succeeded.

"Ghosts, spirits . . . different people give them different names."

"Do they come?"

"Most definitely," said Sabine, and she seemed to really mean it. "You see, the sukkah acts like a doorway. It is a liminal space, one in which transition is possible. A portal, so to speak. It allows us to draw more closely to our past—as wanderers—and to the earth itself, as we ask for rain, and our dead."

Another breeze swept through the tent and I shivered. The sun was setting.

Ziva had returned with my soda and a glass full of ice. The perfect hostess, she cracked open the can and poured the soda into the glass before handing it to me.

"Do you really live on an island?" she asked.

"I do."

"And are you really Will's girlfriend?" She sounded fascinated.

I cleared my throat. "I guess. . . . Yes, I am."

"Lucky," she said with a sigh. Then she wandered over to

where her brothers were playing on the grass and joined in, tucking her long skirt into the waistband and attempting a handstand.

"Ziva is in a liminal space, as well," Sabine said. Her voice was thoughtful. "She perches on that threshold between girl-child and woman. Her time grows close. But right now she's free to flit back and forth between the two worlds as she pleases—playing the lady of the house and then joining again with the children."

I thought back to the summer I'd traveled up the coast to visit colleges with my father and brother. I hadn't thought about it in those terms, but I had already crossed that threshold myself.

"The meat is ready," David called, bringing the steaming platter to the table. The kids cheered, and even Sabine and I clapped. When everyone was seated, we linked hands as David said a prayer over the food. I didn't understand the words, but I recognized the language—Hebrew, the same language spoken by Martin to say his prayers.

Hearing David's blessing made me homesick—not for my own home but for Will's. For those evenings I'd spent with him and his father, listening to them bicker and laugh and, eventually, joining them in conversation. Now that they were gone it felt as if a black hole had opened on my island, a void I could do nothing to fill.

Dinner with the Rabinovich family wasn't really all that different from eating at Lily's; the boys fought over who got the last piece of bread, and the voices of all three children seemed to vie for their parents' attention.

Along one of the canvas walls was a smaller table, on

which sat a tall earth-colored ceramic vase. It held a strange arrangement: a group of tree branches, none with flowers. In front of the vase was what looked like a giant lemon.

"Those are nice," I said, waving my fork at the plants.

"You like them?" said David. "That's our *lulav* and our *etrog*."

I nodded like that made sense to me. Ziva smiled, obviously pleased with my ignorance. In her best "teacher" voice, she said, "The *lulav* is made of the branches from the willow, palm, and myrtle trees. The *etrog* is a citrus fruit." Then the tone of her voice changed, turning conspiratorial. "Mama says the *lulav* is symbolic of a penis and the *etrog* is shaped like a womb. But I've seen my brothers' penises and I don't really see the similarity."

I choked on my soda and struggled not to spray it across the table.

"The *etrog* looks like a boobie," Ari said, dead serious.

"Some people do interpret it as such, son," David said, repeating Ari's serious intonation. "But a nicer word is 'breast.'"

"Boobie," said Ari.

Now I couldn't help but laugh, and the others laughed with me.

After the plates were cleared, which no one would let me help with, David and Sabine stacked wood for a fire in the round pit just in front of the sukkah and we pulled our chairs around it. Ari and Daniel fetched skewers and the makings for s'mores from inside the house, and then Ziva lit the fire.

Orange flames licked up into the darkening night, and I felt the warmth blaze up around me. As the kids set to roasting the marshmallows, it occurred to me that Ronny would have loved this place. The holiday, too, and celebrating the arrival of guests—that would have been right up Ronny's alley. He loved playing host, making sure everyone was having fun, refilling trays, pouring drinks. How sad that he'd died without ever knowing about this tradition.

There was an empty chair in the corner of the sukkah. No one had told me what it was for, but I'd have bet it was left open in case any other guests showed up. The kind you *can't* see or offer a drink to. Of course I didn't believe Ronny was sitting in that chair, but we weren't far from where he'd died. Maybe it wasn't far-fetched to think a piece of him still floated around. At least I could pretend.

I hated that my eyes still filled with tears at the thought of Ronny. On the other hand, maybe it was better than the alternative—forgetting about him, hardening to his death. It *was* easier now than it had been a year ago. I could think about the fun things we'd done together, like the trip up the coast, like those hot summer afternoons in our yard as he and Dad dug the pond, without falling to pieces.

But I would never have what these kids had, ever again—a sibling: someone to fight with for the last marshmallow, as Daniel and Ari were doing right now, someone to remember with me our parents' happier times, when they were still in love, before their marriage fell apart.

"Okay, kids," David said when the fire had softened into embers, "upstairs to get ready for bed. Then we'll bring the air mattresses out to the sukkah." He followed the three children into the house, leaving me and Sabine by the fire.

By now the night was velvety and cool, and we both edged our chairs close to the embers. "How about one more log?" Sabine offered, and she retrieved one and added it to the fire pit. After a few minutes it caught fire and we were warm again. Above us a full moon filled the sky.

"So Martin sent you to me," she said after she'd reseated herself, pulling her legs underneath her and wrapping her scarf around her shoulders. "He thought I might have answers to your questions."

I nodded. "He said you know about Kabbalah. About experiencing God." The words sounded stupid as I said them.

"Martin is a generous man," said Sabine. "Actually, I am still a student myself. Most likely I will always see myself as such. But there is something in my nature, I think, a willingness to let go, that perhaps suits me to the ecstatic practice."

Ecstatic practice. That sounded like a paradox to me. "How do you *practice* ecstasy?"

"The word *practice* can mean many different things," she said. "Most commonly, it's used as a verb, and means to work at improving a skill, the way one practices the violin. And that is always true of my ecstatic practice—I do try to improve and deepen my understanding, of Kabbalah, of God, of myself. But that is not the way I mean to use the word at this time. Scarlett, I am sure you realize that there is more to the world than what we can see with our eyes, hear with our ears, or even touch with our hands. My practice is to receive—and to receive, I must be open to what may come to me." She leaned toward me, the fire gleaming two hot points in her eyes. "There is another world, Scarlett, right here in this one. Only we must search for it."

"But how?"

"I want you to visit me again. Will you do that?"

I nodded.

"Good. But between this visit and the next, I want you to focus on opening yourself to the possibility that there is more than you know, more than you have experienced. Open yourself to the possibility that you may be wrong about the way you see the world. And try—try very hard—to say yes to new experiences, to listening to new perspectives. See what you can see."

"All right," I said, though it sounded like new age bullshit to me. "I'll try."

"But, Scarlett," Sabine said, her voice growing serious, "be careful, also. For it is in those spaces—thresholds between old and new, inside and outside, known and unknown— where danger lurks."

Mostly her warning sounded silly to me, but one word caught my attention. "You mention thresholds," I said. "That reminds me, on your doorframe you have this little thing. Martin has one too, at his house—"

"A mezuzah," she said.

"Mezuzah," I repeated. "What is it for?"

"I've spoken to you twice tonight about liminal spaces— that union between two disparate areas. A door is just that—a liminal space. These points of transition, we believe, can be dangerous. Has Martin told you about the Zohar?"

"It's a book, isn't it? One of the central texts of the Kabbalah. He said it means 'splendor.'"

"Good," she said. "The Zohar is a source of much of our knowledge. It tells us that dark forces—demons—dwell in the area near a door, because that's where they find sustenance. The Zohar goes on to state that by fixing a mezuzah to the doorway, those harmful forces will be denied entry into the home, turned away."

I fought the urge to roll my eyes. Dark forces? Magical tokens? But I asked, "These dark forces. The demons. Do they have a name?"

"*Mazzikim.*"

"And why does the mezuzah stop them, exactly?"

I thought Sabine heard my incredulity, but she continued just as seriously. "The mezuzah is not just a pretty piece of metal or ceramic. Inside each mezuzah is a rolled piece of special parchment. Traditionally it should be made of the skin of a deer, and the words it bears should be scripted under specific conditions. One set of directions about making a mezuzah instructs that the words be inscribed only on Monday, in the fifth hour, with the angel Raphael presiding, or on Thursday, in the fourth hour, presided over by Venus and the angel Anael."

This was sounding downright freaky. *Deer* parchment? But I was curious. "What do the words say?"

"The scroll quotes twice from the Torah, reaffirming that there is one true God and that God has commanded us to write these words on the doorposts of our houses. Then there is a section from the Torah that tells us that our destiny is linked to our fulfilling of God's will. Outside the mezuzah is written one of the names of God—*Shaddai*."

I poked the dying fire with one of the spears the kids had used to roast marshmallows. Honestly, I felt more comfortable in Martin's world of abstractions and book learning than Sabine's world of demons and magical tokens. But then Martin, too, had a mezuzah on his door.

"As you pursue your own practice of Kabbalah," Sabine said, her voice pulling my gaze from the fire to her eyes, "realize that the things we do matter. The things we *say* matter." She was silent for a moment but didn't look away from me. It seemed like she wanted me to know that what she was saying was important. Finally she spoke again. "Be careful which doors you open, Scarlett. And be careful of what you invite inside."

SEVEN

Creatures of the Night

The visit with my mom was pretty much exactly as I'd anticipated. Weird. Awkward.

I thought about what Sabine had told me—to open myself. But honestly I had no desire to do that with my mother. It was hard enough even to be in the same small apartment with her. I didn't want to experience her point of view. I had tried that with her once already, after my accident on the trail; I'd forgiven her for disappearing into herself after Ronny's death. I'd given her a second chance, and look what she'd done with it.

So the weekend was forced and strained, with me saying no to pretty much everything she offered—dinner out, shopping for new clothes (though I needed them, but I could always paw through Lily's castoffs), going to the movies.

She got stiffer as the weekend went on, and by Sunday afternoon, when she took me to the ferry, she seemed as uncomfortable as I felt. We hugged goodbye, but there was no warmth, not from either side. And she didn't ask how soon I'd be coming back, though she did say, with shining eyes, "Take care, Scar."

When my phone rang mid-crossing, I couldn't manage to answer without the quaver in my voice giving me away.

"Hey, Will."

"Yikes. That bad, huh?"

"Yeah. It was pretty terrible."

"I'm sorry, Scarlett." Will was quiet for a minute, but it wasn't uncomfortable the way the silence between me and my mom had been. It felt nice, knowing he was out there waiting, in no hurry, just there.

"She painted a wall in her living room *purple*," I said. "My dad hates purple."

"Ah. Must be a statement of independence."

I didn't want to talk about it. "How's college life?"

"Good. Really good. Totally better than high school. I miss the island, though. I miss *you*."

I smiled. "I miss you, too."

"How much?"

"A lot."

"What do you miss?" His voice grew soft.

"I miss your thumb brushing my palm," I said.

"Anything else?"

I glanced around the deck to see if anyone was looking at me. No one was; everyone was fascinated by the pod of dolphins that swam alongside the boat, leaping and diving.

"I miss your lips," I said. "The way they fit against my collarbone."

"I miss that too."

"I miss the way you pull me tight after we kiss for a while."

"Mm-hmm."

"I miss the way it felt that day on the trail . . . the weight of you on top of me."

He made a sound like a groan.

"What do *you* miss?" I asked.

"I miss your hair," Will said. "The smell of it when you let it down, the brush of it against my arm."

"Is that all?"

He laughed, throaty and deep. "If you only knew everything I miss."

"Tell me."

He was quiet, and this time I was the one who waited.

At last he said, "I miss your smile. I miss the way you look in those jeans of yours—the ones with the ripped knee—both coming and going."

I was blushing now.

"I miss your eyes. The way they close partway when I kiss your collarbone. I miss the way you hold your breath sometimes, when you want to feel something deeply, when you're really paying attention to my hands. I miss watching you ride your horse. I miss your laugh."

"That's a lot to miss," I said at last, warm to the core and full of pleasure. "Maybe you should come home."

"Maybe I should," he said. "Or maybe you should come visit me."

I laughed. "Yeah, I'm pretty sure my dad isn't putting me on a plane and sending me all by myself to my sexy boyfriend on the East Coast."

"You think I'm sexy?" He sounded pleased.

"You're all right," I said.

"All right?"

I laughed again. "Come on, Will," I said. "You know you're dead sexy."

"As long as you think so, Scarlett, that's good enough for me."

"I *know* so."

The next day after school, I rode my mare to Will's house. Martin had been gone from the island for more than a week now, and I hadn't been over yet to check on things. That was kind of a joke, though, really; what was there to check? I knew everyone who lived on the island, and no locals were going to mess with the Cohens' house. Tourists weren't anything to worry about, either; barely anybody who visited Catalina made their way to Two Harbors, and those who did stuck pretty close to the beaches.

So I saw through Martin's request that I keep an eye on his place. It was for me, not for him, that he'd given me his key.

Turning it in the lock was a strange feeling. The door swung open and then there I was, in their space, only without them. I didn't stay long; I just looked around to make sure that nothing was out of place, which of course it wasn't. The last room I checked was Will's. I pushed his door open gently and stood in the doorway, looking in.

There it was—his neat single bed, its gray flannel blanket pulled tight and tucked underneath the mattress, military-style. His desk, cleared now except for his green-glass-shaded library lamp. His books, the paintings on the wall that his mother had made for him. I didn't go into Will's room, not that day.

Instead I browsed the bookshelves in the front room. I was amazed by the breadth of subjects: psychology, science fiction, popular culture, religion (of course), and a pretty staggering collection of Agatha Christie books. Maybe Martin had her complete works, even. This was a surprise; I hadn't really considered Martin the mystery type, but then I thought about what his main goal had been for the past few years—to solve the mystery of Will's abilities, to find an answer and maybe even a cure.

So I guess there was something satisfying about a book that told you the answer at the end, all neat and tied up with no loose strings, when in real life answers didn't come so easily, if at all.

I had read a couple of Agatha Christie's books, one because it was assigned freshman year, and a couple more because I'd liked the first. Now I found myself scanning the titles. I pulled a collection of her short stories from the shelf and tucked it—along with another book that caught my eye, *Kabbalah Magic*—into my jacket before locking up the cottage and retrieving Delilah from the backyard, where I'd left her to graze.

"Will would want us to."

I shook my head, again. "No way, Lily."

"Will's a fun guy. He'd appreciate the opportunity."

We were in Lily's room, listening to music and weeding through her closet, trying to find inspiration for Halloween costumes. And Lily was desperately trying to convince me that it was a good idea to throw the party at Will and Martin's house.

"Come on," she said, sounding desperate now. "This is a once-in-a-lifetime opportunity."

"It's a *never*-in-a-lifetime opportunity," I corrected. "It's not going to happen, Lil."

She sighed and balled up the yellow chiffon scarf she'd been arranging around her waist, then threw it. It drifted benignly to the floor, not exactly the impact she'd probably been hoping for.

There was a knock on the door. *"Entrez,"* Lily called grandly.

Her mom poked her head inside. "We're going to start a round of Pictionary downstairs. You girls want to join us?"

I started to say "Sure" just as Lily answered, "We'll pass."

Laura looked disappointed.

"Hey," I said, "maybe we could have the party *here*. What do you say, Laura? A Halloween party?"

Lily groaned and flopped back onto her bed. "Great," she muttered.

"That sounds like fun." Laura perked up immediately. "Can the boys and I help decorate?"

"Absolutely," I said.

After Laura had gone downstairs, Lily said, "A party with the folks wasn't exactly what I had in mind, Scar."

It sounded just right to me. Honestly, no party at all

would have been my first choice, but I knew Lily would never stand for that. After last Halloween, I was content never to see another costume as long as I lived.

But Lily loved parties. And I loved Lily. So I wasn't about to wreck Halloween for her, even though Andy had come close to wrecking it for me. And ever since Lily's Dutch guy had blown her off, she seemed kind of fragile, mopey. Not like her. Maybe a party *was* what she needed.

"It'll be fun," I said. "I'm sure your parents will stay pretty much out of the way."

"It would have been way better at Will's place," she said, but I didn't answer. Finally she brightened. "Well, if I'm the hostess, then I'd better have the most fabulous costume there."

Two weeks before the big night, Lily came to my place and barged into my bedroom, her dark curls wild, breathing hard as if she'd been running. Of course this immediately got my attention—Lily never ran. ("It makes me sweat" was her rationale.)

"Brainstorm," she said. "I've manifested the theme for our Halloween party."

"Isn't the theme Halloween?"

"Oh, Scarlett, there you go again. Always so *obvious*."

"Okay," I said, setting aside *The Thirteen Problems*, the Agatha Christie book I'd borrowed. "What's the theme?"

Lily held her hands out as if she was framing a billboard. "Picture this: 'Creatures of the Night.'"

"Isn't that pretty much synonymous with Halloween?"

She shook her head vehemently. "You don't get it. See, usually people dress up like all kinds of things: ballerinas, athletes, characters from video games. It's all over the place. There's nothing *unifying* about a party full of all that. No *harmony.*"

"Uh-huh," I said, "so how will your party be different?"

"*Our* party. You have to help decorate."

"Our party, then."

"Everyone has to come as a creature of the night—you know, strictly things that don't show their faces during daylight hours. Or things that get their strength from darkness. Like witches. And vampires."

"Could I be an owl?" I was warming up to the idea.

"If you want to be a completely unattractive ball of feathers, I guess," she said. "Or you could be a fox. They're nocturnal, and way hotter."

I have to give credit to Lily's parents; they jumped in with both feet. Laura pulled Lily and me out of school on Monday to go shopping on the mainland for costume supplies and decorations.

"We can ask your mom to meet us for lunch," she suggested, but I shook my head.

"She's too busy right now at the office," I lied smoothly, as if we talked on a regular basis and I was intimately aware of her schedule.

It was good to see Lily and her mom enjoying each other—shopping together and laughing—like old times. Since their return from Amsterdam I had watched Laura trying so hard, only to be shut down by Lily over and over again.

It took us two full days to decorate for the party. We did the whole downstairs—the kitchen, the living room, the dining room, even the bathroom—and both the front yard and the back.

Laura made Jack move out most of the living room furniture, and what was left we draped in white sheets. All the black frames on the walls that showcased family pictures were filled instead with creepy old-fashioned portraits with eyes that looked like they were following you.

We stripped the games from the shelves under the front window and replaced them with layers of spooky and amazing decor: black vases filled with beautiful flowers, little rubber spiders and snakes and worms crawling across their satiny petals; tree limbs, leaves and all, spray-painted black and silver and arranged across the shelves and in tall urns that flanked the fireplace; a row of heavy crystal punch bowls, each waiting to be filled with either a bloodred concoction or a bizarrely bright toxic-green punch; decanters stuffed with what looked like body parts preserved in formaldehyde (they were really rubber and plastic, of course, but it was almost impossible to tell); domed glass cloches perched atop antique pedestal stands piled with skulls and the skeletons of small animals.

In the dining room, we draped the chandelier in cheesecloth spiderwebs and wrapped each arm of it with tiny strands of connected spiders until the whole thing looked infested. We spread a heavy black velvet cloth over the table and made a centerpiece out of gourds we'd spray-painted silver and gold, then interspersed them with black-dipped branches and leaves. On the branches we perched creatures of the night: tiny owls and mice and more spiders, spiders, spiders.

But the inside of the house was nothing compared with the outside. In the front yard we went for the traditional graveyard scene: tall headstones, an open casket off to one side with a full-sized mannequin corpse resting in it, and black lanterns, each with a candle, lining the path to the door. We taped black-paper silhouettes of spooky figures in each of the upstairs windows and left the lights on so they'd really stand out. In one window was the outline of a hanging body, in another was an arched-back cat. On either side of the front door perched an ominous gargoyle.

The backyard was the pièce de résistance. Right outside the back door, Jack set up a witch's cauldron full of dry ice, and on Halloween night it released a steady flow of slowly spreading smoky fog that hovered just above the ground. Jack really got into the decorating, and with the twins' help he strung long thin ropes back and forth across one corner of the veranda to form a massive spiderweb. In its heart they placed a giant, red-eyed, fanged spider bigger than my head.

The boys had a great time making ghosts; they wrapped foam balls in white gossamer fabric to form the ghosts' heads and then trailed yards of it to make the bodies. Jack hung them in the trees.

And he left the lights on in the pool to showcase the body in it. Dressed in a pair of Jack's old trousers and a jacket, it was made from foam so that it wouldn't sink. Lily staple-gunned a ratty old wig on its head. Floating facedown, it made a creepily convincing body.

Lily put up a pretty strong fight against my costume

choice, but finally she gave in. Being an owl just sounded like too much fun to let Lily talk me out of it.

"Fine," she said at last, "if you insist. But you have to let me help you design it."

Of course this was code for "make the costume more slutty," but okay, whatever, if it made her happy. And I had to admit, it turned out pretty amazing. We dyed one of her old ballet leotards brown ("I can't fit the girls in it anymore, anyway, but you won't have that problem, Scar"), and then whipstitched yards of feather boas—brown, black, white, and creamy yellow—around and around it. She let me wear brown tights under a pair of feather-wrapped leg warmers that she had me pull just above my knees ("Some owls have feathers on their legs, isn't that cool?"), and she fashioned a pair of talons out of strips of leather glue-gunned to ballet slippers. I don't know why she thought it was owlish, but she French-braided my hair and wound it around my head, pinning the braids at the nape of my neck. Then she went to work with loose feathers, bobby-pinning them in my hair, concentrating on forming two points on the top. ("You're a great horned owl," she informed me.)

The face paint was last. Mostly she focused on the eye makeup, brushing on dark feathery lines close to my lashes, then yellow a little farther out, and finally white.

"Okay," she said. "Close your eyes. I have a surprise."

Groaning, I obeyed. I felt her affixing something to my eyelids and silently gave thanks that she seemed to have nothing more bizarre in mind than fake eyelashes.

"There," she said, in her particularly satisfied Lily way. "Open your eyes and look."

She was holding a mirror. It took me a minute to understand what I was seeing. Above each of my eyelashes was a row of tiny, delicate feathers, black and white and brown and gold. They were beautiful.

"Lily, I think I am the sexiest owl ever," I said.

"Damn straight," she said. "There was no way I was going to let you look lame at your own party."

I loved Lily. The party was *her* idea, at *her* house, populated largely by *her* friends—I'd never felt really close to anyone since I'd disappeared the year before—but still, Lily called it my party, too.

"So, what are *you* going to be? Will you tell me yet?"

"Nope. You know I work solo. Go downstairs and try not to screw up your makeup. I'll be ready soon."

Downstairs I took a couple of pictures of myself and texted them to Will.

He replied almost at once—*I'll be your prey anytime!*— and then a couple of minutes later—*Be careful.*

Lily's brothers were skeletons in matching black long-sleeved shirts and pants that Lily had painted with glow-in-the-dark paint. She'd done their faces, too, and they were having fun shining a flashlight in each other's faces and then closing themselves inside the closet to see their bone paint glow.

Of course Lily's first choice had been no parents or brothers at her party, but she'd finally relented; as long as they stayed in the kitchen, they could refill trays and platters. Jack rolled his eyes but bit back his comment and promised to stay well hidden. Even so, he and Laura were fully costumed—Jack as a dead butler, his face painted white and his throat slashed across with red, and Laura as a raccoon, complete with ears and a fluffy tail.

Finally Lily came down the wide Tiffany-blue staircase. My mouth fell open, literally. My first thought was, *Damn.* My very next thought was, *There's no way Jack's letting her wear that.*

She was dressed in what I can only assume was modified lingerie; the milky domes of her breasts crested fabulously from a tight black corset cinched over a diaphanous black skirt that reached less than a third of the way down her thighs. Her legs were poured into shimmery black fishnets and shoes she must have bought off a fetish website: mid-calf, black patent leather or maybe vinyl, with silver grommets all the way up the front and steampunk-inspired metal casings over the three-inch heels.

"Well?" she said when she reached the bottom of the stairs, and then turned around to show me the rear view. A pair of iridescent black wings splayed across her back, and her impossibly short skirt was bustled up even shorter to reveal something that took me a minute to wrap my mind around: her ass, glowing yellow. She had somehow attached rows of tiny LED lights across her panties.

"What do you think?" she asked, looking over her shoulder at me, grinning. Then I noticed she was wearing a pair of glittery yellow antennae; her face was dusted with shimmer and her eyelashes were two inches long and gold.

"You're a firefly," I said, impressed.

"Bingo."

Jack and Laura came out of the kitchen. For a second, as I watched Jack's whitened face turn a murky shade of red, I thought maybe he would go into cardiac arrest. But then Laura laid her hand on his arm and whispered something in his ear, and gradually the pounding vein in his forehead receded.

"Wow, you girls look fabulous!" Laura said.

"Won't you be . . . cold in that, Lily?" asked Jack.

"Nope. I run hot," she said.

I choked back a laugh.

Mercifully, the doorbell rang. And then the party started.

I had to hand it to them; the teenage population of Catalina Island brought their best game that night. The first bunch of guests included Jane Maple, whom I'd always liked, looking really pretty in a white Grecian gown and lace-up sandals, carrying a bow and arrows as Artemis, goddess of the hunt and the moon. With her were Kaitlyn Meyers—a predictable, if undeniably adorable, black cat, whiskers and all—and Katie Ellis dressed as a gray mouse.

Just after we got them drinks, and while they were still admiring the decorations, a bunch of other kids poured in, loud and boisterous. Andy led the pack, of course, dressed as a werewolf, his teeth gleaming like a canine's when he smiled.

"You sure look good, Scar," he said.

I thanked him but didn't return the compliment and scanned the rest of the group. "Where's Connell?" It was rare to see one of them without the other.

Andy shrugged. "I don't know. He'll get here when he gets here."

He sounded irritated, but I didn't think about it for long. Not my problem.

"Hey, Lily, could you back that thing up over here?" called Josh Riddell, the guy she'd dated briefly last year after winter formal. He was a bat; he wore a black long-sleeved tee and tight black jeans, and he'd made a pretty tricky pair of wings out of a dismantled and repurposed umbrella. "I'm having trouble reading this label. . . ."

Gamely, Lily aimed her rear near Josh's hand; he was holding a bottle and pretending to make out the words printed on it.

By eleven, the party had moved outside onto the back patio. The music was thrumming loudly. Occasionally, Jack appeared to turn it down, but as soon as he'd gone back inside, someone would crank it up again.

Of course Lily's parents' intent had been to host a dry party, and there were plenty of nonalcoholic choices—tubs full of sodas and water bottles, along with the disgusting-looking punch inside—but they sat largely untouched after Mike Ryan, dressed as Frankenstein's monster, replete with stitches and screws in his neck, arrived with several cases of beer and a few bottles of something stronger.

"We can't let those kids drink at our house," I heard Jack telling Laura in the kitchen when I headed inside for more chips.

"Oh, Jack," she said, "don't be such a hypocrite. We both know how much you drank in high school."

"Well, you weren't exactly captain of the sobriety club yourself," he shot back at her.

"I didn't say I was. But come on, Jack, you know it's better to let them drink here than to send them off to party who knows where. And it's not like they'll be *driving* anywhere."

I backed away from the door without the chips, not wanting to hear them fight. *I* wasn't drinking, and I kept diluting whatever was in Lily's glass with soda every chance I got.

The party got louder and louder, and the dancing got more and more questionable. At the center of the crush of bodies was Lily, Josh Riddell's bat wings extended around her, and someone else—a green horned goblin in a red-and-black striped tee and an open vest. Even painted green, Connell's thick neck was recognizable. Lily tilted her head back, making the long line of her throat even longer, the slope from her chin to her breasts hypnotizing. As she raised her hands above her head, all eyes were on the black lace of her corset, and everyone seemed to be wondering if it would slip low enough to reveal her nipples.

I shook my head and turned away. Even though I was already outside, I needed some air. Along the back of the Adamses' yard was a row of palm trees, each tree lit from below, casting their long shadows, spear-like, across the grass. I headed in that direction, taking a few steps away from the music and the bodies.

There was a smell—something spicy, smoky. I didn't know where it was coming from. And then, from the shadow of the farthest palm, stepped a figure. A guy.

A plume of smoke rose from his hand as he brought his

cigarette to his lips. In the glow of its ember, I saw his lips—full, somehow giving the impression of a smile even as he smoked. A clove cigarette; it glowed more brightly as he sucked, and I inhaled too.

I stepped closer. He was dressed in black, head to foot—a silk collared shirt, open at the neck, and black slacks pleated down the front of each thigh. He wore black wing tips, not tennis shoes or flip-flops, but grown-up shoes, freshly shined.

He was tall. His hair, longish, dark blond, was brushed back from his forehead, glistening with pomade. As he stepped toward me, I saw his eyes—the right one was light blue, like a piece of sky; the left green and brown, mottled like a marble.

"What are you?" I asked.

He took the cigarette from his lips and tapped ash on the grass. "Do you mean what, or who?" His voice was clipped, British.

"Who, of course," I said, but I wasn't completely sure.

"Gunner Montgomery-Valentine, at your service," he said with an ironic little bow.

"Where did you come from?"

"No introduction in return?"

Dropping his cigarette, he ground it out. The smell of cloves still wafted around him. When I didn't answer, he shrugged. "I came from the ferryboat. And before that, a taxi. Before that, two airplanes, with an uncomfortable layover in Houston. If you want to go all the way back, I suppose you could say I came from a twinkle in my father's eye." He stepped forward again, so close that I could see exactly where the brown met the green in his left eye. Then he held out his hand.

I shook it. His fingers were long and smooth, and when I pulled away I knew my hand would smell like his cigarette.

"I'm Scarlett," I said. "Pleased to meet you."

"The pleasure is mine, I'm sure."

"Hey, Red Hot!" Connell came bounding toward us like an oversized goblin-dog. "You met Gunn."

Ah, so this was Connell's exchange student. I'd heard his family was hosting one this year. "You're from England," I said.

Gunner smirked at me. "Just so."

"Why didn't you come at the beginning of the school year?"

"Full of questions, isn't she?" Gunner said to Connell. Then, to me, "There was a holdup with my passport. But I'm here now. Anything else you'd care to know?"

I shook my head.

"Then maybe you could introduce me to your friends."

"I'll introduce you," Connell offered.

"We'll all go," Gunner said, linking his arm through mine. "By the way, you make a lovely owl."

"Thanks," I said. "You didn't wear a costume."

"Not really my thing."

A slow song was playing, and pretty much everyone was paired off. The dry ice released a steady flow of misty fog. Lily was dancing with Josh, again; his chin rested in her curls and his hands around her waist crept a little lower than I knew Jack would approve of.

"Um . . . they look busy," I said. "Do you want a drink or something?"

"I could use a cup of coffee," Gunner said. "Jet lag, you know."

"Oh. Well, I'm sure we could find something in the kitchen."

I didn't know exactly how I'd become the official tour guide for Connell's guest, but Lily had said this was my party, too, and seeing as she was otherwise engaged, I figured the responsibility fell to me, especially as Connell had been pulled into the crush of dancers.

"Should we go inside?" Gunner asked.

I felt a flash of something, like a warning, a tingling up my spine. The hairs on my neck prickled. But I looked around, and everything seemed fine. "Sure," I said, pulling open the French door to the kitchen. A finger of dry-ice fog swirled inside. "Come on in."

EIGHT

Lines Straight and Curved

"*O*hmygod, Scarlett, he's like an answer to my prayers."

"You don't pray, Lily."

"But if I did."

The party hadn't ended until two a.m., at which point Jack had finally pulled the plug—literally—on the music and announced, "It's two o'clock in the morning. Halloween is over. *October* is over. Go home."

After the last guests had left, Lily and I scrubbed off our face paint and fought our way out of our costumes before hitting the hot tub. My hair was still twisted up in braids and I watched a brown feather drift down from it and float on the bubbling, steaming water.

"He looks like Adrian. But with muscle tone. And his accent . . ." Lily sighed. "British accents are so much sexier than Dutch ones, don't you think?"

"I don't know, Lil," I said. "I don't think I've ever heard a Dutch accent."

"Huh," she said. "Well, British accents are *way* hotter."

"I'll have to take your word for it."

We hadn't bothered with bathing suits, which had been fine with me until my gaze landed on the still-floating body just feet away in the pool. With a jolt of fear, I suddenly felt overexposed. Around us the ghosts swung gently in the trees. Our guests gone, the music silenced, Halloween seemed at last to have arrived.

"Are you ready to go inside?" I asked.

"In a minute," said Lily. The steam made her curls even curlier, if that was possible. "What do you think is up with his eyes?"

I shrugged. "It's rare, but some people have eyes like that."

"I've never seen anything like it."

"Someone's got a crush," I teased, but I didn't feel playful. Not really.

Lily looked at me appraisingly. "More than some*one*," she said.

Of course that was ridiculous. "Come on, Lil."

"I'll bet every girl here tonight is dreaming about Gunner Montgomery-Valentine. Not to mention a few of the guys." I got the distinct impression that she was letting me off the hook. "It was a good party, don't you think?"

"The best," I agreed. "Everyone will remember it for a long time."

"Except for Mike," she said. "Did you see how drunk he got? So gross. I think it's sad that he's got nothing better to do than hang out with a bunch of high schoolers."

Less than five months had passed since Mike Ryan had graduated. But already he had worn out his welcome.

"I wonder why on earth Gunner would want to spend his senior year on Catalina Island," Lily said.

I frowned at the way Lily had practically spat the name of our home. "Catalina has got to be a lot warmer than winter in the U.K.," I said.

Lily shrugged.

"The U.K. is an island too, you know."

"Everything is an island," Lily said, sounding bored. "Almost the whole world is water. We're all just floating on it."

At that moment, her statement seemed especially accurate as we steamed, jets pumping streams of hot water at our backs.

"The girls in our class can want Gunner all they want," she said, changing the subject in her gunshot-Lily way. "*I'm* going to get him. No matter what."

Maybe it was just me. Maybe it was the body floating facedown a few feet away. Maybe it was the ghosts in the trees all around us. But Lily's words sounded like a warning.

At school on Monday, it was clear that the girls were all taking it up a notch. For once, Lily wasn't the only one in heels, and Jane Maple was wearing her hair in a new way, parted on the side and combed across her forehead like long bangs, then pinned in place.

Lily surprised me with the relative casualness of her outfit. She was wearing a Levi's jean skirt—which she'd made extra short by turning up the bottom an inch or so, like rolled-up jeans—and a plain white tee. Well, it was plain in *color,* but it wasn't the kind of tee you buy in a plastic-wrapped three-pack at Target. The neckline was loose and swingy and wide, exposing her shoulders. Little cap sleeves tied up with bows revealed her arms. The fabric was soft and cloud-light. On her feet were white leather platform sandals ("No one pays attention to that stupid Labor Day rule anymore," she told me).

"You like it?"

"Sure," I said. "You look great. Just not as fancy as I would have guessed."

"I'm going for pure Americana," Lily said seriously. "For a British boy to come all this way, he must have a thing for American girls. So look." She pointed to her head. Perched in her hair was a pair of red heart-shaped sunglasses. "Red," she said, then pointed to her T-shirt and then her skirt, "white, and blue."

"Ah. I guess I didn't get the memo," I joked. Lily popped open a little compact to check her lipstick.

"Oh, come off it, Scarlett," Kaitlyn said from behind me. "We all know those aren't your everyday jeans."

I hated that I blushed. Lily raised one eyebrow and said, "Well, it's nice to see that at least one of us hasn't gotten all silly over the new boy, Kaitlyn. *You* look perfectly average, just like always."

Kaitlyn, who'd clearly spent her Sunday touching up her highlights, flushed angrily before stomping away.

Lily snapped the compact closed. "Some girls don't present enough of a *challenge*," she said. Then she looked at me. "Those jeans *do* look great on you, Scar."

It turned out that Gunner was in almost all of my classes— English, AP French, Anatomy, even Psychology. There was no drama class this year—Mrs. B, pregnant with her first child, was having what they called a "complicated pregnancy." She'd moved to the mainland to be closer to her doctor and was reportedly on bed rest. So that was a huge downer, but at the last minute Mrs. Antoine, the French teacher's wife, offered to hold a class at the same time that Drama would have been. Unfortunately, she didn't know anything about the theater, so instead she was teaching an intro psychology class. Pretty much everyone who'd been enrolled in Drama signed up for it, mostly because it was more convenient than changing around the rest of our schedules. Connell didn't take it, of course. It didn't sound like an easy A, so he was out.

Lily, who had never showed any interest in the subject, sailed into psychology class the day after Gunner arrived at our school. She gave me her famous innocent, wide-eyed look, like there was nothing at all suspicious about her voluntarily adding a class that involved writing two term papers. I was more than willing to cede my chair—which was right next to Gunner's—to her. It was the least I could do.

And it wasn't just the girls who were affected by Gunner Montgomery-Valentine. From the very first day, the crowd of guys who'd followed Andy around campus for the past three years changed their allegiance. Even Connell jumped on the Gunner bandwagon. Josh started combing his hair straight back like Gunner, but he used way too heavy a hand when applying pomade and ended up looking like a mortician. In the lunchroom, at the table where Andy and his boys always sat, no one seemed to question that Gunner should sit at the head. It was like they could all smell the leadership on him.

It was there, undeniably. The way he wore his shirts—tucked in, belted. The shoes he chose—never casual. The tilt of his head as he listened to the others joke around—like a beneficent warlord. The way the rest of the table seemed to wait a beat to see if he'd laugh at a joke before they'd join in. Creepy.

And, in a way, compelling. I couldn't figure out why my gaze kept tracking him. He caught me looking at him more than once, and each time that slow smirk of his would spread across his face, making me want to smack it right off.

Or something.

Mid-November, I finally made it back to the mainland. Sabine invited me to spend Saturday evening and Sunday with her family, which was a relief since I needed a break from the island but didn't want to repeat the visit with my mom.

I'd gotten pretty good at having normal-seeming phone conversations with her. If I didn't pay too much attention to what we were talking about, I found I could keep the animosity out of my voice almost completely. Eventually I'd have to visit her again, but I wasn't in a hurry.

"Try to take it easy on your mom," Alice said to me out at the stable. I'd just hosed down Delilah and was scraping water off her red coat with a plastic sweat scraper.

"Sure, Alice," I said. I didn't want to fight with Alice. I didn't want to fight with anyone.

"It's tempting to think you know her whole story," Alice said, trying again, "but try to be open to the idea that you might not know everything."

Alice didn't *look* like she was trying to be insulting. "I don't think I know everything, Alice."

"Of course you don't think that. That came out wrong. It's just . . . your mom is a good person, Scarlett. And she loves you."

If I hadn't been in a hurry to finish up with Delilah and catch the ferry to meet Sabine, maybe I would have paid more attention to Alice. She seemed ruffled. A very un-Alice-like state.

Later, on the ferry, her words came back to me. *Try to be open.* That made two people who'd given me the same advice.

The sukkah was gone from the yard and no children were playing. For a moment, standing at the gate, I wondered if the magical feeling I had experienced during my last visit had been imagined. The empty chairs, angled toward each other as if in conversation, felt kind of sad. The little canal behind me seemed stagnant.

But then Ziva opened the door and smiled out at me and I felt the magic all over again.

It occurred to me as I looked around the Rabinovich living room, open to the dining area and kitchen, all one big space, that homes reveal the character of the families that occupy them. This wasn't an original or particularly deep insight—Will and Martin's cottage was appropriately book-filled, the Adamses' space was shrine-like in its worship of family, and this house, full of color and light and art, brimmed with warmth.

What hit me, though, was the thought of my own house and the fact that it wasn't really a home. It was a hotel. A stop-off point for tourists. Our upstairs space suddenly struck me as an afterthought.

In contrast, everything about the Rabinovich house sang of forethought. Of planning. Of intention. Clearly, it was an artist's home. For one thing, the light was fantastic. Even I could see that. And there was art everywhere, not just the hanging kind, but sculptures, collections of seashells and glass, even the fruit seemed artfully arranged. In the center of the house, like a tiny sun, hung this incredible light fixture. It was maybe four feet across, oval, and inset with dozens and dozens of spirals, each composed of even smaller spirals, cross sections of shells. I recognized them from my freshman-year geometry class.

"Those are nautilus shells, right?"

"Yes," said David. Sabine was upstairs, he'd told me, with Ari, who had a cold. She would be down soon.

"The golden ratio," I said.

"What's that?" asked Daniel. He and his dad were playing a wrestling game on the TV. Both of them, the whole time they talked, kept their eyes on the screen.

"It's also called the Fibonacci sequence," I said. "Basically, it's a series of numbers where you get the third number by adding the first two. So it starts with zero, then one, then another one, because zero plus one equals one, then two, because one plus one equals two, then three, then five, then eight . . ." I drifted off because Daniel didn't really seem to be paying attention.

But Ziva was. "Then thirteen, right?"

"Yeah," I said. "Then what?"

She thought for a second. "Twenty-one. Then . . . thirty-four."

"You're good with numbers."

She shrugged, obviously pleased with herself. "Well, knowing about numbers is important. In Torah, every word has another meaning, did you know that?"

"No," I said. "I didn't."

"It's true." She sounded a little smug now. "We study it in our group at the synagogue. It's called gematria. See, in Hebrew every letter of the alphabet has a numerical value, so every word has a number meaning, too."

"Like a code?"

"Uh-huh. Like the number eighteen is important, because it's the numerical value of the word *chai*."

She waited a minute for me to ask what *chai* meant.

I did.

"It means 'life,'" Ziva said. "Are you eighteen?"

"I will be in April."

"I'll be twelve in July," she said. "Then I'll have my bat mitzvah."

I assumed this was the female equivalent of the bar mitzvah, which I knew about because of Will. "I thought you have to be thirteen for that."

"That's just for boys," she said. "Girls mature faster."

She went over to the couch to watch Daniel and David's game. I stayed where I was, looking up at the light fixture. It was beautiful; the whole thing glowed, each nautilus segment so thin that light permeated it.

"Ari fell asleep," Sabine said, coming down the stairs. She looked tired, like maybe she'd fallen asleep for a little while herself.

"Good, good," David said, still glued to the game he was playing.

Sabine smiled at him, indulgently. Then she turned to me. "Scarlett," she said, "we're so glad you've returned."

"Thanks for inviting me."

"Are you hungry? We're ordering Thai for dinner."

That sounded delicious.

"Are we getting lettuce wraps?" asked Ziva.

"Of course," said Sabine. "Why don't you go upstairs and order for us? Be sure to get lots of soup. It'll be good for Ari."

Then she joined me in looking at the light fixture. "You like it?"

"It's amazing."

"Thank you," she said with the pride of a mother.

"You made it?"

She nodded.

"Wow," I said. "It's really cool."

I started looking around the house, wondering what else Sabine had made. The more I looked, the more circles and spirals I saw—in a mosaic around the fireplace, in the backsplash behind the kitchen sink, in the stack of dessert plates on the countertop. "You really like circles."

She smiled. "Yes, but not singularly."

Then I noticed more—the way the nautilus shells on the light fixture were arranged in rays, shooting from the heart of the sun; the angular rigidity of the metal screen in front of the fireplace; the massive dining table, rectangular and heavy in mahogany wood.

"Lines, too," I said.

"You have an artist's eye," Sabine said. "Really, though, it all boils down to curved and straight lines."

"What do you mean?"

"Well," she said, "take a curving line, and continue its curve. What do you have?"

"A circle?"

"Yes. A circle. And any straight line—horizontal, vertical, diagonal—extend it indefinitely, and it's still a line. It projects. It reaches outward, whereas a curved line—a circle—is, by its nature, self-reflective."

"I guess so," I said. "I've never really thought about it before."

"I've spent way too much time thinking about it," Sabine said, "as evidenced by my artwork."

"Well, does it matter?"

She looked at me dolefully. "Everything matters, Scarlett."

I must have looked doubtful.

Sabine went on, "Much in Kabbalah centers on interpretation, symbology."

"So what do circles mean?" I asked. "And lines?"

"Feminine and masculine," she answered promptly. "Take

our ancient rite of circumcision—the cutting away of the foreskin. The shaft of the penis—the line—is masculine. By removing the foreskin, we reveal the corona—which means 'crown,' or 'circle,' the feminine. Some say that circumcision is the ritual act of revealing the sacred feminine within each man."

I shuddered, and Sabine laughed. "Too graphic?"

"Maybe a little," I admitted.

"Perhaps," she said, "but it's important. Even God is both masculine and feminine."

"Then why do we call God 'he'?"

Sabine shrugged. "Most probably as a result of patrilineal society," she said, "but Genesis tells us God is both. It's written, 'So God created man in His own image, in the image of God He created him; male and female He created them.'"

I remembered reading something in the book Martin had given me, about how the Sefirot act as a map of the body of God. And the Sefirot had masculine and feminine elements, too.

"Anyway, in spite of all that, David and I chose not to circumcise the boys," Sabine told me quietly, so that Daniel wouldn't overhear her talking about him. "When it came down to it, we just couldn't cut our children."

Briefly, I wondered about Will. I had never seen him naked, and I didn't know whether or not I'd be able to tell if he was circumcised.

"Here's something else that's circular." Sabine reached into the refrigerator and withdrew an egg. She handed it to me.

The light brown shell was decorated with symbols, which I recognized as Hebrew. It reminded me of an Easter egg, decorated as it was.

"Is it hard-boiled?" I asked.

"It is. It's for you, Scarlett."

"For me?"

Sabine nodded. "And it's no ordinary egg. This egg is a *first* egg."

"A first egg?"

"Yes. It's the first egg laid by a young hen."

"How do you know that?"

"A friend of mine raises chickens. I told her it was important that she give me a first egg."

"But why?"

"You wish to learn about Kabbalah?"

I nodded.

"Scarlett, Kabbalah is a lifetime of study. It is not a hobby. And normally I wouldn't advocate the pursuit of it by a student so unpracticed. But I feel, somehow, that you may have a special talent for it. And I want to help you."

I rolled the egg between my palms. It was smooth, cold.

"I've told you before to open yourself, Scarlett. This egg is special. I think you're special, too. So does Martin."

"Thank you." It made me feel embarrassed and kind of happy to think that she'd spoken to Martin about me. "So . . . what do I do with it?"

"You eat it, of course."

The answer was too pedestrian. "That's all?"

"What did you expect?"

"I don't know," I said. "Something else, I guess."

"The words on the egg constitute an incantation," Sabine told me. "It's a *petihat ha-lev*, or 'opening the heart.' It's meant to help you in your quest to take in what Kabbalah has to give you."

The egg had warmed in my hands while Sabine had spoken. I looked at it carefully—the words, of course, but also the egg itself. It curved perfectly into the palm of my hand. It was a promise.

"I just . . . break it?"

"The strength is in the *intention*, Scarlett, not the words themselves. Crack the egg, and eat it."

Gently, I tapped the egg against the countertop. A spiderweb of lines spread across the shell. I peeled it away.

"As the egg loses its shell, so too should you free yourself of what binds you, holding you back from manifesting your latent abilities. Open the egg, Scarlett, and open yourself as well."

In three bites I ate the egg, focusing on the smoothness of the white, the graininess of the perfectly round, golden yolk. I chewed. I swallowed.

The doorbell rang. I felt myself stiffen, as if maybe that ringing heralded the arrival of some great truth.

Ziva ran loudly down the stairs. "The food's here," she called.

After dinner David watched a movie with the kids. Ari had woken just after we'd finished eating, and demanded soup. His hair stuck up in all directions. Again he was bare-chested, clothed in a pair of orange sweatpants.

"Does he ever wear a shirt?" I whispered to Ziva.

"Not if he can help it."

"What about school? He has to wear one then, right?" Honestly, I couldn't imagine anyone making Ari do anything he didn't want to do.

"We don't go to school," Ziva said. "Our parents say they don't want us to be institutionalized."

I checked her expression to see if she was joking. She wasn't.

"So you're homeschooled?"

"We don't do school," she said. "We live our lives."

The movie they watched was in Hebrew, but it seemed to be something funny. All four of them laughed loudly, and often.

Sabine and I cleared the dishes and then she showed me a little room off the kitchen where I'd be sleeping. Together we put sheets on the foldout bed.

"Tomorrow I'll take you with me to meet my prayer group. But first, maybe I should tell you a little more about us."

I nodded. We spread the quilt across the mattress and then sat down.

"Do you know anything about Hasidism?"

I didn't.

"Have you ever noticed how young people—teens, and people in their twenties—tend to rebel against the generation before them?"

"Yeah, sure, like with politics and fashion, things like that?"

"Exactly. Well, Hasidism, a movement in Judaism, is something like that. It began as a pull away from the meticulous observance of the religious rules and regulations that some believed were smothering the very life from our faith. It was begun in the eighteenth century. Hasidim chose to embrace laughter, revelry, singing, and dancing. Their goal was direct contact with God. But, like many good things, it grew to look a lot like the group it rebelled against—much the same way children, in their adulthood, come to act like their parents."

I laughed a little, wondering which of my parents I might turn into. Neither seemed plausible.

"The group of which I'm a member keeps what we believe is the best of Hasidism and sloughs off the rest. But like the Hasidim, we, too, gather to discuss the Torah and its mystical interpretations. We sing, we chant, we dance. We drink wine. We attempt to feel God, to see the face of God."

"Does it work?"

"It can," Sabine said. "We look not only outward but inside ourselves, as well. We believe that there is a spark of God within each of us. We search for those sparks. We celebrate them."

"It sounds all right," I said.

"Others have searched for God," Sabine said. Her voice grew serious. "Not all have returned."

"What do you mean?"

"One of our sacred texts tells the story of the four sages. They sought the face of God and entered paradise."

"What does that mean, 'entered paradise'? Like, heaven?"

Sabine shrugged. "That's one of the mysteries of the story," she said, "the meaning of that phrase. I think that to enter paradise is to come face to face with the energy, the life force, that we call God. And for three of those four men, it was too much."

"What about the fourth?"

"Ah, is that one more interesting to you than the other three?"

I nodded.

"He returned, transformed."

"Then that's the one I'll be."

Sabine opened her mouth to speak, then closed it. She smiled at me and brushed my hair back from my cheek. "I think you may be right."

In the morning Sabine woke me early, before the kids were up, and we drove to Laurel Canyon. After we left Venice we traveled on the freeway for a while. It was quiet and we moved quickly. Then we made our way back into the canyon and the roads grew twisty. I thought about our discussion from the night before—straight lines and curves. The freeway and the canyon road—or the roads on our island, for that matter—were like that. The first, direct and straightforward, a clear shot; the latter, circuitous, roundabout, complicated.

Finally we turned onto a street called Wonderland. That really was its name.

The house we parked in front of was pink stucco, two stories, with a red tile roof. When I pushed open the car door, I shivered at the cool air and wrapped my sweater more tightly around me, cinching its belt. I was glad I'd worn my boots, but as we rounded the corner of the house into the backyard, I saw a row of shoes outside the door of a small, rough-hewn structure.

"No shoes, huh?"

Sabine slipped hers off and added them to the collection. "End of the line for worldly things," she said.

I unzipped my boots and abandoned them with the others.

"Come on in," said Sabine. "Meet my friends."

I don't know what I was expecting. Long dresses and tunics, maybe, or witchy-hippie chic. What I *didn't* expect was a room full of perfectly normal-looking women.

They all greeted Sabine warmly and welcomed me in a way that made me pretty sure Sabine had cleared my visit with them before she invited me. There were six women— "We believe that prayer should be done in a group, not in isolation," Sabine had told me on the drive—and they had the air of people who knew each other really well. Like members of a family, they seemed comfortable together— touching one another casually, cutting into one another's sentences, leaning into their conversation.

The room was nice. Windows had been pushed open in spite of the cool air and light spilled into the room, creating long, bright rectangles on the wood floor. The curtains undulated in the breeze. It was funny—now that I was looking, I saw straight lines and curves everywhere: in the pattern of sunlight on the floor, in the billowing curtains. Even the lines on the faces of the women surrounding me: around their eyes, fine straight lines; around their mouths, curved semicircles that accentuated their smiles.

After the obligatory introductions and niceties, Sabine said to me, "Feel free just to watch if you want, Scarlett, and join in anytime. We're glad to have you here."

Then we all sat in a circle, and one of the women—Melissa—led us in a chant. I didn't understand a word of it. It wasn't English; in fact, I don't think the words were from any language. It was a chant, a melody, and it was rhythmic in an almost hypnotic way. Another woman beat gently on a drum. As they chanted I began to feel the circle of sound they were looping through, and though I couldn't join their tune I started to feel lulled by it. Around me, the other women closed their eyes, relaxed their heads, and swayed in rhythm with the chant.

They went on like this for some time, losing themselves in the sound of their own voices. I felt myself loosening, too, as their wordless chant filled my head, crowding out other thoughts—of Will, of my anger at my mother, of Lily and Gunner—that fought for my attention.

I don't know who stood up first, but suddenly all around me the women were dancing, spinning and weaving, some with their eyes still closed but somehow no one colliding.

I wanted to stand and dance too. I wanted to close my eyes and move my body to the rhythm of their tune. But something prevented me—I don't know what—and so I sat, alone on the floor, while all around me the women undulated.

There was one woman in particular who caught my atten-tion. She didn't look anything like Lily, but I recognized her as being cut from the same cloth as my best friend. Maybe it was in the tilt of her chin. She had it—or some of it—that

Lily energy that I loved so much, that I so admired. She danced like Lily, too—like she was setting herself free.

I thought of the Agatha Christie book I'd borrowed from Martin. It featured an elderly spinster who lived in a little village not dissimilar from my Avalon. She believed that human nature is basically the same everywhere, but that in a village you can view it up close, as if it's under a microscope. Someone else had said something similar to me once. I struggled to remember who it had been.

Then it came to me. Andy. It had been Andy, at our lunch table last fall. We'd been wondering about Will Cohen and what his life might have been like in New Haven. Andy had said, "You can learn quite a bit about human nature without ever really going anywhere. This little island is a microcosm. If you pay good enough attention, you see things."

I watched the women dance and wondered if it was true. Were there only so many types of people in the world? And were all of us simply variations of those types?

Suddenly I saw a face. Without warning, it flashed into my consciousness for just a sliver of a moment. But it was *not* the face of God. It had one blue eye and one marbled eye, and it smiled, slow and easy.

Around me, the chanting and dancing went on.

He'd started out just walking, restless. Home seemed far away and he was irritated with his father for bringing him here. In his head he was going over the same argument, again, looking for a new way to convince his dad that one semester would be plenty of time for him to get things under control. They could still get back to New Haven by spring.

The beauty of this island irritated him. The winding shoreline, the chaparral, the disorienting view of the ocean—irritating, all of it. He wanted to see ugliness to match the way he was feeling.

And then, suddenly, there was no room in his head for any of these thoughts—the irritation, the sulkiness—for the hook had dug its way once more into the meat of his brain and he had no choice but to follow its pull.

He didn't notice when his body went from walking to running. He barely saw where he was going; pain was his everything. Only by running, tripping one foot in front of the other to go faster, faster, could he keep pace with the tug of the hook in his brain.

He ran on and on, one hand extended, stumbling many times and even falling once. A cramp tightened his right side, but the pain of it was an almost welcome diversion from the tugging of the hook. The trail wound up a hill, curving around a gnarled tree.

Thunder. He heard thunder, but it seemed to be pounded out from the dry packed earth rather than from the sky. He stopped abruptly; the pulling pain had slackened. But the hook was still there. If he tried to turn *away, it would yank him back. He knew this from experience.*

Not thunder. Hoofbeats, coming fast. No time to think, no time to move aside. He held up a hand just as a horse careered around the tree.

The girl who rode the horse had hair the color of wheat. It flew loose behind her; she leaned forward in the saddle, her heels pressed low in the stirrups. Her eyes widened as they connected with his.

"Stop," Will said, and he stood his ground.

NINE
Lies of Omission

I sat straight up in bed, my heart pounding. For a moment I was on that trail again, where Will had found me, only . . . I hadn't been *me*. In my dream, I'd been Will.

I'd felt the pain he'd described, the pain pulling him to crime scenes, the pain pulling him to me that day. Strung out and miserable, I'd *been* the crime scene. *And* the victim, *and* the criminal, all rolled into one.

Through his eyes, I saw myself. I could see myself now—wild-eyed and shocked by his sudden appearance, my face wan, my arms too thin, my collarbones sharp under my skin.

I glanced at the clock and added three hours. It was just after ten a.m. in New Haven. And this was a Tuesday; Will would be in class. I decided to call him anyway. Just hearing his voice on his message, I thought, would make me feel better.

But he answered. "Scarlett."

"Will," I said. "Are you all right?"

"I'm fine," he said.

He didn't *sound* all right. He sounded exhausted, like he'd been sick.

"What's the matter?"

"I'm okay. It's just—last night, things kind of got out of hand."

Breathe, I told myself. We'd known something like this would happen. He'd gotten through almost two months of school without a problem; it had been only a matter of time.

"Where are you?" I asked.

Silence. Then, "It's okay, Scarlett. Don't freak out."

I stayed quiet, shivering even though I was still in my warm bed.

"I'm at the hospital."

I exhaled. "But you're okay."

"Yeah. I'm fine."

"Okay," I said. I made my shoulders relax and unclenched my toes, unwound my tangled legs. "Tell me what happened."

He sighed. "There was a fight. A guy. A girl. Nothing that different. Only . . . I was different."

"What do you mean?"

"There wasn't any pain. I didn't have to go. I was looking for them."

"Looking for them? For *who*?"

"For *what* is probably more accurate," he said. "I was looking for a problem."

I didn't get it. Martin had spent the past year trying to

140

protect Will from his abilities. And he'd been so relieved when Will had told us last spring that things were changing for him, that the pulling was gone, shifted.

"It's been too quiet in my head."

His words sounded like a confession. A terrible thought occurred to me. "Will, this was the first time you've gone looking for trouble, right?"

No answer.

"Will?"

"No," he said.

Now I was quiet. I think he could hear my anger, but he didn't try to talk me out of it. We were quiet together, but it wasn't comfortable like it usually was.

Finally I had to ask. "What did you do?"

"You've got to understand, Scarlett. When you know you have the ability to help someone, it's torture to just *sit* there and do nothing."

"Okay," I said. "I'm trying to understand. But how do you find them?"

"If it's quiet out and I can quiet my mind, I can still feel them. Only it's not like it used to be, that pull. Now it's like an invitation."

"An *invitation*?"

"Yeah."

"Do you do it a lot?"

Silence. Then, "Every night."

Now I was furious. I tossed back my quilt and spun myself out of bed, pacing as soon as my feet hit the wood floor. "And what does Martin think?"

Of course I didn't really think he'd told his father. We both knew what Martin would think.

Will didn't bother answering the question. "I'm sorry I didn't tell you, Scarlett. I didn't want you to worry."

"So you just lied to me instead."

"No. Well, yes, I guess—I lied by omission."

"What happened last night?"

"The girl had a knife. She was going after the guy—her boyfriend, her husband, I don't know. I managed to get between them."

"And now you're in the hospital." Slowly I sat back down on the bed. "How badly are you hurt?"

"I'll be fine. The nurse says I'll be released this afternoon, as soon as the doctor makes her rounds."

"You said there was a knife."

Will sighed. "Yeah. There was. She was going for the guy—his neck, it seemed like. I got between them and deflected the knife. But I couldn't knock it out of her hand. She got me in the thigh."

"How deep?" I heard my own voice and noted that it sounded calm.

"The doctor said I was lucky. It'll leave a scar, but I'll heal."

I closed my eyes. The image from my dream—of myself astride Delilah, barreling toward Will on the trail—returned to me. It was the reason I'd called Will this morning. But it didn't seem important anymore.

As if he knew what I was thinking, Will said, "I'm really glad you called. My dad has been reading me the riot act for the past three hours, and he finally stepped out for a cup of coffee. It's nice to hear someone else's voice. Someone who's . . . not mad at me?"

There was definitely a question there, in the upward cadence of his tone. Was I mad at him? No. I wasn't his parent. I was his girlfriend.

I wasn't angry . . . I was scared.

"I had a dream about you last night," I said, avoiding answering what he'd asked.

"Was it a good one?"

"It was strange. It was like I was in your head. Looking at *me*."

"That does sound weird," said Will. But he didn't push me for more details.

"So with a wounded leg, I guess you won't be chasing after any bad guys for a while?"

Will laughed. The warm richness of it, the familiarity of the sound I loved, from the boy I loved, took the edge off my fear.

I stood again and parted the curtains. The sky was wide and blue. It was going to be a beautiful day.

"I'm bored of talking about me," said Will. "What's going on with you?"

"Not much," I said. "But I've got to get going. School."

"Yeah," said Will.

It wasn't until after we'd hung up that I realized I still hadn't told Will about our new foreign exchange student, Gunner Montgomery-Valentine. But it wasn't like Gunner really constituted *news* of any kind, I told myself.

I dressed in a pair of fitted gray cords with lace-up

moccasins and a soft pink wrap sweater. Underneath I wore a T-shirt in case the weather lived up to the promise the blue sky seemed to be making.

As I clicked closed the front door and started down the path, Will's words returned to me. *I lied by omission.*

Grimly, I thought, *That makes two of us.*

In front of the school, Gunner seemed to have taken a break from smoking his clove cigarettes long enough to instruct the island boys in the finer points of rugby. As far as I could tell it wasn't all that different from football but involved less padding and maybe slightly more profanity.

Andy sat on the steps of the main building, watching glumly.

Since last Halloween night, when Andy hadn't wanted to hear my change of heart about having sex with him—and Will had helped clarify my decision with a few well-placed blows—Andy and I hadn't had a lot of cause to speak. I'd kind of expected Andy to make another move now that Will was gone, but ever since Gunner had shown up, it seemed like the wind had been knocked out of Andy's sails.

"Not into rugby, huh, Andy?"

He looked up at me. "Hey, Scar. Nah, I wanna play baseball next year for Stanford. I can't risk getting hurt by one of those stupid assholes." He raised his chin in the direction of Gunner, Connell, and the rest of the guys. Gunner was leaning into Connell, whispering something to him as he pointed to a couple of the others. Then he tossed the ball underhand to Connell and clapped twice.

When the two lines of boys crashed a minute later, Connell was on top of the dog pile and Gunner was nodding, a half smile on his lips.

A group of girls, Kaitlyn front and center, cheered loudly. As if they had any idea what had just transpired. At least Lily wasn't among them.

"Gunner seems to fit right in," I said.

"Son of a bitch," murmured Andy.

I raised an eyebrow and waited for him to say more, but he wasn't forthcoming. He stood and headed up the steps, yanking hard on the door.

The bell rang loudly a moment later.

As I made my way to my locker and exchanged the books I'd needed for homework for the books I'd need for morning classes, I knew I shouldn't feel sorry for Andy. Not after the way he'd treated me. But I *did* feel sorry for him. Kind of the way I might feel sorry for a dog that had once bitten me and now found itself the target of a rival pack.

I guess I wasn't an "eye for an eye" kind of girl. Never had been.

"Morning, Scar," said Lily. I closed my locker. She was gazing into hers as if she expected to find something way more interesting than schoolbooks inside. Then she turned her head in my direction and grinned. "Hey, we match."

Only a mind like Lily's would call our outfits "matching." I guess they were from the same basic color palette—pinks and grays—but that was where any resemblance ended. Hers involved pink ballet tights, above-the-knee cream-colored woolen socks, gray lambskin ankle boots, and a fluffy pink thigh-length sweater that she seemed to be passing off as a dress.

It wasn't a dress.

"See?" she said, pointing to her shoes. "We're both wearing boots."

"Ah," I said. "Yeah. We're practically twins."

"Well, I wouldn't go *that* far," she said. "Have you seen Gunner?"

"You mean since the rugby exhibition on the front lawn? No."

"Was he playing *rugby*? I missed it. Damn."

"I'm sure there will be a repeat performance," I consoled her, "given how popular today's seemed to be."

"Kaitlyn?" she asked.

"Uh-huh. She's going to need a new set of pom-poms if she keeps bouncing around like that."

Lily smiled devilishly. "She's going to need more than a set of pom-poms if she thinks she has a chance with Gunner," she said. "I happened to overhear her asking him to the movies on Saturday. He abjured."

"He *abjured*?"

"Gunner's word. Not mine. He said, 'Thank you for the invitation, but I must abjure a liaison with you.' I'm pretty sure Kaitlyn had to go home and look it up before she figured out he was turning her down."

We laughed together and headed down the hall to our first class, French. The only reason Lily stuck with the class for another year was because I let her copy my homework. In her opinion, the rest of the world should just get over itself and learn English.

"Hey, you want to stay at my place this weekend?" Lily asked.

"I'd like to," I said, "but I'm supposed to go to the mainland to see Sabine."

"*Again?* Jeez, Scar, I'm going to start getting jealous pretty soon."

"No need for that, Lily. No one could ever replace you."

"Well, as long as we both understand that," she said. "I guess I could see if Gunner is busy. . . ."

We slid into our seats. Monsieur Antoine looked up disapprovingly at us from his desk. His mustache twitched. Seconds later the bell sounded. It was uncanny, the way his mustache always seemed to know just when class was about to begin. You could set your watch by it.

"*Silence, s'il vous plaît,*" he said.

At lunch, Andy wasn't sitting at his usual table. Connell was there, and Gunner. Gunner didn't have a tray of food in front of him; his chair was pushed back from the table and his legs were sprawled into the aisle, crossed at the ankles. His neat black trousers were creased; he wore argyle socks with a laced pair of mahogany leather shoes. His white shirt had a crisp collar. Over it he wore a charcoal-gray sweater-vest.

Every other boy at the table was wearing either flip-flops or tennis shoes. Except for Connell, I saw. He was wearing oxfords. They looked like the same pair Gunner had worn that first night, at the Halloween party. They must wear the same size, I thought.

In his left hand, Gunner held an apple. He bit into its flesh.

I had been standing with my tray, not sure where to sit. There was an open seat next to Gunner, but it felt strange to sit there. Then Lily arrived.

"I am *famished*," she said, "and *this* is what they're serving." She shook her head and her pretty curls bounced jauntily. Unaffected by the uncertainty that had kept me standing, Lily plopped down into the seat next to Gunner. "Come on, Scarlett, sit next to me." I made my way around the table, noting with amusement that the place she cleared for me was *not* between her and Gunner, but rather on her other side.

"So," she said, turning the full blaze of her Lily glory onto Gunner, "tell us what it's like to live somewhere cool."

Gunner laughed. "Your island isn't cool?"

"Don't be ridiculous," Lily said. "This island is like a holding area for cattle that aren't quite ready for processing. We're stuck here with the buffalo until June when we'll be set free. I, for one, will never look back."

Honestly, I was a little annoyed. "It's not like you've really got it so terrible here, Lil," I said. "Your parents adore you, you can get whatever you want shipped two-day delivery, and you go on regular, fabulous vacations all over the world."

"With my *family*." Lily practically spat the last word.

"Family's not such a terrible thing to have," I argued.

"I have to agree with Lily," Gunner said. "Family can be a royal pain in the arse."

"Isn't it cute how he says 'arse' instead of 'ass'?" gushed Kaitlyn. Anything to be part of the conversation. All three of us ignored her.

"What's so terrible about family?" I asked Gunner.

He lifted and dropped his shoulders, the laziest shrug I had ever seen. "They're fine at holiday, I suppose, and when you need someone to clean up a scrape you find yourself in. But other than that, they're not a very good ROI, are they?"

"ROI?" asked Connell.

"Return on investment," Gunner clarified.

"What do you have to invest in them that is so valuable?" I asked.

"Time," he answered. "And really, that's the only commodity we truly have."

"I agree completely," said Lily. Her curls were nearly *quivering* with agreement.

"Gunner, are you rich?"

Down the table, I heard Kaitlyn gasp.

Connell chuckled. "Smooth, Big Red."

"Scarlett!" hissed Lily. "You can't just come out and *ask* something like that."

"Why ever not?" said Gunner. "I find it refreshing. Very American."

I remembered Lily's theory that Gunner must have a real thing for Americana as I felt her deflate a little next to me.

"I suppose by any measure, the answer would be yes," said Gunner. "I am well-to-do."

"You mean your *parents* are rich," I said.

Gunner shook his head. "That isn't what I mean. They *are* well-off, yes. Father is in parliament—he's running for reelection this year—and Mum comes from old money. But I have my own wealth. Mum's father died several years ago and he left me a very generous legacy, along with a sizable art collection."

"Well, there you go," I said. "It's fine to be cavalier about family when everything is easy for you. You don't rely on others so much, to pull together." I was thinking about the summer Dad and Ronny had dug the fishpond. They hadn't hired anyone to help, and Mom and I had been busier than usual inside without them. The four of us worked hard, all summer. Looking back, with my brother dead and my mother gone, I realized that had been the happiest summer of my life. "Not to mention," I said, "you wouldn't have your money at all if it weren't for your family."

"Touché," said Gunner, his smile spreading like warm honey.

I guess that meant I won, but it didn't feel like it. Because I wasn't trying to say that family is valuable because of what it can do for you or give you. What I *meant* was that family is important in some other, not-so-easily quantified way.

"Well, with all that *money* and *art*," I said, saying the words like they were something dirty, "what are you doing *here*? There's not much of either of those things on our little island."

"Come, Scarlett, don't sell your island so short. I've seen the art deco murals at the casino; quite lovely. And your friend Lily is moneyed, at least comparatively. But I've plenty of my own. I needn't look here to fill those needs."

"Then what need *does* our island fill?" I got the feeling he was avoiding my question.

Gunner pulled his legs in from their sprawl, sitting up

straighter. "It's not *my* need that this island fills, but my father's."

"Your father needs our island?"

"You recall I said my father was running for reelection?"

I nodded. So did Lily, and Connell, and the rest of the table. I guess all of us were wondering what could have brought Gunner Montgomery-Valentine to Catalina.

"Well," Gunner continued, seemingly oblivious to the table's collective focus on him, and speaking just to me, his marbled eye almost hypnotic, "there was an incident with a girl. My father found it convenient for me to disappear for a while. Your island is a good place to become invisible."

I was thinking of how Will had come to Catalina the year before for a similar reason—to disappear from his abilities.

"Didja bang her?" asked Connell. "Didja knock her up?"

Gunner turned his attention from me to Connell, who looked a bit uncomfortable by the intensity of Gunner's focus.

"Very American," Gunner said as he pushed back his chair and stood up. Before walking off, he dropped his apple core on the table. It was beginning to brown, and one clear imprint of his bite faced upward like a crescent moon.

TEN

Uninvited Guest

"Up, down, up, down, keep the rhythm, that's right, heels down, shoulders back, up, down . . ."

I stood in the middle of the arena, tethered to Delilah by a longe line. She trotted around me in slow circles, her ears rotated to hear my voice drumming out the rhythm of her pace. Her hooves carved an endless loop into the sand around me. I was the circle's center; the longe line, the radius. Here they were again—the curve and the straight line, the two shapes Sabine had told me constituted everything.

Henry, properly helmeted, sat astride my mare. To Delilah's credit, she didn't really seem that annoyed by the way he flopped and flailed as she trotted. I was trying to teach him how to post—how to stand and sit in rhythm with Delilah's trot to mitigate its bounciness.

As an Arabian, Delilah had an especially bouncy trot, and the situation probably wasn't helped any by the fact that both Henry and Jasper, who was hanging on the arena's rail and watching, were dealing with a serious case of the giggles.

"You're gonna bruise your nards!" called Jasper.

"I . . . already . . . did!" Henry laughed.

Delilah looked annoyed. It seemed her tolerance had found its limit. Nard jokes. She slowed to a walk and then stopped. I flicked the longe whip at her hind fetlocks, but all she did was swat her tail at it. She wasn't moving.

Normally I wouldn't have let her get away with that sort of insurrection, but I couldn't really blame her. I'd been putting up with the twins for close to twenty-four hours, and I was about done with them, too. And now that the sun had finally made an appearance, I wanted to get Delilah cleaned up before it got chilly again. The forecast called for evening rain.

"All right, Henry, go ahead and slide on down." I gathered the longe rope, folding it back and forth across my palm as I crossed the arena toward Delilah.

Henry did more of a jump than a slide and landed on all fours in the sand, which sent both him and Jasper into another round of laughter. Delilah didn't kick him in the head, though, so that was something.

"Let's take her to the washracks and give her a bath, okay, guys?"

This sounded like fun to the twins, who ran out of the arena whooping and hollering, in direct opposition to the rules I'd laid out before driving them to the stable—no running, no sudden movements, no loud noises.

Rather than yelling after them, I just sighed and patted

Delilah's neck. "Pretty soon you're going to have one of those of your own to chase after," I told her. "Just be glad it's not twins."

Delilah snorted as if she agreed and followed me to the washracks. The boys had a great time spraying each other with the hose and thumping the lathered sponge against each other's backs. Idly, I wondered if I could count this activity as their evening bath. They seemed to be getting wetter and soapier than Delilah.

It was Saturday, around two in the afternoon; I was halfway though the weekend.

"Whatever doesn't kill you makes you stronger," I told Delilah. She looked incredulous, a line of bubbles trailing down her forehead.

Laura had called me two days earlier, after dinner on Thursday night. "Scarlett, hon, are you busy this weekend?"

I'd told her that I'd had plans to visit the mainland.

"Oh," she'd said, disappointed, "to visit your mom?"

Not the type to lie unnecessarily, I'd told her that actually I was going to visit some friends of Will's family.

This brightened her mood considerably. "Well, then maybe I can ask you after all. . . . Any way you could switch your visit to another weekend?"

She and Jack wanted to go away for a couple of days with just Lily. "We think it would be good for her, you know, to have some real one-on-one time with us. Jack thinks I'm silly, but . . . I worry, Scarlett, that she's changing."

I'd wanted to say no, I couldn't shift my plans, but the hitch in Laura's voice stopped me. "Sure, Laura," I'd said. "No problem."

So after school on Friday I'd met the twins as they came out of their classroom. We'd walked back to their house for snacks, followed by video games, followed by more snacks, followed by dinner and a movie on their giant flat-screen TV, followed by more snacks.

To break the monotony of snacks and screen time, I'd dragged them out of the house after lunch on Saturday and we'd driven to the stable. I'd made each of them wear a sweatshirt, which they protested loudly, but the mid-November air had a distinct cold snap to it. They thought it was bad enough that I forced them into long pants; I tried to explain that you don't ride in shorts, but logic held very little interest for them. I think it was the fight they relished, more than anything. It gave them something to do.

Planning ahead, I decided we'd have pizza for dinner that night; feeding the twins two nights in a row seemed too herculean a feat to expect of myself.

The night before I'd offered choice after choice—mac and cheese? Chicken? Sandwiches? But getting Jasper and Henry to agree on a meal was impossible. Just as with the fight over the sweatshirts, it was almost like they were *trying* to thwart me.

Finally, I'd fried up a couple of eggs for Henry and nuked a frozen burrito for Jasper before flopping down on the Adamses' enormous couch and feigning sleep so that the two of them would have to work out which movie to watch without me running interference.

They'd chosen something with zombies and had laughed hysterically as the undead ate their way across greater Manhattan. So clearly I should have offered brains for dinner.

On the way back down the hill, I told them we'd order in pizza. When they hollered in excitement, I miscalculated and asked them what toppings they'd like, setting off a ten-minute fight—pepperoni versus sausage.

"We'll get half of each," I said.

A perfectly reasonable resolution, I'd thought, until Jasper said, "As long as the pepperoni is on the *right* side."

"No way!" whined Henry. "I want *sausage* on the right side!"

"A pizza is *circular*, guys. Either side can be the left or the right, depending on how you look at it."

They didn't believe me, or they didn't care. Finally, I ordered two pizzas—one pepperoni, one sausage. They could eat the leftovers for breakfast.

Watching them tear into the pizzas, I smiled. As annoying as they were, I liked these kids. I'd been around them all their lives. They probably thought of me more as a cousin than their sister's friend.

Really, it was a shame that Lily didn't seem to take much interest in the boys. I tried not to compare our situations, but if I'd been as lucky as she was—to have brothers, alive and breathing, even if they *were* giant pains in the ass—I think I'd appreciate what I had instead of being so irritated by them.

Of course, this was easy to *say*, I reflected, looking at the boys' sauce-stained faces as they lay crashed out on beanbags in front of the TV. Who knew what I'd actually *feel* in Lily's situation? After all, I'd wanted to strangle them myself more than once over the weekend.

But Lily was always rolling her eyes at them and closing her bedroom door whenever they walked down the hall. She hadn't been like this forever; when the boys were little she'd played with them a lot. I tried to put my finger on when, exactly, she'd grown so annoyed by her brothers—and her parents, too, come to think of it.

Really, it hadn't happened overnight, more like over the past couple of years. Pretty typical, probably. I tried not to feel preachy or judgy about it. I wasn't Lily. I'd never been Lily—not that anyone else *could* be. I was just me, and my experience was all I knew.

Still . . . it seemed that if I were in Lily's shoes, I wouldn't take it for granted. All of it—the brothers, the home, the warm feeling, and the smells in her kitchen. Food prepared just for me rather than for the people we called "guests" but who were really customers.

And parents who noticed what the hell was going on in my head. Parents who wanted to spend the weekend alone with me.

Maybe that wasn't entirely fair; my mom *had* been trying. She'd left me two messages last week asking—timidly—when we could get together again. I hadn't returned either call. So maybe I *could* understand Lily. Maybe none of us can really appreciate what we have.

I wrapped the leftover pizza in foil and slid it into the refrigerator. With the twins asleep, the house seemed cold and quiet. Outside, the promised clouds had gathered, darkening the sky before its time. The heater clicked three times; then warm air filtered down from the registers. I realized I'd never been in Lily's house like this before—without the noises and rhythm of the family filling it.

Images from the zombie movie came back to me. I wasn't the kind of girl to freak out over scary movies or being home alone. Actually, I was pretty levelheaded. But tonight I felt jumpy. Maybe it was the latte I had downed when we'd gotten back into town after riding Delilah. I'd felt like I needed something to get me through the afternoon with Jasper and Henry, but now I was regretting it. My stomach turned slow flips, and I suddenly wished I weren't alone.

As if in response to my wish, a slow knock beat against the front door.

I waited a moment in the empty kitchen to see if the sound would repeat; it did not. I crossed the room and made my way to the front hall, peering first into the family room to see if the boys were still sleeping. They were.

I flipped on the porch light, then unlocked the door and pulled it open.

He was facing away from me. Still, there were so many ways I recognized him—the slanted set of his shoulders, the left pulled slightly lower than the right; the silky soft fabric of his black shirt—different than the others I'd seen him wear, but beautiful; the tight slimness of his hips. The smell of him—spicy, smoky.

I felt a flash of heat radiate from my stomach downward and I hated myself for it.

Then he turned and smiled at me. In his hand he held a satchel, the dark leather one I'd seen him carrying around school. "You're not Lily," he said.

"Gunner. Hi. Um . . . no, I'm not Lily."

158

"But this *is* her house." He peered over my shoulder, as if looking for proof.

"Yeah," I said. "Lily and her parents are out of town. I'm babysitting the boys."

"Ah," he said. "The boys." Then, smiling, "Well, do you have room for one more?"

I led him into the kitchen. "Do you want something to drink?"

"Anything."

In the refrigerator I found apple juice, sodas, a couple of Jack's energy drinks. I grabbed two sodas and filled two glasses with ice.

Gunner had sat himself at the table.

"So," I said, pouring the sodas over the ice, "what are you doing here?"

He shrugged. "Maybe I have the wrong night. Lily and I were going to work on a project together. For economics."

I'd taken Econ over the summer, online through a junior college on the mainland; Lily, of course, didn't believe in summer school, so she was stuck taking the class this year.

"Maybe Lily forgot," I said, knowing as I spoke that there was no way Lily would forget a date with Gunner, for a school project or not.

"This is fine too," he said, as if it didn't make much difference to him one way or the other. He reached into his satchel and pulled out a silver flask. He unscrewed the lid and poured a stream of honey-brown liquid into his soda. Without asking if I wanted any, he poured some into my glass, too.

I wasn't much of a drinker. The one time I'd gotten really

drunk hadn't ended well, and I could still remember the particular pain of the headache that followed. But a little alcohol wasn't such a big deal, I told myself as I pulled my glass across the table and took a sip.

Gunner wasn't watching me. He'd leaned back in his seat in that way he tended to do, scanning the kitchen. His gaze landed on the book I was reading. It was another Agatha Christie; I'd exchanged it for the first one I'd borrowed when I'd last visited Martin and Will's house. That day I'd sat for a while in the living room. It had been quiet, like an invitation for introspection.

I'd used the time to practice some of what I'd been reading about in other books I'd helped myself to over the past few weeks, techniques for finding God. Actually, I was surprised how closely what the writers recommended mirrored the practices I'd taken up the year before: attention to the details of living; mindful enjoyment of my own body, like when I ran a brush through my hair or let hot water course down my back in the shower. At the Cohens' house I practiced sitting quietly and breathing regularly, and tripped across the mantra-like Hebrew name of God one of the books encouraged the practitioner to repeat. It still felt awkward, but easier each time I said it.

"Is that yours?" Gunner asked, raising his glass in the direction of the mystery novel.

"No. Yes. Sort of—I borrowed it from a friend." It felt strange talking with Gunner about anything even remotely connected to Will.

He laughed. "You sound as guilty as one of Dame Agatha's murderers."

"I'm not guilty."

"That's what all the criminals say," Gunner said.

"Have you read any of her books?"

"Of course. A few of them. She's one of my own, you know. Another Brit."

I nodded.

"And the most popular novelist of all time," he went on. "She's only outsold by the Bible and Shakespeare."

I hadn't known that. "Really? Are you sure?"

"Positively."

I considered this. "Why do you think she's so popular?"

He answered immediately. "People like simple answers to complex questions. They like everything neatly tied up. Resolution and all that. And they like to see the wicked punished."

His glass was empty now. He poured more liquid from his flask atop the clinking ice cubes and added another splash to my glass, though I'd barely sipped my drink.

"What about you?" he asked, leaning across the table. His dark blond hair, pushed back from his face, looked tantalizingly soft. "Do you like to see the wicked punished?"

"Who doesn't?" I tried to keep my tone light and leaned away. His breath had a sweet-sharp scent of liquor. And his eyes, blue and green and brown, were hypnotic.

"*I* don't, particularly," he said. Maybe it was the lilt of his accent, or maybe it was the dizzying effect that sitting this close to him seemed to produce in me, but I found it hard to tell whether or not he was kidding. "I think it's much more interesting when the wicked walk among us unchecked. It makes for more . . . possibilities."

"You don't mean that."

"Don't I?"

He swirled his drink in his glass, making a little whirl-pool.

"I find it interesting," he said, "the similarity between our names."

The rapid change of subject left me a little confused. It took me a moment to respond. "Gunner and Scarlett?" I finally said. "They're both two syllables, if that's what you mean."

He shook his head. "No. Not that. It's their reductions . . . Gunn and Scar. You see it now?"

I did. One could cause the other. Both could be violent. Ugly.

"Why are you here?"

He smiled, slowly, and my stomach did a slow circle of fear . . . or anticipation. "I knew I'd find you."

I shook my head, though he'd confirmed my suspicion that maybe he hadn't really planned a study date with Lily. "That's not what I mean. Not here at Lily's. I mean why are you *here*—on the island?"

"Ah. You want a different answer." He rolled his glass on its edge across the table, leaving a wet line like a snail's trail. "I told you already—my father found it convenient for me to disappear."

"What did you do?"

There was nothing warm in his eyes now, or his gaze. He was thinking about home, and his father. "There was a mis-understanding about a girl," he said at last. "There was a

162

party, and she and I were both in attendance. There was an accident—I wasn't there when it happened, but I was close enough to the scene for it not to look good for my father. The media, you know, they like to create stories that embarrass public figures."

"What happened to the girl?"

"Sadly, she died."

"She *died*?"

"People do so every day."

"What did she die of?"

"Such an American sentence construction, 'What did she die of,' don't you think?"

I said nothing but took a nervous pull on my drink. The ice had melted slightly, thinning it.

"She fell, some say. Or perhaps she jumped. Either way, the result was the same. She was, you know, several stories up."

I felt sick. "You don't sound all that upset about it."

"Should I be? I barely knew her. And people die every day. Do *you* feel emotionally invested in all their deaths? I doubt it. It was merely my bad luck to have been in the same place at the same time as that girl, that's all. And worse luck that my father learned about it. So, here I am—exiled, as it were, to your island until such time as my father sees fit to call me home again."

I shuddered. His cavalier attitude—the way he spoke of the girl's death. As if it was an *inconvenience* to him.

But though I didn't like to admit it, I felt the truth in some of what he said. People did die every day. And most of those deaths didn't affect me. I didn't mourn them all, only the deaths of people I loved. Really, the only death I'd ever truly mourned was Ronny's.

Gunner said these things out loud. Things most people didn't admit, even to themselves. Did that make him worse than me, or better?

But it seemed like something was wrong with his line of reasoning, something I couldn't quite quantify. I hadn't had more than a few sips of the alcohol he'd added to my glass, so I couldn't blame my lack of clarity on drink.

It's not the alcohol that's intoxicating, my inner voice whispered. I ignored it and focused on how I felt about his cold logic. I didn't like it.

"I think you'd better go," I said, pushing my drink away from me. "I'll tell Lily you stopped by."

He smiled slowly, as if he could feel the rhythm of my quickened pulse, as if he read my thoughts in my expression. He didn't argue with me. He just slid his flask back inside his satchel and stood.

I followed him to the door, opening it for him and standing aside for him to pass.

He didn't leave, not right away. Instead he leaned in close, bringing his lips down to my ear. His breath stirred my hair and I shivered.

"You can tell her whatever you want," he whispered. "But we both know I came for you."

ELEVEN
Tête-à-Tête

On Monday in psychology class, Mrs. Antoine announced that our next unit of study would be on dreams. "The first thing you should know," she told us, "is that there is virtually no consensus about the meaning of dreams. Some researchers claim dreams are solely the result of physiological changes that occur during sleep, and that any interpretation of them, while fun, is scientifically unsound. Freudians, on the other hand, argue that dreams are the gateway to the unconscious mind."

Next to me, Lily wasn't even pretending to take notes. She held her phone just under the desk and was doing something—reading a text, maybe—so she didn't notice when Mrs. Antoine started up the row toward her seat.

I tried to warn her by coughing loudly, but whatever she was doing had her complete attention. Mrs. Antoine stopped next to Lily's desk and stood quietly, waiting for Lily to notice her.

165

The whole class waited along with her to see what would happen next.

Finally Mrs. Antoine cleared her throat.

Still not looking up, Lily said, "Just a minute. I'm almost done."

She typed something quickly and hit the send button. Then she looked up at Mrs. Antoine and smiled.

"I'll take that," Mrs. Antoine said, holding out her hand for Lily's phone.

"Sure," Lily said. "Perfect timing."

Lily's complete lack of chagrin seemed to amuse Mrs. Antoine rather than annoy her. After she'd walked back to the front of the class, Lily's phone in hand, I grinned over at Lily. But she wouldn't meet my eye.

Mrs. Antoine went on about dreams, filling the board with an overview of the psychiatrists and psychologists we'd be reading about, outlining each one's core arguments. I took notes mechanically, filling up two pages in my notebook. But I wasn't really paying attention, even though the subject matter was of particular interest to me.

What was up with Lily? Again, when Mrs. Antoine's back was turned, I tried to get Lily's attention, this time by flicking a little piece of wadded-up notepaper at her head. It stuck in her curls, where she left it. She didn't even flinch, her pen moving smoothly across the paper she'd laid on her desk.

That was when I knew something was really wrong. Lily never took notes, if she could help it, which meant she never took notes in any of the classes that we shared. She always borrowed mine.

So if she was taking notes—and ignoring me—there was only one conclusion to draw.

The text had been about me. And Gunner's weekend visit.

I had meant to tell her that he'd come over. But when Lily and her parents had gotten back to the island on Sunday, the atmosphere had just been all wrong. Jack's forehead vein was pulsating again, and Laura, despite her excitement over seeing the boys, emitted a wave of fatigue.

Lily had seemed steely and had pulled me by the wrist up the stairs to her room without even saying hello to her brothers.

"Some weekend," she steamed, as soon as the door was closed. She flopped backward onto the bed.

"What's the matter, Lil? Where'd you guys go, anyway?"

"Oh, they took me to San Francisco. We stayed at this little boutique hotel in Union Square. Here . . . I got you something."

She reached into the purse she'd discarded next to the bed and pulled out a long scarf. It was dark red, swirled through with tiny yellow-gold spirals. It was beautiful. The silk reminded me of Gunner, which reminded me of his visit. That moment would have been a good time to tell Lily about it.

But I didn't. Instead I said, "Wow, Lil, it's amazing. Is it from India?"

She shrugged. "It's from Neiman Marcus."

I laughed. "Yeah, but before that."

"Maybe," she said. "It reminded me of you."

"Well," I said, winding the scarf around my neck and

admiring it in her mirror, "Frisco, shopping, how bad could it have been?"

"You can't call it *Frisco*, Scar," she said. "Everyone knows that."

I ignored her tone. "Whatever," I said. "What was so terrible?"

"Just *them*."

"Ah. Them."

"Scar, seriously, sometimes you're as bad as they are."

"I'm sorry, Lil. Tell me about it."

"Well, it wasn't anything in particular, you know? It's just . . . everywhere I looked, there they were."

I suppressed my laughter. "Well, you were on a trip together, weren't you?"

"Yeah, of course, I get it. But, like, they wouldn't leave me alone, not for a minute. It felt like I was on lockdown."

"Maybe they're still upset about Amsterdam."

"No shit," said Lily. "So am I."

I suspected that different aspects of the trip bothered Lily and her parents.

"Scar, in three months I'll be eighteen years old. A legal adult. And they still treat me like I'm a little kid. They don't *trust* me, Scarlett."

I didn't know how to put it delicately, so I just said it. "Lil, last time they trusted you, you ended up sleeping with some random tour guide."

Lily looked at me dolefully. "You really don't get it, do you?"

I didn't say anything. I just waited for her to enlighten me.

"I don't want them to trust me not to sleep with tour guides." She spoke slowly and carefully, as if to make sure that her words got through my thick head. "If I want to sleep with tour guides, I'm going to fucking sleep with tour guides. That's *my* decision, not theirs. I want them to trust that if I'm sleeping with a tour guide, I've thought through the implications, I've balanced the risk against the possible reward, and I've made an educated decision. That's what I want."

The scarf Lily had given me had been cool when I'd first wound it around my neck. It had warmed as she'd spoken and I'd listened.

"Do you think that's too much to ask for?" Lily asked.

I didn't know. I'd never been a parent. Hell, it seemed that I'd barely been anyone's *child* these past couple of years. Like it or not, I was a free agent. In a way, Lily's point sounded strangely compelling.

So why was I angry?

"Maybe that's asking a lot, Lil, of any parent."

"I don't think it is."

"Well, when you're a parent you can let your daughter sleep with all the tour guides she wants."

Exasperated, Lily said, "You totally missed the point, Scar. It wouldn't be up to me to *let* my daughter sleep with anyone, or forbid her from it, either. It would be up to me to support her and be there if she needed me."

"That sounds good in theory," I said, "but in practice that might be nearly impossible."

"They shouldn't have kids if they're not up to the

challenge," she said. "There *is* such a thing as abortion, you know. Anyway, I'm not having any kids."

That had been yesterday. And this was today. Someone, in between then and now, had told Lily about Gunner's visit to her house, I was sure of it. And it hadn't been the person who should have told her—me.

After class I waited while Lily collected her phone from Mrs. Antoine. She brushed by me on the way out of the room and I had to rush to keep up with her.

I didn't bother asking her what was wrong. "I should have told you he came over," I said as we pushed through the double doors at the end of the hall. The afternoon air was crisp and the sky was bright blue in that particular way of fall days. I was wearing the scarf Lily had given me and I wound it once more around my neck.

No response.

"Lily, I'm sorry. But it was no big deal. I swear."

We were off campus and halfway down the street before she stopped to speak to me. When she finally did, it was to ask a question. "Scar, do you remember last year? When Will first showed up at school?"

I thought back to that day—the way he'd leaned up against the wall of the front building, the way his eyes had found me across the quad. The way his gaze felt upon my face. "I remember."

"And do you remember what I asked you, just before the party at Andy's?"

I swallowed hard. I did.

"I asked you if you wanted to keep him on the back burner. Remember? Even though you were with Andy."

"I know, Lil."

"So what did I do?"

"You stayed away."

"Damned right. Friends first."

"But, Lily, it's not like I asked him over. He didn't even stay that long. It wasn't like that."

"Bullshit," she said. "If it wasn't like that, you would have told me."

There was nothing I could say to this, because she was right. If it wasn't like that, I would have told her. I would have told Will. Instead I'd told no one. A lie by omission.

"I'm sorry," I said, but Lily had already turned away.

I couldn't make Lily forgive me. I knew her too well. She'd forgive me in her own time, in her own Lily way. But she wasn't the only person I wanted to apologize to.

Will answered on the second ring. I guess it had been a little strained between us since he'd told me that he'd taken things into his own hands, so to speak, going out looking for trouble rather than waiting for it to find him. But just the day before I'd gotten a letter from Will in the mail—a real, old-fashioned love letter, written by hand, full of his particular voice and the amazing news that he and Martin would be coming to the island over winter break.

"Hey, Will," I said when he answered. "I got your letter."

"Did you like it?"

What was not to like? "Mm-hmm," I said. "But I don't think I deserve it."

"Of course you do," he said. "Why would you say that?"

"There's this guy," I said. The words caught in my throat, coming out more like a whisper. So I forced myself to say it again, louder. "There's this guy."

He was silent for a moment, but I knew he'd heard me. Finally, he spoke. "Oh."

Tears stung my eyes. I was down by the beach and a bunch of tourists whose cruise ship was anchored just off our island were milling around, sipping lattes and snapping pictures of one another.

"Do you want to tell me about him?" Will said. His voice was tight.

I nodded, then remembered that he couldn't see me. So I said, "I guess so. Nothing happened, Will, it's not like I kissed him, or—anything. It's just that . . ."

"You like him."

"No!" I laughed, bitter. "I don't actually. I don't like him at all."

"I'm confused."

"Me too," I said. Then, "His name is Gunner. He's a foreign exchange student from England. He got here at the end of last month. And I didn't tell you about him," I blurted out, and the tears flowed down my cheeks.

"Okay," said Will. "You didn't tell me . . . what, exactly?"

"That he's *here!*" I sounded hysterical now, and a little cluster of tourists looked at me quickly before taking a few steps away. "And that I like him."

Will laughed, but it didn't sound like he really found the whole thing funny. "I thought you said you *didn't* like him."

"I did. I mean, I don't. I don't like him; he's kind of a bastard. But I'm attracted to him." There. I'd said it. It hurt coming out, the truth.

After a minute, Will answered. It was a long minute, waiting for him to speak. Finally, he said, "Scarlett, you don't have to tell me that you're attracted to some guy. I don't own you."

"I know," I said, "but it felt like a lie, not saying anything."

"I see girls around campus every day. Attractive girls. Girls I'm attracted *to*."

I had no words for this. Logically, of course he did. He wasn't stuck on a tiny island; he wasn't me. I felt a flame of jealousy shoot through me.

"Do you talk to them?"

"Sometimes," he said. "But I don't *sleep* with them."

"Do you want to?"

Silence. Then, softly, "Sometimes."

We were both quiet for a long time. I watched the water. It was dark blue under the day's bright sun. *Entirely wrong weather for this conversation*, I thought.

"So now what?" I finally said.

"In three weeks, I'll be back on the island for winter break," said Will, "and all I want is to smell your hair and kiss your face and hold your hand."

I choked a little on my sob. "Even though I like that guy?"

"I don't care if you like *all* the guys," said Will. "As long as you want me to smell your hair and kiss your face and hold your hand."

"I do," I said.

"Then it's a date."

When I got home, my dad was out somewhere. We didn't have any guests, so the place was empty and I took my time going up the two flights of stairs to our flat. In the kitchen I made myself a cup of tea and took a couple of cookies from the batch that Alice had dropped off the day before. She'd been doing that kind of thing a lot lately—bringing us food, offering to pick up supplies from the mainland when she went across. It was nice of her to want to help fill in the gap created by my mother's absence.

I took the tea and cookies to my room and set them on my desk. Then I found one of the books I'd borrowed from Martin—*The Encyclopedia of Jewish Myth, Magic, and Mysticism*.

I'd flipped around in the book a little bit, but mostly it had just sat by my bedside in the weeks since I'd brought it home. But today, after Mrs. Antoine's lecture on dreams, I began to wonder what the Kabbalists had to say about dreaming.

My own dream—the one I'd had about Will, on the trail—seemed different from any other dream I'd had. In fact, it seemed too clear to even count as a dream. It had been more like a memory.

And it seemed there were others, before that one. Maybe if I cast my mind and searched for something that felt just past my reach, I'd pick up the translucent fishing line of memory that strung other dreams together.

I couldn't do it. I knew there were more of them. I knew they were connected. But I didn't know *what*, or *why*, or *how*.

The book told me that dreams were considered "one-sixtieth of prophecy" and also "one-sixtieth of death." According to the author, the sages of old believed that both prophecy and death "give a person access to the divine mind."

The divine mind. Did he mean the mind of God?

For the rest of the week, Lily ignored me. She was really, really good at it. Kaitlyn Meyers had this ridiculous simper that made me ninety-eight percent sure she had been the one to tip off Lily about Gunner's visit.

So I was pretty surprised when, on Friday afternoon, Connell slammed his tray down next to mine and said, "Hey, Red Vine. Lily's still pissed over that text Andy sent her, huh?"

I turned to look at him. His wide face showed no hint of duplicity. "*Andy* texted her?"

He nodded. "Yeah, I guess after I told him that Gunner had gone over there, Andy thought Lily would want to know what was going on in her own house."

Really, I shouldn't have been surprised. Andy *had* always loved a juicy bit of gossip. Probably if he'd had Will's number, he would have texted him, too.

"It doesn't matter," I said. "It wasn't a secret, anyway."

"Su-ure," Connell said, winking at me conspiratorially. "That's what Gunner says, too. Still, though, even you've gotta admit that Gunn's a pretty big step up from the Jew."

I felt heat flush my face in anger. "Connell, you are such an asshole."

He laughed. "Whatever."

"I shouldn't waste my breath explaining this to you," I said, "but I'm not looking to 'trade up,' as you call it. Not that Gunner would *be* a step up."

"More like a *floor* up," he scoffed.

"You know, Connell, I'm beginning to wonder if maybe you're a little bit jealous that Gunner wanted to hang out with me last weekend. Maybe *you're* the one looking for a step up."

"Whatever, Scar," he said, but his ears were red, so I knew I'd embarrassed him. "See ya." Then he spotted Gunner across the quad and loped off after him, abandoning his tray. I remembered how he'd seemed the night of Lily's party— like an oversized goblin-dog. Even out of costume, the metaphor still seemed fitting.

There *was* something slavish, I guess, about the way Connell traipsed after Gunner. The way he'd followed after Andy, too, before Gunner showed up. Maybe some people are just born to be led.

I couldn't put off the visit to my mother any longer, and with Lily still mad at me, the island felt smaller than usual, so the next day I caught the early ferry to the mainland. My mother was waiting for me when I got off, my backpack slung over my shoulder and the red scarf trailing behind me in the wind.

"Scarlett," she said, and before I could really prepare myself for it she pulled me in, close and tight.

At first I held myself stiff, not really wanting her hug, but she didn't let go. Finally I wound my arms around her waist and hugged her back.

She looked good, I admitted to myself as we drove away from the water and to her apartment. She'd cut her hair; it was a long bob now, with bangs, but it wasn't a "mom" haircut. Cute.

The plan was that I would spend Saturday with her and then Sunday with Sabine. I wanted to go with her again to her prayer group.

My mom was dubious. "Who is this woman again? How do you know her?"

It was annoying, the way she seemed to feel that she still had a vote on whom I saw, on where I went, even though she'd checked out and moved on herself. But I didn't want to fight with her. So I said, "She's a friend of Will's family, Mom. She's a nice lady."

"I'm sure she must be," Mom said. There it was again, the same tone I'd heard in Lily's voice, when she'd confronted me about Gunner's visit, and earlier, when I'd been angry at Lily's distress over her parents' hovering.

"Mom," I said, "are you jealous?"

"No," she said quickly. Then, "Well. Maybe. A little."

We were in her apartment, sitting by a big window in her kitchen. It had a view of Westwood. Outside, people hurried busily along, each in a separate bubble, many wearing earbuds, several walking and texting.

"It's kind of funny that you're jealous," I said, "considering that you're the one who left."

It seemed that this was my week for saying painful things out loud. As with Will, it felt better to have said it.

She grimaced. "I left your father, Scarlett, not you."

And there it was. The truth. She had left my father. At least it was out in the open now, like an oversized slug dumped onto the table between us.

"So needing to go back to work because business was slow on the island . . ."

"That wasn't untrue, Scarlett. The only way we've been able to pay the mortgage since August is with the money I've been sending to your father. But it's not all of it. You know that."

Yes. I did. I just didn't have the particulars.

"So what's the rest of it?" I prodded.

"Have you spoken with your father?" she asked.

I shook my head. First my brother's death, and then my mom leaving him—I didn't want to be confronted by his pain.

"Your father is a good man," Mom said, which I certainly didn't need *her* to tell me. "Sometimes," she added, "people have to make the best of what they have."

"Are you talking about Dad?" I asked. "Or you?"

"Both of us," she said. "*All* of us."

"Well," I said, looking around the kitchen, into the small neat living room with the one purple wall and the new furniture, "it looks like you've certainly been trying."

Sabine picked me up early the next morning. Mom hugged me again before I left, and I tried to give her back some of the same warmth.

On the ride out to Laurel Canyon, I told Sabine about the dream I'd had. I wanted to hear what she thought of it. "It was like *I* was Will," I said.

"Have you had similar dreams before?" She had listened intently as I described the dream to her, and she seemed amped up by it.

I shook my head, trying to remember. "I think so," I said. "I feel like I can almost remember. . . ."

"When we're together today," Sabine suggested, "place your intention to remember. We will remember with you."

"How can you remember *with* me?"

"We are all made of divinity, Scarlett. Each of us has within us, waiting to be found, a hidden spark of God." Then she said, "Theosophical Kabbalah, as you know, is the study of the Sefirot, in which Martin is an expert. Ecstatic Kabbalah is an attempt to know God physically, and intimately. But there's a third form, practical Kabbalah, that seeks to transform the world through our knowledge of God. The egg I prepared for you—that was an example of practical Kabbalah. There are many aspects of practical Kabbalah. One of them is oneiromancy. Have you heard that word before?"

I hadn't.

"Oneiromancy is the practice of interpreting dreams to predict the future. I wonder if you might have a particular talent for it."

I thought about that and remembered something else. "Once," I said, "last year, when Will first told me about his mom and the car crash, I said something to Will."

"What was it?" Her voice was eager.

"I told him it was a good thing that he was sitting behind

179

the passenger's seat, not the driver's. But I don't know how I knew that. Will hadn't mentioned *where* he'd been sitting."

"And now you tell me of this dream you've had, about Will. About seeing the world through his eyes." Sabine's excitement was palpable.

"It's true," I said.

"I wonder if these things are connected. If perhaps you and Will are connected in a way that makes itself clear to you in dreams."

It was tempting to believe this. It sounded romantic, and exciting. Like Will and I were soul mates, woven together on some higher spiritual plane. But if that was true, then I wouldn't have the hots for our creepy island visitor. Right?

TWELVE

Dissection

$\mathcal{M}$r. McCormack stood at the front of the classroom. He wore a white lab coat over his polo and jeans. His usual loose, goofy expression was uncharacteristically sober. Next to him were two stacks of metal trays, each holding a plastic-wrapped shape.

From my seat in the second row of tables—next to Gunner, my lab partner—I had a good view of the packages but couldn't clearly see what they contained. I could imagine, though.

"Before we begin," Mr. McCormack said, "let's have a little chat about respectful handling of the dead."

Over the first two months of school, anatomy class had progressed from dissecting worms to frogs, and today we'd be meeting the fetal pigs that would carry us through the rest of the first semester. In the spring we'd focus on human physiology.

Lily wasn't in this class ("Formaldehyde stains," she'd said) or she would have been my lab partner. Each of us had gotten our own worm and frog, but I guess fetal pigs were more expensive. We had to share.

Mr. McCormack had spoken with us briefly about how to handle the worms and frogs, too, but as soon as he distributed the piglets, each looking waxy and under a sleeping enchantment beneath its plastic shroud, I understood why he'd made a bigger deal about it this time.

These were mammals. Their pale pink skin, sparse hair, and death grins seemed almost human.

At least there was nothing even remotely romantic about dissection. And Gunner was smart—he'd make a good partner. He'd missed worm dissection, but I couldn't help but admire the clean incisions he'd made on his frog corpse. He didn't hesitate, just gently placed the scalpel and sliced right in. Steady hands.

I was a little wary of what Lily would say when I told her that I'd been paired up with Gunner, but after the past weekend maybe she wouldn't be too worried anymore.

I'd only been back from my visit to the mainland for about an hour when Lily texted that she was coming over. So at least the silent treatment hadn't lasted long. I didn't really know what kind of Lily to expect, but when she breezed into my room twenty minutes later it was like she'd never been upset with me at all.

"Guess who took me out on Saturday?" she sang happily.

He sat next to me at the lab table, waiting patiently for our specimen to be delivered.

"We went to the new little French place over by the casino," she gushed.

He sliced cleanly through the plastic, sliding the little body onto the dissection tray.

"And when we got back to my house he walked me to the door and ohmygod, Scarlett, he is an *amazing* kisser."

He held the limbs still as I tied them to the tray—first the left front leg, then the right, and then each hind leg in turn until the piglet lay spread and helplessly dead and exposed on the table.

"Congratulations," he said, handing me the scalpel to make the first incision. "It's a girl."

But before we could begin cutting, we had to measure and examine the body. Mr. McCormack had distributed packets of papers along with the piglets, slapping them down on our lab tables with considerable heft.

I flipped through the packet, getting a feel for the main components of the assignment. We were to work in pairs, mostly at our own pace. Mr. McCormack would roam the classroom answering questions and assisting when necessary.

The first section of the packet dealt with the pig's external anatomy. Our first task was to establish its age. I laid the scalpel aside and picked up the small measuring tape from our supply basket. It was wound into a spiral.

"Snout to rump," I told Gunner. "We don't include the tail."

Our specimen was 21.2 centimeters long. Checking against the chart, I found that it was about one hundred days since fertilization. The chart terminated at one hundred fifteen days. Had the fetus's mother lived just two more weeks, this animal would have been a piglet rather than a lab experiment. And she would have been a mother rather than a pile of bacon and pork chops. Neatly, I wrote *100* in the space Mr. McCormack had left on the worksheet for gestational age.

A row behind me and to the left, Jane Maple was making little sniveling sounds like she was trying to hold back tears. Her partner was Andy. I knew from experience that he didn't deal well with crying girls.

"I'm glad I got partnered with you instead of Jane," Gunner said conversationally as he rewound the measuring tape. "Some girls are quite emotional."

"I have emotions."

"Do you?" I heard—and ignored—the smile in his voice. "Everyone does."

"You have the whole wide range of them then: happiness, sadness, anger, jealousy. . . ." He trailed off, inviting reaction. I thought about him and Lily kissing on her front porch and shifted my attention deliberately to the dissection packet.

The next question asked us to mark whether our pig was male or female. I checked the appropriate box. Then, we were supposed to find another pair whose specimen was the opposite gender of ours so that we could compare. All of us would be responsible for knowing the reproductive structures of both sexes for the final exam.

I turned to Andy. "Male or female?"

"Male," he said.

We took turns examining the piglets. Andy and Jane's had all the male markers: a urogenital opening just behind the base of the umbilical cord; a penis, not yet fully formed but palpable under the skin; and scrotal sacs, two, just behind the hind legs. I watched as Andy examined the vulva of our piglet, making notes on his worksheet. Jane stared upward at the light fixtures.

"You'll need to know all this for the test, Miss Maple," Mr. McCormack said as he passed by.

"I think I might be sick," she said.

"There's a sink at the back of the class." Mr. McCormack grinned, like this wasn't the first time he'd seen one of his students turn green.

Jane hopped down from her stool and headed for the door instead. Mr. McCormack didn't stop her.

"There's always one," he hummed.

Next on the worksheet was the digestive system. We'd examine the mouth and tongue and then begin making incisions to look inside. This piglet, I considered, probably wasn't much smaller than Delilah's foal. Delilah was five months along now. In a month I'd have to stop riding her, and already we'd slowed our work to gentle walks on the trail. Traveler—the horse I'd fallen from last winter—had become my more regular ride.

Right now, Delilah's foal was about the size of a rabbit. According to my equine pregnancy book, her foal should have hair on its chin and muzzle. It had developed eyelids and eyelashes.

I thought about Delilah standing in her stall, munching

on hay. Her coat had grown extra shiny during the pregnancy, most likely due to the corn oil I'd been adding to her feed over the past few weeks. Her hind end had dappled up beautifully. Her belly had begun to swell with life. Inside her, her baby lay warm and safe and wet, listening to the rhythm of her heartbeat.

I was looking at the specimen in the tray in front of me—cold, antiseptic, and dead—but I imagined Delilah's foal, and it was as if I could hear the *whoosh, whoosh* of my mare's heartbeat, and then I was remembering something else—a dream I'd had of a baby in the womb, listening to his mother's heart, knowing warmth and safety.

The scalpel slipped from my hand. I heard the tinny sound of it hitting the edge of the metal tray. I stood and turned toward the door.

"Scarlett?" I heard Gunner's voice behind me, but I didn't answer.

"Funny," Mr. McCormack said, as I pushed open the classroom door. "I wouldn't have pegged Scarlett as the puking type."

I needed air. Mechanically, I made my way down the empty hallway lined with lockers, past the other classrooms, and out the double doors at the end of the hallway. Of their own accord, my feet carried me to the tree where Will and I used to sit. My legs were shaking. I lowered myself to the ground and sat very still, waiting for more memories to surface.

They came.

I remembered the crushing press on my head, my chest,

as I emerged from my mother, the feel of her warm hands on my body, the flash of fear as the beat of her heart faded and the happy comfort of its return as she laid me against her chest. The smile she gave me. The green of her eyes.

The green of her eyes.

My mother's eyes were blue.

Will's eyes were green. His mother's had been green; I'd seen them in a picture. And in my dream. It seemed so clear now, as the images rushed back—Will in his mother, Will being born, Will in the car, behind his father's seat, as his mother's eyes connected with his in the rearview mirror before the crash that ended her life. Will coming to me on the trail. Will, Will, Will. He lived inside my dreams, coming to me as I slept, but more than that—I saw the world through his eyes. I became him.

Devekut. It was a word I had read, more than once, as I studied Kabbalah. It meant to cleave to God—to become one with him—and it felt like what I had done, except with Will. In my sleep, deep in the night, I had somehow cleaved to Will.

In as intimate an act as sex, my consciousness had cleaved to his. I had seen inside his memories; I had felt inside his soul.

And I had no idea how this had happened to me, or why.

A breeze rustled the dried leaves; they rained down around me, brown and yellow. I watched one of them settle on the grass. Another breeze twisted it over onto its back and then it lay still.

Someone was coming. I heard footsteps, and a cheery

whistle. Last year, I had imagined more than once that I could turn my head and find Ronny grinning at me, ambling toward me just as if nothing had changed, as if he'd never died. Those fantasies had faded as time marched further from his death. On this day, under the elm where I had once sat with Will, I found myself wishing that the footsteps I heard were my boyfriend's.

Of course I knew they weren't. Even before I turned to look, I knew who was coming for me—my lab partner, Gunner.

The breeze lifted and turned his dark blond hair, playing it across his brow and then sweeping it back again. His hands were in his trouser pockets; today he wore wide-wale corduroys in deep brown. He had on a chambray shirt, collarless, and over it a brown vest, unbuttoned, with fine gold threads woven through it. I had to hand it to him— Gunner Montgomery-Valentine was a snappy dresser.

He looked down distastefully at how I was sitting, cross-legged on the ground. Then he sighed as if resigning himself and squatted next to me, not quite lowering himself to the dirt.

He took a slim gold case from the pocket of his vest and shook free a dark brown cigarette. Before he spoke, he placed it between his lips, replaced the case, and retrieved a lighter, and brought the tiny flame to the cigarette, pulling on it until an ember glowed at his cigarette's tip. Once his lighter was safely tucked back in his pocket, he settled his weight more comfortably on his heels.

I liked the smell of his clove cigarette. Hot and spicy, not gross like a regular cigarette, even though it was probably just as cancerous.

But why, exactly, did it turn me on to watch him? The way he held his cigarette—not between his index and middle finger, but instead the way people held a joint, with the index finger and the thumb, and in his left hand—bringing it to his mouth, inhaling deeply, then pulling it away, resting his wrist on his knee as he exhaled the plume of fragrant smoke. It was like he was consuming the spice and the fire . . . as if the smell of it, the taste of it sustained him, nourished him.

Maybe it was because every action he took seemed so sensual, so pleasure-filled; he smoked because he wanted to, without considering the implications or worrying about the future cost of this decision. At least, that was how it seemed. And he was unapologetic about it.

He never asked anyone around him, "Do you mind if I smoke?" Gunner didn't seem particularly concerned about offending.

I guess I was watching him too closely, because Gunner shifted his attention from middle distance to my face. For a moment I felt lost in his marbled gaze, like I was falling, like I had lost all sense of direction, actually—falling or flying or sitting still, I couldn't tell.

"Would you like one?"

I shook my head. "I don't smoke."

"How do you know? Have you ever tried?"

"No," I said. "I've never smoked anything."

But suddenly I wanted to—not because I wanted the

cigarette, but because I wanted his kiss. His lips. His hot breath, spicy and wrong.

Instead I held out my hand and took his brown cigarette, ignoring his smirk and bringing it to my mouth, wrapping my lips around its tip and pulling gently, bringing its hot dry fragrance into my lungs.

I don't know what I expected. What I got, though, was a flaming pain in my chest as the smoke filled me. I thrust the cigarette back at Gunner as a coughing fit overwhelmed me.

He didn't laugh at me, I'll give him that, though the smirk he continued to wear was bad enough. "Not for everyone."

When I'd recovered enough to speak, I said, "Why on earth would you *choose* to smoke those things?"

He shrugged. "I like the burn of them," he said. "I like the way they hurt." He turned his gaze on me again. "But I don't suppose you could understand that, a good girl like you."

My eyes flitted down to the crescent smile-scar on my left wrist and an image of myself—cold, empty, hollowed out— flashed through my mind.

Maybe he read my thoughts on my face, maybe he saw me glance to my scar, because he raised an eyebrow and mused softly, "Or, perhaps, you can."

"No," I lied. "I can't understand that. It seems like an awful waste of time."

Gunner saw through my lie, I could tell by the amused tilt of his lips, but he didn't call me on it. Instead, as if he believed me, he said, "Yes, Lily told me that you're not a lot of fun when it comes to parties."

Betrayed. That's what I felt. Lily was *talking* about me to this guy?

"I guess I'm not," I said. "I'm pretty dull, really. So what are you doing out here?"

"Checking on my lab partner," he said. "I don't want to fail the assignment, after all."

"You couldn't care less about an assignment."

He laughed. "Astute," he said. "I guess I'm curious—what could have gotten you all worked up like that? You're made of tougher stuff than Jane, I'd wager. Not like you to run off."

He'd smoked his cigarette down to a nub and ground it into the dirt by his shoe.

I didn't feel like confiding in Gunner. "I guess the formaldehyde was making me dizzy."

"Bollocks."

"Is that even a word?"

"Indeed it is. Roughly translated into American English, it means 'bullshit.'"

"Ah." I couldn't help myself—I liked his wry sense of humor, his ironic, jaded perceptions. "Well, I guess you'll just have to live with the mystery."

"You won't tell me?"

I shook my head. Share with *Gunner* my revelation that I seemed somehow connected to Will through my dreams? Absolutely no way.

"Well, can I hazard a guess?"

"Sounds entertaining. Be my guest."

"Hmm . . ." He rocked gently on his heels, thinking. "Well, there was a corpse in front of you. A room full of them, actually, tiny little corpses. And Lily told me that your brother died a year or so ago. . . ."

Had they spent their whole date talking about me?

"So perhaps the little piglets turned your attention to your brother. Also dead."

I had come a long way, I noticed, as if I were an impartial observer. Gunner was talking about Ronny, about his death, and his cavalier attitude, though irritating, didn't make me physically ill. So that was something.

"I wasn't thinking about Ronny."

"Hmm . . . ," he said. "The boyfriend, then. Away at college . . . Yale, is it?"

"Let me guess. Lily again?"

"A veritable fount of information."

Somehow the conversation had turned to Will, though I hadn't brought it there. "Actually," I said, "I was thinking about my horse. She's pregnant."

"A pregnant horse and a dead piglet. Interesting. You *are* complex, aren't you, Scar?"

"No more so than anyone else, I guess."

"That is most likely true. But your particular complexities interest me."

"Why?"

"*That* is a very good question."

I waited for his answer. It was easy to pretend that we weren't at school, that the bell to announce the end of this period wasn't due to ring in a few minutes, that nothing we said or did under this tree was part of our real life.

"There is something about your energy," he said at last. "Something about you that seems to speak to me. To call to me."

It was tempting to lose myself in the romantic idea of

Gunner's words, but ultimately, they were meaningless. This tree, this moment in time, was not isolated from the rest of my life, from the people I loved. Everything, and all of it, was connected. The things I did mattered. If I let myself fall into Gunner's marbled eye, that would matter. It would resonate. Even if no one saw me do it.

From the distance, I heard the harsh call of the school bell. I stood and wiped the dirt from the back of my jeans. "I'm not *calling* to you, Gunner," I said. My voice was even as I looked down into his eyes, looking up at me. "I'm just a girl, and I have a boyfriend."

Then I walked back toward the building. Behind me, I heard the flick of Gunner's lighter. And I took a deep breath, inhaling the sweet scent of his next cigarette.

Usually on Mondays, I headed straight to the stable after school. Alice had consistently been my ride until this year, but as Dad had gotten more comfortable with my driving, I had begun taking the old Volvo. If I'd driven directly from school (where I'd parked the car that morning, packed with my riding clothes and boots), maybe another month would have gone by without my discovering Dad's secret. Or maybe longer. Maybe I could have avoided it forever.

But the car wouldn't start. The battery was dead; it took me only a minute to realize that I'd left the headlights running and they'd slowly, silently drained the battery.

The jumper cables weren't in the trunk, and somehow no one else seemed to have a set, either. Dad didn't answer my call—it went straight to voice mail, which meant his phone was either off or dead—so I decided to walk home and find him.

He wasn't on the main floor; he wasn't in any of the guest rooms. I made my way to our flat on the third floor, but I knew before I walked through it that he wasn't there, either. The space had that strange, particular sensation of emptiness. Even so, I poked my head into the kitchen and his bedroom and tapped on the bathroom door. My bedroom door, at the end of the hall, was open, but before I headed there to set down my backpack, I found my hand on the doorknob of Ronny's room. I hadn't really intended to put it there, and as I watched with strange fascination, my hand twisted the knob and pushed open the door.

I hovered on the threshold. Inside, the curtains were pulled; the room was in shadow. Then my hand reached into the room, found the wall switch, and flipped it.

It had been a year and a half since I'd last stepped into Ronny's bedroom. At first, as I took a cautious step across the threshold, I wondered if I would be able to breathe. But my lungs filled just the same, though the weight I had felt on my chest in the long months after Ronny's death threatened to descend upon me again.

I was a girl with a dead brother. For the rest of my life, this would be true. There was nothing I could do to change it. Dead was dead, whether or not I entered Ronny's room, whether or not I visited his grave . . . which I hadn't done since the day we buried him.

Ronny's room didn't smell like Ronny, but this didn't surprise me. Even before his death his room had already become a shade of its former self; most of his time had been spent on the mainland in his dorm room, so he'd taken all his favorite possessions with him. They'd been returned, of course, but we'd just stacked the boxes inside the room and no one had touched them since.

I blinked and took another step. There. That was far enough. The blue-and-white quilt was pulled up over the pillows on his bed. There was the oversized armchair Mom had wanted to throw out, which Ronny had appropriated for himself. One side of it had been clawed by a cat we'd had, Applesauce. She was dead, too, of natural causes, having lived a long and happy life; it was her death that prompted Mom to redo the great room. Applesauce had had a thing for clawing the furniture. With her out of the way, Mom decided it was safe at last to buy nice things.

Maybe I would look through the boxes, I mused. There must be some stuff in there that I would want to take with me when I went off to college in the fall. I was almost done with my applications—I was applying all over California, nowhere far because I knew my parents couldn't afford out-of-state tuition.

But not today.

It was good to know that I could handle Ronny's room. And I decided that it was past time that I visit his grave. Maybe Dad would go with me.

I switched off the light and stepped back into the hallway, closing the door quietly, listening for the click as it shut.

My own room was cold—I'd opened the window that morning to see what the weather might be like and hadn't shut it when I'd left. Quickly, I crossed to the window and reached for the sash to push it closed. But when I saw movement in the garden, I froze. There was my father, sitting on the bench next to the koi pond, the pond he'd dug with Ronny, just beyond our gazebo.

I often saw him sitting there. It had become his private space in the time Since Ronny Died, a place where he went to think, to stir the water slowly with a stick, to gaze into the evening—but on this day, he was not alone.

Next to him was Alice. They sat close, with their heads together as if they were discussing something serious. A fleeting thought passed through my mind that they must be talking about me. I was, after all, their common interest.

But as their faces closed the distance between them, as my father dipped his head down toward Alice and she tilted her face up to him, as his hand buried itself in the brown wings of her hair and he clutched her close, tight up against his body, and as a little sound like a whimper came from my heart, it occurred to me that maybe they had something other than me at the forefront of their minds.

THIRTEEN

And Then There Was One

I stepped back from the window. I left my room. I made my way down the two flights of stairs on quiet cat feet and closed the front door as gently as I could. Then I ran. I ran and ran, not caring where my feet took me as long as it was *away*.

I tripped over a slab of concrete that had been displaced by a tree root, falling hard and skinning my hand. The pain of it was sharp and welcome. Pulling myself back to standing I went on, walking fast now rather than running, watching blood pulse up to the surface of my palm where the skin had been shredded by the rough concrete.

First Ronny, dead. Then my mother, AWOL. And now Dad—kissing Alice, a friend, a married woman.

I strode quickly up my street, the ocean behind me. At first I was just trying to put distance between myself and what I'd seen from my bedroom window, but after a while it became clear that I was heading to the graveyard.

The curved iron gate of the cemetery was closed but not latched. The graveyard was built on a hill, so it had been terraced into two sections. Ronny was buried on the lower terrace. I entered through the gate at the top of the cemetery, as far from Ronny's grave as I could get.

I stood there breathing quietly for a few minutes, trying to calm down. I knelt and passed my hand along the damp grass. My palm felt better. Standing again, I made my way over to the head of the cemetery, where there was a verse inscribed onto a large piece of bronze framed by rocks. I remembered having read it on the day of Ronny's funeral. It was a fragment of Tennyson's *Idylls of the King*.

I read it again now:

BUT NOW FAREWELL

I AM GOING A LONG WAY . . .

TO THE ISLAND-VALLEY OF AVALON:

WHERE FALLS NOT HAIL

OR RAIN OR ANY SNOW

NOR EVER WIND BLOWS LOUDLY:

BUT IT LIES

DEEP MEADOW'D, HAPPY, FAIR

WITH ORCHARD LAWNS

AND BOWERY HOLLOWS CROWN'D

WITH SUMMER SEA

WHERE I WILL HEAL ME

OF MY GRIEVOUS WOUND.

When I had last stood in this spot, I hadn't found solace in the words, though I'm sure that had been the hope of whoever had chosen the poem.

I'd tried to imagine Ronny, his spirit, his soul, arriving after death to some more perfect version of our Avalon, an Avalon deep meadow'd, happy and fair. I'd tried to imagine him healing from his grievous wound. I'd stood at this plaque wishing fiercely, willing to barter away *anything* if only Ronny could be returned to us.

This time, though, I could look at the poem more dispassionately, analytically, even as the vision of my dad and Alice beat against the backs of my eyes. And this time I was struck not by the images the poem painted but rather by the placement of the specific words.

One line stood out in a way I hadn't seen before:

BUT IT LIES

Grammatically, these words should be connected to those beneath them:

BUT IT LIES DEEP MEADOW'D, HAPPY, FAIR

They weren't. Those three little words comprised their own line. Maybe Tennyson had placed them that way. I didn't think so, though; I would bet money that it was the engraver who'd chosen to set them on a line of their own. It could have been a matter of convenience, to break the phrase into two groups of words.

Reading that line, my hand stinging, though not nearly as much as my heart, I saw a message, not hidden at all, terribly obvious and searingly true—BUT IT LIES. All of it, everything lies—the promise of a happy, safe escape after death, the promise of family.

So ugly, the truth: the image of my father and Alice, the particular shade of my mother's purple wall, the memory of Ronny's freshly dug grave.

I turned away from the plaque and wiped angrily at my eyes. Then, because I was already there and already in pain, I descended to the lower terrace and found my brother's grave.

In the third grade, my teacher, Mrs. Flannigan, had taken us on a field trip to this cemetery. We'd made grave rubbings of some of the oldest headstones. The one that had most fascinated me belonged to a girl from another time, a girl who had died at just seven years old.

Her headstone was made of chalky, crumbling white marble. It looked a lot like the fake headstones we'd used to decorate Lily's front yard at Halloween, except this one marked the bones of a long-dead girl. MARY EDITH AULL, declared the neat printing on the headstone. DEC. 18, 1912–JAN. 19, 1920.

A lamb was carved into the marble, and across the top of the headstone were the words OUR DARLING.

Ronny was buried not far from Mary Edith Aull. His grave marker was the modern kind: a flat rectangle of brass set into the grass. Though it looked different from hers, the particulars were pretty similar. There was his name—Ronald Jonathan Wenderoth—and the dates of his birth

and death. Beneath these facts was the inscription LOVING
SON AND BROTHER.

He was someone's darling, too.

All of us are, until we aren't anymore.

I stood next to his grave. The last time I had been here,
there had been a gaping hole in the ground, a coffin set inside it, and I had thrown in a handful of dirt. My father had
thrown one in, too, but my mother couldn't bring herself
to do it. That, I understood. To rain dirt down upon your
child's body . . . to know that was *the end* of the baby you'd
birthed, the child you'd kissed and consoled, the young man
you'd cheered and rooted for—and that his body was in the
ground in a box in a suit. . . . It sickened me, thinking of it.

But it wasn't so bad here, now. There were squirrels; there
were birds. If you could ignore the bodies decomposing beneath your feet, the cemetery might make a pretty sweet
picnic spot.

Some people talk to their dead. Some people visit their
graves and put fresh flowers on them, and little Christmas
trees in the winter and heart-shaped balloons on Valentine's
Day. Personally, I found this nauseating.

Dead is dead. Balloons don't fix dead.

As the week progressed, Gunner and I took our piglet ca-
daver to pieces. We made a great team; he watched as I cut
down the length of her abdomen and then made two lat-
eral incisions to create a flap that we peeled back to peer
into the abdominal cavity. Together we examined the liver,
stomach, gallbladder, and pancreas. We explored the large
intestine, the small intestine, the rectum.

I watched as Gunner took the piglet's hind legs in his glove-encased hands and cracked the pelvic bone, splaying her legs even wider apart so we could more clearly see her reproductive organs. There were ovaries; there was a uterus.

We took notes and dutifully filled out our packet. Mr. McCormack held up our work more than once as an example. Behind us, Jane Maple grew by degrees indifferent to the death before her. One day, she squealed with delight upon properly identifying the aortic arch as she held her piglet's tiny heart in her hand.

As we worked I trained my thoughts carefully away from visions of my father kissing Alice, and from Gunner kissing Lily. I focused on the pale lips of our piglet and concentrated on the work in front of me.

And I counted the days until the weekend. At last Friday arrived. I managed to avoid my father most of the evening, and on Saturday I locked myself in my room, trying desperately to focus on studying.

I hadn't really spoken with my dad all week; he'd written off my disconnection to midterms and college applications. I'd been fine with that assumption. And I didn't even really tell him my weekend plans, just left a note for him before I headed to the ferry Saturday evening. The note was vague enough to let him assume I would be staying with my mother, but I hadn't called to tell her I was coming to the mainland, and I had no intentions of seeing her this weekend.

It was to Sabine's house that I was headed. I was done with my own family for a while.

Finally the ferry was full and we pulled away from the dock. I stood at the bow of the boat, itchy to get away from the island as quickly as possible. Even the length of the ferry felt like a welcome relief from the island's shore. As the boat shifted out of the harbor and onto the open ocean, the cold wind cut through my layers of clothing and I shivered. But I didn't cross my arms over my chest; I let them hang at my sides as the wind assaulted me. It wasn't a pretty day. The mottled gray-blue sky recalled to me Gunner's eyes, and I felt glad to be leaving him behind, too, and Lily.

I looked back over my shoulder at the island shrinking behind us and remembered again the Agatha Christie book in which, one by one, each character perished on a vacation island. Philip Lombard was the second-to-last to die. I remembered the poem's last lines:

> One little Indian boy left all alone;
> He went out and hanged himself
> And then there were none.

In Christie's book, the "he" who hanged himself was a "she"—Vera Claythorne. It was a stupid poem—*alone* and *none* didn't really rhyme—and it was a stupid ending. She shouldn't have killed herself. She should have signaled for help and gotten her ass off the island. She should have *survived*.

I was not Vera Claythorne.

When I got to the Rabinovich house on Linnie Canal, I found Ziva in the yard. She was sitting in one of the Adirondack chairs, surrounded by a voluminous quilt, head tilted down into the pages of a book. Behind her, the house was full of sounds: I heard Ari's screech and Daniel's answering yell; they were either murdering each other or playing another video game. There was music, too, something classical.

Ziva seemed to register none of this; the book had all of her attention.

"What are you reading?" I asked, after I had stood quietly next to her for a minute, waiting for her to look up.

Without raising her eyes, Ziva replied, *"Black Beauty."*

"I've read that," I said. "Did you know I have a horse?"

"Mm-hmm," she said, turning a page. "Will told me."

"Do you like horses?"

"Not particularly."

I didn't know what to say to this. Don't all girls like horses?

"I like books," she said. Then she looked up at me. "My mom's inside," she added, clearly an invitation for me to move along.

I took the hint. "Thanks."

The sounds and smells of a full household—the warmth of the lit fire, the sizzle of fat on the stove top as David began dinner—were bittersweet. I joined in, though, with a cheery "Hey, everyone," and Ari even paused his game to come across the room and give me a bare-chested hug.

The next morning, David took the kids to their cousins' house for a birthday party.

"There'd better be a piñata," Ari grumbled as his father pulled a shirt over his head and herded him out the door.

Sabine and I went for a walk on the beach. Venice's

boardwalk was a totally different experience than Catalina's; at home we had a small row of tourist shops mixed in with restaurants. It felt a little old-fashioned. Benign.

Not so Venice. Even early as it was, the boardwalk was crowded: tourists snapping pictures with their phones; hopeful rap musicians clamping their headphones over your ears, imploring you to listen to their tunes, then buy their CDs; stoned girls no older than me in hip-slung skirts and triangle-top bikinis, holding out their hands dispassionately for spare change. Across the boardwalk was Muscle Beach, a square of asphalt dotted with weight-lifting equipment and surrounded by chain-link fence. Two men—one mahogany-skinned and completely bald, about forty years old, the other well into his eighties and weathered so his skin looked like beef jerky, both dressed in little more than underwear and tennis shoes—lifted weights to the complete indifference of the passing crowd.

We stopped at a little coffee shop and Sabine bought us each a chai tea. Then she led me away from the boardwalk and down toward the water. Sipping our hot, fragrant drinks, we sank side by side into the sand and looked out at the ocean.

I could see the curve of Palos Verdes Peninsula to our left and, across the swath of ocean, my own island.

I got the feeling that Sabine was waiting for me to speak. I'd been pretty quiet all morning and the night before, too, so I was sure she knew I wasn't in the best of moods. To her credit, she didn't press me but seemed content to wait for me to be ready to share.

She'd be waiting a while. Even though I was furious with

my father, it would feel traitorous to share his secret with Sabine. But there were other things I did want to speak to her about.

I had told her before about the dream I'd had of seeing myself through Will's eyes. Now I told her about the other dreams that I'd remembered, visions that I realized I had been experiencing. She didn't ask questions, just listened as I explained, but I could feel her energy quivering, growing more intense and focused.

It was nice that she was so interested in me. My parents seemed pretty wrapped up in their own extracurricular activities, so Sabine's attention felt especially warm. And she seemed to really think I was *special*, that I had a talent, even though the dreams made no sense to me, even though they weren't something I had to work for, like my skill in the saddle or my grades.

"Have you told Will about this yet?"

I hadn't—not really. He would be back on the island in a couple of weeks, and I wanted to talk to him in person.

"It would be nice if you and Will could visit together when he's in town," Sabine offered. "I know the kids would love to see him again, and Martin, too."

"Yeah," I said. "That would be nice." Inwardly, I thought that any excuse to spend time away from my parents was a good one.

"Would you like to practice some chanting?" Sabine asked.

"Here? Now?" My eyes scanned the beach; it wasn't as crowded as the boardwalk behind us, but it was hardly what I'd call private.

"That's all we have," Sabine said, smiling as if pleased with her little joke. "The here and now."

No one seemed to be paying attention to us.

Sabine pushed her cup into the sand to steady it, and I did the same. Then she closed her eyes and rolled her neck, slowly. "Join in whenever you're ready," she said.

I had been practicing the chant that Sabine had taught me. It wasn't difficult, just hard to keep straight. It involved moving my head—to the left, to the right, up, and down, and back to center between each turn—and breathing in and out as I moved, as well as vocalizing a series of sounds.

"The true name of God is a mystery," Sabine had told me. "The ancients believed the power of God's true name was so strong as to be potentially devastating, so they rarely spoke it aloud. But after so many years of the name being veiled in secrecy, we forgot how to say it at all. All that is left are the consonants that form the name: *Y-H-V-H*. But the vowel sounds that connect them—those are lost. Still, if we work our way through all the possible permutations of vowel sounds, we will at some point speak the name . . . even if we do not know we have spoken it. And just the act of meditating on the sounds, of moving our heads and breathing in rhythm, with focus and concentration, brings us closer to God, to our highest and truest selves, to an ecstatic experience."

So there on the beach, I joined her. I closed my eyes and touched my thumbs to my middle fingers, as Sabine did, and I breathed with her, moved with her, made the sounds with her.

At first I had to force myself not to open my eyes and

check if anyone was staring at us. I felt my face flush at the possibility that a line of onlookers might have formed to laugh and point.

But Sabine's voice was clear and fearless, and by the third round of head movements—up, center, left, center, right, center, down, center—my voice rang clearly, too.

It was as if I'd stepped away from the things that had been bothering me—my anger at my father, my confusion over the way I felt about Gunner, my yearning for Will—if only for a little while.

I stopped counting the rounds of our chant. With Sabine's strong voice at my side, I found it easier to slip into each syllable, matching my tone to hers, knowing without looking that her head moved along with mine, that her breaths crested and released in tandem with my own. Direction ceased to exist, and slowly I separated myself from the sun above me and the sand beneath me. Slowly I felt warmth spreading through me, a sweet, radiating tingle that seemed like something I could almost reach, I could almost become, if only I concentrated more intently.

But the more I concentrated on reaching that sensation, the more it seemed to elude me, frustrating me, and I became aware again of the sounds I was making, the way I moved my head, the breaths I took, and the moment was gone as if a spell had broken.

Then I realized that I didn't hear Sabine's voice any longer; I chanted alone. My voice faltered and flagged, and I stopped.

When I opened my eyes I found Sabine watching me. Her eyes seemed eager.

"You felt something," she said.

I had. Nodding, I said, "I think so. I felt—not me, for a minute, if that makes sense."

"Yes," she agreed. "It does make sense. But you never stopped being you. Anything you may have felt . . . it was you. It *is* you. That reaching out that you felt—toward the universe, toward God—it's a reaching *inward,* a form of touching your truest self. There can be profound joy, Scarlett. Even ecstasy."

Until that moment, sitting on the beach with Sabine, the warmth of our chant fading from me, I hadn't clearly articulated to myself why I was interested in the study of Kabbalah. Last year, reading Martin's books, my research had been a way to heal myself, a way to channel my energy into care rather than harm, as well as a way to learn more about Will's strange abilities. But since Will had left the island, my focus had become less clear. Maybe I studied Kabbalah because it made me feel less detached from Will, who was separated from me by the length of a continent. Maybe I studied to avoid thinking about my family. But nearly grasping that elusive sensation—now I had a new reason to study, and a positive one at that.

It felt *good.* That surge of warmth and energy—whether something I channeled or something I created—I missed it already, and it had only been a moment since it passed. I wanted more of it.

I smiled at Sabine. She smiled back. I asked, "Can we try that again?"

I took the last ferry home Sunday night, and during the whole ride I sat in the open bow of the boat, feet tucked beneath me, fingers and thumbs gently touching, weaving my way through the permutations Sabine and I had practiced. Everyone else stayed inside, but as we plowed through the ocean toward home, the sun extinguished as it dipped into the water, I practiced ecstasy.

"Your mother called."

Dad was sitting in the kitchen, waiting for me. The lights weren't on; I'd thought maybe he wasn't home. Maybe he was out with Alice.

"Jesus, Dad, you scared the crap out of me!"

"Really?" he said.

I flipped the light on.

His face looked drawn; his hands were clasped on the empty table. "Where were you?"

The anger I'd been feeling for almost a week now simmered inside me, daring him to push me further. "I told you," I said smoothly. "I was on the mainland."

"You knew I'd think you were with your mom."

"Frankly," I said, "I'd think you'd have been glad for some time without me hanging around, regardless of where I went."

He looked confused. "What are you talking about?"

I sighed. "Forget it," I said. "What did Mom say?" I'd gotten calls from both of them, one after the other, while I was on the ferry, but I'd ignored them and hadn't listened to the messages.

"She was looking for you. When I told her you'd gone to the mainland, it took her a while to calm me down, I'll tell you that much. She said you must have gone to those friends of Martin Cohen—is that where you were?"

I didn't want to answer him. I didn't want to check in with him. So I just stood there in the kitchen, my backpack slung over my shoulder. "I'm tired," I said. "Can I go to bed?"

His eyes were pained. "Scar—" he said, but I'd already turned away.

In my room I slammed my pack on my bed. All the warmth and comfort I'd felt with Sabine and by myself on the ferry—all of it was gone, replaced by a mean emptiness and anger.

I could feel Dad steaming in the kitchen, and I stood waiting for him to follow me, willing him to, planning what I would say if he dared to darken my doorway.

But he didn't come.

And then there was one.

The buildings and the paved streets, the cars with their agitated drivers, the traffic signals and flashing lights—all of it formed an animated concrete labyrinth. He didn't know this cityscape; it was not his home. He tried to get free of it, tried to get to a place where he could take a breath of air.

She was behind him, clasping his hand, which felt like a beacon of hope in the throbbing crowd. But he couldn't clearly see where he needed to go. So, even though he knew it might mean losing her in the crowd, he squeezed her fingers and let go.

Then the path he needed to take lit up in front of him—not with lights, but with sensation, as if a long golden wire snaked through the web of bodies, through the twists and turns of the streets and the towering buildings.

He heard a word behind him—Will. A call to him, or a question, or a command. But he couldn't turn to answer it, so he chose to hear it as an order—use your will, find your way, set things right.

And he would do it. He willed it to be so. A mighty flame of vengeance stoked his heart and he broke into a run, the echo of the word—Will—calling him back, urging him forward.

FOURTEEN
Thin Ice

I woke with a gasp, sitting straight up in bed, my hair wild around my shoulders as if I'd been thrashing in my sleep, or running hard. My heart thrummed in my chest like a hummingbird and the whole world seemed to vibrate in the aftermath of my dream.

The red numbers of my alarm clock read 4:23. The sky outside my window, still black. I should go back to sleep; I should pull my quilt back over my cold shoulders. But I felt the restless pounding of feet on pavement from my dream and needed to get up. Outside my bedroom, the house was heavy with sleep. I heard my dad's even, deep breaths from his room down the hall. My long white nightgown tangled between my legs as I tiptoed down the stairs to the first floor.

It was midweek; we had one guest, a loud snorer we'd put in the Purple Room just off the front hallway. I passed his doorway quietly and found myself in the Yellow Room, the place I'd once sat with Will. No one was in it now. I found myself staring into the yawning maw of the darkened fireplace, remembering when this room had been bathed in firelight as Will shared with me his story.

It was like there was a hook in my brain and it pulled me like a fish on a line through the dark streets of the city.

In my dream I had felt the tug of that thin golden wire he had described, reeling me toward an unavoidable destination. But in this dream it hadn't been painful; it had been intoxicating, heady, a siren song.

Next to the fireplace squatted a basket of split logs. I arranged three of them in the hearth along with some loosely crumpled newspapers and struck a match. When the fire caught I lowered myself in front of it, pushing away the chairs where Will and I had sat and settling cross-legged on the floor. The fire's fingers reached and splayed, warming my chest, my face, my hands. I closed my eyes and tried to recapture the feeling I'd had in my dream, the thrilling urgency I'd felt while running in Will's body. But I couldn't grasp it now; I was too awake.

So I fell to chanting again, almost without intending to do so, softly stretching my head up, then back to center, then turning left, center, right, center, down, and back to center. The more I did it, the better it felt, and I added the breaths—in and out, deep, chest-opening breaths that left me light-headed and somewhere just above my body, the way hyperventilating had when I was a kid.

And the sounds—Y-H-V-H—strung together with each vowel in turn, wound together in a loop of sound as strong as the golden wire from my dream but this time all my own.

Time passed. The fire turned to embers, but still I was warm, an internal conflagration replacing the heat from the logs. The room grew lighter, and undefined shadow shapes around me became chairs, a little end table, the lamp upon it. Everything seemed tinged with pink and orange. Day had come, and though I registered this fact, it seemed that I wasn't attached to it. I at once saw and set aside the details of the room, the details of dawn. The tingling thrill I had felt on the cusp of embracing when I'd chanted side by side with Sabine returned to me. Again I focused my energy on reaching that place, grasping that specific vibration.

But as before, as soon as I placed my intention and reached for that sensation, it eluded me. I wanted to cry out to it as if that feeling was another person or a tame animal. But there was nothing tame about it; it was wild and feral and beautiful and would not belong to me, not that day. Then I suddenly noticed my legs beneath me. They felt stiff.

The moment was lost once more.

To shift from that sensation back into the mundane activities of a school morning—tooth brushing, shoelace tying, breakfast eating—felt disappointingly pedestrian. Even Lily's appearance at my front door as I latched it behind me, dressed in cords and a hoodie, my backpack slung over my shoulder and a bagel balanced on the rim of my coffee cup, didn't fully recall me to myself.

"It's such a *bore* the way you've been taking off on the weekends," she complained as we headed up the street toward school. "Thank *god* I've had Gunner to keep me entertained, or I don't know what I would do."

"You guys went out again?"

"That boy," Lily gushed, "is like *catnip* to parents. Jack and Laura *adore* him. He came over Saturday morning—he *said* he was returning a book he'd borrowed, but of course I hadn't loaned him one—and they invited him to stay for breakfast. Maybe it's his accent. Or his smile . . ." She sighed, remembering. Then she asked, "Do you think he'll like my outfit?"

She held her arms out and did a little spin. I don't think you could really call what she was wearing *pants* . . . *tights* would be a more accurate word, though I'd never seen a pair made out of fabric like that. They were textured velvet, I think, plum colored, and fit Lily like a second skin. They disappeared into yellow Hunter rain boots; I guess there were some clouds in the sky, though the ground was dry. But whatever . . . Lily could pull it off.

Really, her sweater was demure: positively no cleavage. But the way it wrapped across her chest, a long thin rope of twisted ribbon passing twice around her torso like a Grecian goddess's before ending in a little bow just beneath her right breast, belied its baby-girl shade of pink.

"Who wouldn't like it?" I said. "What's not to like?"

"Exactly."

"So what did you and Gunner do after breakfast?" My voice sounded light and tinged with best-girlfriend interest. I hoped only I felt the subtle edge of my words that gnawed at me.

"We took a walk."

That sounded pretty innocuous.

"Back to Connell's place. He and his folks were out for the day, so Gunner and I had the place to ourselves."

Ah.

"Did you . . . have fun?"

Lily laughed. "We didn't *do it,* if that's what you're asking."

I hated that it kind of was.

"We just hung out. Talked. Smoked a bowl of this killer weed he had. And, you know . . . fooled around a little." She grinned and looked around before stopping and turning toward me, angling her back to the school just up the road. Then she stretched open the neck of the sweater, pulling it down to reveal the milky crest of her right breast. And I saw why her fabulous cleavage was under wraps.

"He gave you a *hickey?*"

"Shhh." She laughed, yanking her sweater back into place and shaking her dark curls. "The whole *world* doesn't need to know!"

"Sorry, sorry." I had taken only a few sips of my coffee, but I felt jittery, on edge, like I'd downed a whole pot.

Her grin threatened to split her face.

"So does that mean you're official?"

She shrugged. "Gunner isn't really into labels," she said in a tone that revealed they'd definitely talked about it.

We'd arrived at school. Just ahead, standing under a tree in front of the main building, was Gunner. He could have been dressed for a trial; he wore a blazer and a sweater-vest, and the neat knot of a tie peeked out.

"He's waiting for me," Lily said, and I could feel her

217

contained energy at my side. She was practically vibrating, and as Gunner caught sight of us and ambled our way, I wondered for a second if she might explode from the sheer thrill of it.

"Good morning, ladies," Gunner said when we reached each other. His smile landed on Lily briefly but then turned to me. "Scar," he continued, "might we chat for a moment before class? I have a question about our little joint autopsy."

"Um . . . okay," I said, and only as we were walking away did I think to turn and say, "See you later, Lil."

But the words froze on my lips. Her gaze was venomous.

That afternoon I was relieved to escape to the stable. I turned Delilah out in the smaller arena and watched as she trotted a little ways before lowering herself with a grunt to her knees and then rolling in the sand. It seemed to take her more effort than usual to fling her legs up and over so that she could rub her other side.

She stood and shook off the sand; it puffed out around her. Then she strolled over to an edge of the arena where she could best reach grass across the fence and settled in to her snack.

It was the second week of December. Delilah looked definitely pregnant. Her belly stretched beneath her in a round taut curve. Her gait was more rolling, less up and down and more stretched out. And eating, rather than running, seemed to be her preferred leisure activity.

Even though it had been my idea to get her pregnant— and my hard-earned dollars that had paid for the sperm—I felt kind of sad. Like I was losing my best friend to a stranger.

218

As I thought those words, it occurred to me that they fit more than one of my relationships. I didn't know how much longer I could stand this hot-and-cold Lily; one moment she was pouring out her secrets to me, and the next she was surrounded by people at lunch, barely acknowledging my existence.

It pissed me off, actually, that she could let the attentions of some guy dictate what was happening between us. A little voice urged me to admit that she wasn't the only one susceptible to Gunner's charms; after all, I'd let him lead me away from Lily that morning.

And what for? As soon as he got me out of Lily's sight, he claimed that he'd forgotten what he'd wanted to ask.

But the damage was done. Not only had Lily been too popular at lunch to save a seat for me, she'd disappeared from campus before I'd been able to track her down after school.

Horses were simpler, I told myself. After returning Delilah to her stall and pouring a little extra A&M into her feeder, I decided this would be a good day to see if Traveler had changed his mind yet about trot poles.

I could use a good fight.

At last, at last, at long, long last, the day came that Will would return to the island. School was closed for winter break; Lily and her family had headed off to Australia ("The twins want to see boxing kangaroos," Laura had told me by way of explaining this year's destination); and I paced my bedroom wildly, back and forth, wondering if I'd chosen the right outfit, if Will would be glad to see me, if that feeling we'd shared—that magical electric connection—would still be there when we touched or if I'd somehow ruined it by feeling the way I did about Gunner.

People misunderstand the word *ambivalent*. It had been one of the words on the list I'd studied over the summer, vocabulary words most likely to appear on the SAT. I'd been surprised to find that I'd misunderstood the word for years. People think *ambivalent* means that you don't care about something one way or the other. But that isn't what it means at all. *Ambivalent* can mean desperately wanting two completely different things—being pulled equally in opposing directions.

My mind wasn't ambivalent; it was Will I loved, Will I admired, Will, Will, Will.

But my body didn't feel so certain. It was ambivalent.

I'd seen Gunner the night before. I had gone down to the beach just before sunset, wrapped in a wool blanket and holding a cup of hot tea. I hadn't seen him standing in the shade of the pier; it wasn't until I had made a little nest for myself on the sand and had settled in to watch the final sunset before Will's return that he stepped out of the shadows.

Just then the sun lit the sky in its last triumph and it glowed behind him like a giant fireball, rays of orange blinding me. I couldn't see his face, just his form, the black outline of him.

"Hello, Gunner," I said, but when he stepped closer to me, preparing to sit on the sand, I said, "Goodbye, Gunner."

"Not in the mood for company?"

"Not really." I meant it. Really, I did. I wanted to stare

into the blackening sea and dream about my reunion with Will. So why did my traitor flesh tingle the way it did? Why did my stomach turn in slow flips?

He shrugged. "I just wanted to say goodbye," he said, and started to turn away.

I was on my feet instantly, against my own best intentions. "You're leaving?"

When he turned back to me, his smile was slow. Sardonic. "Does that bother you?"

I didn't answer.

"Connell's parents are taking us to Los Angeles to visit his aunt over the holiday," he said. "Don't fret. I will return."

"I wasn't *fretting*," I said. "Whatever. Have a good trip."

But by noon the next day, the sun full and bright over my head, the day crisp and clear and full of light, I'd pushed thoughts of Gunner far aside and watched with thrilled anticipation as the ferry grew close, then closer, until finally I saw him—Will—at the very bow of the boat, his hand shading his eyes as he scanned the dock for me.

"Will!" I cried. My voice caught in my throat. It didn't matter; he was still too far to hear me. But he saw me, and thrust his hand up in a wave, and I waved back, smiling widely and bouncing on the balls of my feet. The sun shone down right above him and each of his features—his eyes, his nose, his beautiful mouth—was crisp and clear and bathed in light.

At last the boat docked, and all that separated me from Will was the rush of the crowd departing the ferry. Then there he was, his bag slung over his shoulder, his hair a little longer than when he'd left, brown waves cresting around his neck.

I couldn't help myself—I pushed past the last cluster of people that separated us and threw myself at Will. He dropped his bag and reached out for me. We tangled together and kissed, his mouth warm and soft, the whole length of him so present, so absolutely real and solid against my body.

We kissed and kissed and it was like the rest of the world didn't matter at all. There was just Will and me and that was enough, right then, to fill me up and thrill me to my absolute core.

Finally we pulled apart, and I could see his eyes. They seared into mine, and for a moment I was lost in them. Then he leaned in for another kiss.

I laughed. "Your face is all scratchy."

"I can shave if you want," he murmured, kissing me again and again.

"No, don't," I said, running my hand against his cheek. "I like it."

Someone coughed behind Will. It was Martin. I felt bad for forgetting he was on the ferry, too. "Well, Scarlett, so nice to see you," Martin said, and Will had to let me go so that I could greet his father.

"Welcome back, Martin," I said, giving him a quick hug. But only with one arm—Will had ensnared my other hand and wasn't letting go.

"I trust our house is still standing?"

"Mm-hmm," I said. "At least, it was a few days ago when I was last there."

On that day, I had tiptoed into Will's room. I'd run my hand across the gray flannel blanket; I'd pulled the cord to light his green-shaded lamp. I'd lowered myself to the bed and kicked off my shoes, laying my head on his pillow and imagining Will next to me.

It had been difficult to leave.

"You'll have to come have dinner with us soon, all right, Scarlett?" Martin had organized his suitcase and his other, smaller bags and was preparing to step aboard the bus that was heading to Two Harbors.

But Will made no move to follow him. "Dad," he said, "I'm going to stay with Scarlett on this side of the island for a while."

Martin frowned. Clearly they hadn't discussed this. "How will you get to Two Harbors?"

Will shrugged, a little irritated. "I don't know, Dad. I'll figure it out. Maybe Scarlett can give me a ride."

"When should I expect you?"

"Dad, no offense, but I didn't come all the way from New Haven to Catalina to hang out with *you*. I get to see you all the time. I'm here to see Scarlett."

There was a moment of tense, loaded silence, and I could almost feel the unspoken negotiation, the shifting invisible line of freedom and accountability. I wanted Will to stay with me, of course, but it made me uncomfortable to witness their struggle.

"All right, son," Martin said at last as the bus driver cleared her throat. "Just give me a call to let me know what you're going to do. And," he said, almost as if he needed to voice the words, "be careful."

"Always am," Will said, waving to his father as the bus door closed. We watched it pull away from the curb and make its way through town, toward the road that would take Martin to Two Harbors.

I could feel Will's body still tense from the negotiation with his father. "He just loves you," I said.

"I know. But I think I'm pretty safe here with you. Besides," he said, "it's not like he knows where I am every second back at Yale. I live in the dorms and do my own thing."

I almost said something about how his "own thing"— roaming the streets looking for crimes to stop—didn't really sound like the best plan to me, either; his father wasn't the only one who worried about him. But I didn't want to start off our visit that way. Will had a limited engagement on the island.

We decided to swing by my house and drop off his stuff and then figure out what to do from there. But when we got to the house and found it blissfully silent, neither of us felt like going anywhere.

Two couples were staying with us that week, but with such beautiful weather they weren't hanging around in the middle of the day. Dad had mentioned that morning that he planned to give Alice a hand with some paperwork out at the stable as a way to pay her back for all her help around our place. At the time his easy excuse to be alone with Alice had bothered me, but I was glad now that I hadn't said anything and had the house to myself.

I led Will by the hand up the two flights of stairs to our little flat. "Are you hungry?" I asked as we passed the kitchen.

"Not at all," he said, and the tone of his voice propelled

me down the hall toward my room. We walked in and I watched as Will slowly, gently, pushed the door closed.

His eyes were full of intention as he turned to me. I reached out and stroked the dark stubble along his jawline. His hand reached up and took mine, turning it palm up. He kissed me there, on the soft center of my hand, then took each finger, one by one, between his lips.

Circles and lines, I mused, my logic fuzzy and disorganized. The hard press of his erection against my thigh. The straight, flat plane of his chest. The curve of my breasts pushed against him, the arch of my back as I stepped even closer. But Will had curves, too—the bow of his lips, the tilt of his chin. And I had lines—the long sheet of hair that fell across my shoulders, the arrow-straight thrust of my desire for Will's touch.

There were so many things to talk about—my convoluted feelings of guilt and yearning, my anger at my father and Alice over the discovery of their betrayal, everything I'd been reading and doing, all the ways I felt myself stretching and growing and changing as I practiced Kabbalah. But as his tongue looped around my smallest finger, his hot breath warming my skin, and as his gaze asked a question, I wanted to answer him not in words but in action.

My hands found the hem of his wool sweater and pushed it up, catching his white tee, too. Will raised his arms over his head and I tugged off his sweater and shirt, leaving them tangled on the floor. Then my fingers splayed across his chest and I stepped up against him. Will's fingers weaved through my hair and he kissed me so gently.

"I've missed you," he murmured into my mouth. I

225

answered him by sliding even closer, winding my arms around his warm, naked back and tilting my head so he could kiss me more fully.

We stumbled together toward the bed and sat on its edge. Somewhere my brain registered that my long white curtains glowed with the midday sun; some part of my consciousness heard a bird outside. But every part of me that mattered was focused on Will's ragged breath, the sensation of his lips and tongue and teeth, the knowledge that we were alone here in this moment, on this day. Right now.

FIFTEEN

Love, Seen

I had spent hours thinking of this moment—Will returned to me, the two of us alone in a room, just the sound of our mingled breath and our kisses. I had imagined doing with him the things I did now . . . sliding my hands across his shoulders, tracing the line of his neck with my tongue, feeling his hands tangled again in my hair.

I had imagined these things while riding Delilah. I had imagined them in class, staring out the window into rain. I had imagined them while lying alone at night in this very bed, as my hands touched my breasts, my stomach, and reached down into my underwear.

There had been a time—it felt like a long time ago, now—when my body had been almost dead to me. I had punished it, denied it, hurt it, left it hungry and hollowed out.

But *it*—my body—wasn't an *it*, not really. It was me, and I, it. Over the months between then and now I had forgiven my body for living in the terrible wake of Ronny's death; I had forgiven *myself* and come to love my body, even—what it could do and feel, how it could sit astride a horse, how it could relax into the sand, how it could respond to my fantasies and to Will's touch.

I had imagined being in Will's arms over and over again, and now here we were. And I couldn't get enough of him— his smell, his touch, his taste. I felt his hands winding up the back of my shirt, fumbling a little with the clasp of my bra before it came undone. Then he mirrored my earlier movement—sliding up my sweater and the tank top underneath, tangled together with my bra. The air felt cool against my bare skin, but it wasn't that I was suddenly colder without clothing that caused me to shiver, made my skin tighten into goose bumps.

It was *being seen*. Will and I had fooled around before, and he'd touched me under my shirt, but this was the first time we'd been together like this—both of us half-naked, face to face in full light. My first instinct was to shake my hair forward to cover my breasts. But I didn't want to hide from Will, not really. I wanted to see him, and be seen by him in return. So I straightened my shoulders and took Will's hand. Slowly, deliberately, I raised it and placed it over my left breast. His touch was hot and electric and my heartbeat quickened under his palm.

Then Will leaned in close and kissed me again. We fell backward onto the pillows and fit our bodies together, chest to chest, hip to hip, our legs entwined. We kissed and kissed, our hands on each other's flesh, tongues in each other's mouths, my hair tangled around us both.

Finally Will murmured, "What do you want to do?"

I knew what he was asking. I had thought about this a lot—what I wanted to do with him. "I want to be naked with you," I said. "But I don't want to do anything that hurts. I want more of this"—running my fingers lightly up and down his sides—"but just this."

"Okay," Will answered. We kissed again, and he ran his hand down the length of my thigh, but he didn't make a move to unbutton my jeans, or his. I knew why—he didn't want to push me. If pants were going to come off, it would be my decision, not his.

So I slid my hands down between us, and I unfastened the button and then pulled the zipper of my jeans. Will's green eyes stared into mine as I pushed my pants down and snaked free of them. I left my underwear on.

And then, emboldened, I popped loose the five buttons on the fly of Will's jeans and pushed the rough denim across his hips, leaving his underwear on, too. He helped me push off his pants the rest of the way and my gaze flitted down. His underwear were boxers, I guess, but shorter and tighter. They were blue. And they were stretched tight across his erection, a sight that both thrilled and terrified me.

"These are cute," I teased, running my finger along the waistband of his underwear. "Boxer briefs, right?"

"Mm-hmm," he murmured distractedly, kissing my collarbone.

"What, couldn't make up your mind?"

"They combine the comfort of boxers with the support of briefs." He looked up at me and said, smiling in that sweet sideways way of his, "But do you really want to talk about my underwear?"

I ran my finger along the line of his new scar, high up on his right thigh. It was pink still, too new to turn white. Then I shook my head. "No. I don't."

Eventually, as the sun began to lower in the sky, as my room grew darker in the dusk, we stopped kissing and touching and I rested my head against his chest. Will pulled my quilt up over my shoulders and we lay there together, watching the sky out my window transform into night.

It felt so nice like that—Will's arm wrapped around me, his breath warm in my hair. I knew Dad would be home soon—he never missed dinner—and we'd have to get up, climb back into our clothes, make small talk. I wanted to hold on to this feeling longer, forever. The last time I'd felt this exposed had been last year, on the beach with Lily. But that had been completely different; then, my nakedness had seemed shameful, proof of the way I'd neglected myself. This was different—I felt empowered, strong, satisfied. I felt beautiful. And not just because of the way Will reacted to my body—because of the way it felt to *be* this body.

And even though we hadn't needed to pull out any condoms—despite Will whispering yearningly that he had a few in his wallet, in case I changed my mind—I felt as though I had stepped to the other side of the invisible line I had often imagined, the line between virginity and experience. I thought the view from where I now stood was mighty fine.

Downstairs, I heard the shutting of our front door. It could have been the guests, or it could have been Dad. Either way, it was time to get dressed. Suddenly, I remembered that I was supposed to put out the cheese plate and wine.

"Oh no," I said, clambering over Will and retrieving my jeans from the floor. "The guests get cranky if there's no wine."

"So does my dad," said Will. He sighed and threw back the quilt, untangling his pants and pulling them on. "I'll help."

That night, after a pizza dinner with Dad, after straightening up the great room and washing the dishes, after Dad had gone to his room and had finally fallen asleep, his even breaths signaling that it was safe for me to go downstairs, I made my way to the Yellow Room and found Will awake, waiting for me.

It turned out that sleep wasn't as necessary as I'd always thought.

Will had three full weeks off from school. He'd be spending two of them—fourteen days—in California. After that first day and night, we made a pact to spend as much time together as possible. In practical terms, this meant that he spent most nights in the Yellow Room, and when he went to Two Harbors, I went with him. Martin wasn't about to green-light a sleepover at the cottage, so when Will was home, I had to drive back to Avalon alone.

During the days we took long walks when the weather

was nice, and sat curled in front of a fireplace with books, music, and hot chocolate when it was stormy. One day I took Will out to the stable to see Delilah.

He admired the swell of her belly and fed her carrot after carrot, breaking them into pieces and holding them up to her mouth.

Another day we took a picnic lunch and filled our water bottles, heading up Boushay Trail to Silver Peak, the island's highest vantage point. There were a few routes to Silver Peak, and we chose the second-longest route; it was more scenic than the quickest, steepest trail, six and a half miles shorter than the most circuitous path. The first five and a half miles, the trail meandered along the coast. Then we headed inland and wound up and up to the summit. It was a long hike, and hard, and even though I'd started off the day in a thermal, a fleece hoodie, and a cap, by the time we reached the summit just after one o'clock, my sweater was tied around my waist and my cap was shoved into the pack along with lunch. I had my silver water bottle, and though I'd tried to be sparing, I'd drunk more than half of it.

Will made a fabulous hiking partner. He'd told me once that he'd never really been an outdoorsy type before moving to the island, that his mother had always tried to get him interested in hiking but to no avail. It was funny—not in a ha-ha way—that it was as a result of her death that Will and his father had retreated to Catalina, and that Will had come to love long days outside.

I wondered what inadvertent good had come to me as a result of Ronny's death. Maybe I was myopic because

Ronny's death was still too close; maybe in time I'd come to see things that weren't clear to me now.

The farther we climbed, the more barren the peak became. Once, long ago, the whole island had been fertile and green, but in the years between then and now the island had basically been stripped of its foliage by wild boar and cattle, by miners and loggers. It had been a few years since the Island Conservancy had started advocating for protection of Silver Peak, and in time, probably, the place would be beautiful again . . . but this was hard to imagine.

The *view* was beautiful: a panoramic ocean vista, bright blue, with the mainland's peninsula clearly visible, as well as San Clemente Island. Will and I stood side by side and turned in a slow circle, taking in the wide, wild ocean and the peaks of earth across it.

The ground was brown dirt and stunted grasses, dotted here and there by a cactus. We'd brought a lightweight blanket along with our lunch and together Will and I spread it across the ground.

We had to pin the four corners with rocks; up here the wind was strong, with no trees or houses to cut it. So we lay together on the blanket, as close to the ground as we could get, and the wind seemed to soften, passing over us like a caress rather than a gale.

I shrugged back into my hoodie and zipped it up. When we were motionless like this, the warmth I'd worked up while hiking quickly dissipated. Will pulled me into his arms and threw one of his legs over mine. It was warmer like that, and kind of wonderful, too.

We didn't talk for a while or even kiss. We just lay and watched the wind in the grass, watched shadows move across the cobalt water.

"Do you ever wonder where you'll be in five years?" Will's voice startled me, we had been quiet for so long.

I shrugged. "I try not to think about it too much," I said. "I guess I'll be finishing college. Maybe applying to grad school or medical school." Then I asked, "What about you?"

He kissed my hair before he answered. "Wherever I am," he said, "I hope it's right here."

I knew he didn't mean on the top of Silver Peak, huddled on the ground to escape the wind.

There were so many things we hadn't yet said. And I didn't want to say them now. But then Will asked, "Did you finish your applications?"

I nodded.

"Any East Coast schools make the final list?" His voice sounded light, but I knew Will well enough to know he was forcing it.

I shook my head. "All California schools," I said. "The UCs, mostly."

"Ah." He was quiet.

"I could never afford to move Delilah across the country," I said. "And I can't just leave her *here*. Anyway, my parents can't afford out-of-state tuition."

He sighed. "Well, maybe I'll have to see about transferring."

This made me laugh. "No one transfers *from* Yale."

"You want to hear something funny?"

I nodded.

"No one at Yale says straight out that they go to Yale. They say that they go to school in Connecticut."

"That's crazy. They can't be *ashamed* to say they go to Yale?"

Will shook his head. "It's considered gauche. Like bragging, you know? So everyone avoids saying it outright."

"But if that's what everyone does, then isn't it the same thing? I mean, if *Connecticut* is code for *Yale*, and if everyone knows the code, then what's the difference?"

Will shrugged. "No difference. It's just what people do."

"Do *you* do it, too?"

"Sure," he said.

"Like *when?*" I asked. "When does it come up?"

He shifted slightly and brushed my hair back from my temple. "Like a few weeks ago," he said. "Some guys and I went to Cambridge for The Game."

"What's 'The Game'?"

"It's our big rivalry game. You know, football. Every year Harvard and Yale play a game toward the end of football season. Lots of people care more about the outcome of that one game than the whole rest of the season's record. This year it was at Harvard; next year it'll be a home game for us."

"Okay," I said. "So you were in Cambridge for 'The Game.' Who won, by the way?"

"They did."

"Sorry."

"Not a big deal to me, really. But my roommate, Shane—he's a die-hard Bulldogs fan—he was pretty broken up."

"Condolences."

"I'll tell Shane. Anyway, yeah, we went out afterward for some drinks, and we met some people. And one of them asked me where I went to school. And I said, 'In Connecticut.'"

I noticed that Will had been careful not to apply a pronoun to this "person" he'd spoken with at the "place" he'd gone for drinks. "So where did she go to school?" I asked casually.

He laughed. "You're clever," he said, kissing my nose. "She said she went to school there, in Cambridge."

"Code for Harvard?"

"Uh-huh."

We were quiet for a while. Finally I said, "Will? Why did you tell me that story?"

He shrugged. "No reason."

"You're sure?"

After a minute he said, "How are things with the new guy?"

"Will Cohen." I laughed, but it sounded tinny. "Are you jealous?"

"I keep telling myself it isn't fair for me to be," he admitted, "but I am."

"Well, I don't exactly love the idea of you hanging out at a bar with a bunch of girls, either."

He ignored this. "Did you kiss him?"

"No," I said.

"Do you want to?"

"No," I said again, but neither of us believed me.

"You should kiss him," Will said.

"You *want* me to kiss him?"

Will touched his lips to my forehead, my nose, and then my mouth. He kissed me so gently, a hand cupping my cheek. Then he said, "No. Of course I don't want you to kiss him. But you should kiss him anyway."

"Did you kiss that girl at the bar?"

He shook his head, his lips brushing back and forth across my lips. "No," he said.

"Then why should I kiss Gunner?"

"Because you want to."

This time I didn't deny it. Instead I kissed him, trying to show him that right now I was here with him, on the top of Silver Peak, in his arms.

Then I said, "I'm starving. Let's see what your dad made for us."

We sat up and set aside our unfinished conversation as we unpacked the lunch. When Martin had heard our plan to climb Silver Peak, he'd offered to prepare our food. He kept his kitchen well stocked, and the picnic he'd packed didn't disappoint; it consisted of little packages of wrapped cheeses—Gouda and Bûcheron and Brie—along with crusty bread, grapes, salami and prosciutto, and two small bottles of fresh orange juice that he'd frozen to act as insulation for the rest of the food as we hiked. The orange juice had melted most of the way and was slushy and sweet.

We ate. Then, as the wind picked up even more, we packed up the picnic site, laughing as the blanket flapped and tried to escape. Downhill was easier and faster, but still it was past four o'clock when we finally turned onto Olive Lane. Will's brown-shingled cottage seemed like a beacon, a plume of smoke rising from its chimney. Will pushed open the gate for me, but before I walked through, I put my hand on his.

"Did you *want* to kiss the girl in the bar?" I asked the question and found I was terrified of the answer. It had taken me the length of our return hike to gather the courage to ask it, and he must have seen that in my face.

"I did," he admitted.

"Then why didn't you?"

"Because I wanted to kiss you more," he answered simply, and letting the pack slip to the ground, he did.

Too soon, Will's visit ran its course. I comforted myself by remembering that I'd be taking the ferry to the mainland with him, and that he, Martin, and I would spend two days with the Rabinovich family before Will and his dad had to be at LAX for their flight back to New Haven in time for Will's semester to start. Martin's, too; he seemed eager to get back to the classroom.

"There is something so *invigorating* about a live audience," he confessed to me on the ferry. We were sitting inside because a steady light rain was falling.

"I bet you're great in front of a class."

Martin nodded. "I would be lying if I said that wasn't true," he said. "And I try my best never to lie."

Next to me, Will rolled his eyes.

I squeezed his hand. It was cute to see him irritated with his dad, a relief to know I wasn't the only one with issues.

I'd told Will about what I'd seen—my dad kissing Alice. He'd whistled, long and low, before saying, "Well, what did your dad say?"

"I didn't *tell* him I'd seen them!"

"Oh. Why not?"

"I don't know. It was too weird."

"If I were you, Scarlett, I'd talk to him about it. I've noticed that things seem off between the two of you, and you've barely mentioned Alice all week."

"Yeah." I'd barely *seen* her, either. With Delilah officially on maternity leave there wasn't much of a pull to the stable, and Will's presence on the island made a pretty good excuse for me to avoid talking to either my dad or Alice. But it couldn't last forever; sooner or later I'd have to deal with them.

I chose later.

When we got to Sabine's house after walking from the port in the soft, endless mist, we found it ablaze with celebration. It seemed Sabine and David had invited over all of Martin's West Coast friends to spend time with him and to celebrate Shabbat—the day of rest that begins at sundown on Friday night. As with every other aspect of their lives, Sabine and her family celebrated the holy day in their own way. A large awning, which reminded me fondly of their sukkah, had been erected on their deck, and the party poured out from the open French doors.

Loud, joyful music—which may have been cranked up a little loud to entirely suit the neighbors—infused the party, along with the savory scent of garlic and meat. Even in this weather, Ari rolled bare-chested. He danced through the crowd on unshod feet, in a ratty pair of cutoff corduroys, arms spread wide. He hopped on one foot and then the other, weaving and spinning as if in a celebratory rain dance.

"Scarlett!" he called, and ran straight for me. Secretly, I was pleased that he'd singled me out rather than Will or Martin, though it had been way longer since he'd seen either of them.

"Hey, Ari," I said, giving him a hug. "Aren't you cold?" But his bare skin didn't *feel* cold; that kid must have run five degrees hotter than the rest of us.

Daniel came over next and awkwardly presented his hand, first to Martin, then to Will. They each shook it formally, giving due respect to his serious demeanor.

"Ah, Martin, Will!" Sabine called, winding through the crowd, holding a half-full glass of Burgundy. She looked so dressed-up and elegant, her long silk skirt, almost the same shade as her wine, swishing as she walked. David was beside her and each of them embraced the three of us. Ziva, I noticed, hung back; she was dressed, as her mother was, in a long, colorful skirt and a tucked-in blouse. Unlike Sabine, who wore her hair loose, Ziva had hers twisted in braids and then pinned at the nape of her neck. I saw her eyes scanning my outfit and I felt awkward and underdressed in my jeans and sweatshirt. But to be fair, I hadn't expected to walk into a party.

I also saw her gaze flicker down to my hand, grasped firmly by Will's, our fingers entwined. Then she glanced away.

"Looks like someone is jealous of you," Will whispered into my ear jokingly. "Better sleep with one eye open."

I smiled at his joke, but I made sure Ziva couldn't see me. Because I knew what she was feeling. I had felt it, myself. Around me the music and the laughter and the wine rose and crested and rolled like waves. I stood in the center of it, an island in this ocean of family and friends, Will's hand my anchor. And I tried very hard to keep myself in the moment, not counting the hours before Will would be high in the sky, flying home, away from me.

SIXTEEN
Toy District

*T*he next day was our last full day together. The sky, when I woke, was cloudless and blue. I woke alone in the same little room Sabine had given me on my other visits. Will had bunked with Ari and Daniel, and though he'd snuck into my room after the boys had fallen asleep, he'd left me just after three a.m.

"Martin's a light sleeper," he said, kissing me as he pulled on his flannel pajama bottoms. Martin was sleeping in the other room, on the foldout couch, and Will would have to walk past him to head up the stairs.

"I'll bet even when he's sleeping Martin knows what we're doing," I said, only half joking. Last year it was like he could sense a change in barometric pressure when Will and I were about to kiss and was uncanny about interrupting us just in time.

"You're probably right. Sometimes when I'm out wandering

at night he calls me, even if it's really late. I don't answer, but it's like he knows that I'm not where he thinks I should be."

I couldn't be too upset with Martin for that; even though Will and I hadn't talked very much about his nighttime wanderings, he knew I thought they were a really bad idea. To my mind, it was one thing to respond to a danger you knew was there; it was another thing entirely to search it out.

"Speaking of that," I said, reaching out and taking Will's hand, pulling the sheet across my chest, "I've been meaning to ask you something."

"Have you?" Will lowered himself to the edge of the bed. "What is it?"

"It's something I read," I said. "Have you ever heard of *makom sakana?*"

Will groaned. "Not you, too."

I ignored him. "As far as I can tell," I said, "*makom sakana* is a rule that says you aren't allowed to put yourself in a dangerous place to perform a good deed. A mitzvah, right? I read that it's prohibited to endanger yourself in order to help someone else."

"Have you and Martin been talking?" Will was smiling, but I could tell from the tone of his voice that he was annoyed.

I didn't care. I pressed on. "So as far as I can figure out, that rule means that what you're doing—seeking out trouble, putting yourself in harm's way *on purpose*—is against the rules."

"Whose rules?"

Just two little words. A single syllable each. A simple

question. But it tripped me up, and I stuttered out my answer. "I—I don't know . . . *God's* rules?"

Will's laugh carried no trace of humor. "Since when were *you* such a believer, Scarlett?"

I flushed. "That's not the point."

"It's *exactly* the point," Will said, trying to be quiet in spite of his agitation. "My father has thrown that same antiquated 'rule' in my face more than a few times. But even *he* isn't willing to say who wrote the damn thing in the first place. Scarlett, I can't live my life by someone else's moral code, someone else's fairy tales."

I hated how he could take my argument and make it sound foolish, twisting it around until I felt almost compelled to agree with him. The truth was, I was desperate. Tomorrow he would fly back to Connecticut; I would have no control over him there. And I was sick with worry that something terrible would happen to him. Something terrible was *bound* to happen to him, eventually. No one's good luck lasted forever.

"I could understand *before*," I said, struggling to keep my voice even and quiet, "when you got so sick when you didn't give in to the pull. But now—now that you're *choosing* to do it . . . it just seems so reckless."

"All I've got," Will said carefully, "is this one life. This one precious life. But, Scarlett"—his green eyes met mine intensely, seriously—"it's *my* life. And I get to dictate how I spend it."

He left unsaid the rest of what he was thinking, probably to spare my feelings. But I heard it just the same, in the echoing silence that followed: the rest of us—me, Martin, whoever else might hassle him—did not get a vote.

Will was going to do what Will was going to do.

And after he left, and after I cried for a while, for reasons I couldn't clearly articulate, my thoughts turned to his name.

Will.

I remembered what Gunner had said about his own name, and mine—Gunn and Scar. *I find it interesting,* he had said, *the similarity between our names.*

Both carried connotations of pain. Violence.

But Will was different. Will was force. Determination. Intention. Will was not about compromise, or second-guessing, or capitulating.

I lay in Sabine's guest bed wide awake in the dark and I wondered about Will. About us.

Will was extra sweet to me at breakfast, pouring syrup on my waffles and sliding me the last piece of turkey bacon. I could see he felt badly about how we'd left things, but I had gotten over my initial hurt and was trying to be pragmatic about the whole thing. Will seemed determined to martyr himself. That was *his* choice.

My choice? I wasn't sure, yet, what it would be.

After the family returned from synagogue, we spent most of the day hanging out at Sabine's house with the kids. Ari wanted to show Will how good he'd gotten at chess, and he didn't pout too much when Will roundly beat him. After lunch, Ziva shyly asked Will if he'd like to see the poems she'd been working on, and the two of them spent a while outside, chairs pulled close, poring over a notebook together.

I was not invited to join them.

But around four o'clock, Will asked David if we might borrow a car for a few hours, and we headed toward the city.

It seemed that we'd silently agreed to leave behind this morning's conversation and focus instead on our last night together. I had to pry my thoughts away from the ticking clock in my head that relentlessly counted down the minutes until eleven a.m. the next day, when Will and Martin would head for the airport.

But my mind had grown sharper and clearer with the past few months' practice, and when it tried to drift toward worry I measured my breathing and looped through a mantra Sabine had taught me—*Oseh Shalom*, each syllable exaggerated and drawn out. The Maker of Peace.

Traffic was amazingly light, and we made it downtown in less than half an hour. Will hadn't told me where we were going, but he'd said I should wear pants instead of a dress.

We found on-street parking in front of a broken meter, so we didn't even have to put in any quarters. Then we walked hand in hand up a hill, past the Los Angeles Public Library, and into a little Italian restaurant that was tucked, unassumingly, into the side of a parking garage.

Will had made reservations. The maître d' showed us to our table and kind of embarrassed me by spreading my napkin across my lap. He did Will's next, but I was the only one who seemed to think it was weird.

The restaurant served the traditional five-course dinner,

which Lily had raved about after she'd visited Italy, and I'd never experienced before. First came the appetizer—the antipasti—a selection of thinly sliced cold cuts, olives, and roasted peppers.

Then came the *primo*, the first course. Both Will and I had *spaghetti alla puttanesca*, the waiter's recommendation. By the time our *secondo*—veal marsala—arrived, I didn't think I had room for anything else. But it was so delicious that somehow I managed to make room for it.

The restaurant was alive all around us with sound and energy, clinking glasses and laughing, well-dressed families. Across from me, Will seemed to be enjoying his meal as much as I was.

I was about to take one last bite of bread dipped in olive oil and vinegar when I glanced up and found Will looking at me. His eyes were their most brilliant green. He smiled, and I smiled back.

The waiter arrived. *"Dolce?"* he asked.

"Excuse me?" I looked away from Will, shifting my focus to the waiter.

"Have you saved room for *dolce*? Something sweet?"

"Oh. No. I couldn't. Thank you, though. Maybe our check?"

The waiter bowed and left. I turned back to Will, reaching across the table for his hand.

Will paid the bill and we went outside. It was dark now, not terribly cold, but cool enough that I wound my red silk scarf one more time around my neck.

"You're going to be glad in a minute that you brought that

scarf," Will said. He seemed happy, light on his feet, and he walked with intention. I had to trot a few steps to keep up.

"Where are we going?"

"It's a surprise." He grinned. "A goofy surprise, so don't get too excited."

We walked down a long block, the buildings tall on both sides of us, cars backed up at a red light. Someone honked at a bicyclist who raced through an intersection against the signal.

Ahead, I could hear murmurs of live music, and as we crossed one more street and entered a pavilion, a woman's voice, slightly off-key, joined the instrumental, singing a generic country song. There was a big crowd up ahead and they seemed to be moving in a tightly packed circle, which didn't make any sense until I realized that they were ice-skating.

"Corny, huh?"

I laughed. "Totally," I said. "Perfect for the two of us."

We bought tickets for the next session and got in line to rent skates, then found a bench to swap out our shoes. My first set of skates had a broken lace and Will offered to get me a different pair. As I waited for him to navigate through the crowd to exchange them, I watched the skaters do their best to stay on their feet. It was so funny to see a skating rink in the middle of Los Angeles; winter here didn't even mean all that much *rain*, let alone *ice*, so the place was packed with people who seemed thrilled by the novelty of it all. As I watched, a little boy about nine years old went down hard on the ice. His mother tried to help him up, but he shook her off and climbed back up on his own, quickly wiping off the seat of his pants and skating on.

"Red Hot, fancy seeing *you* here."

Groan. Connell. Gunner had told me they were coming to the city to visit some of Connell's family, but in a population of thirty-eight million, what were the chances of running into them *here?*

"Hello, Connell," I said, swiveling my gaze in his direction. He grinned at me, tottering a little on his skates. Next to him was Gunner.

"Hello, Scarlett," he said. "Enjoying yourself?"

I was, I thought, but all I said was, "Mm-hmm."

In a way, Connell and Gunner were a study in opposites. There was something brutish about Connell, in the Neanderthal slope of his forehead, the brawny bulk of his shoulders, the almost constant forward thrust of his hips. Next to him Gunner was all grace and refinement—was that a *cravat?*—neatly shaven, well coiffed, easily balanced in the awkward rental skates.

But of the two of them, I mused, some unspoken quality made Gunner infinitely more dangerous. And even though they seemed so different, tonight they had something in common—a particular look in their eyes, one I'd never noticed there before. A glint, or a glaze . . . something kind of wild, I guess. Looking more carefully, I noticed that Connell's eyes were red-rimmed. I was about to ask him about it when Will returned with my skates.

"Hey-y!" chortled Connell. "It's the Jew!"

"Connell," chastised Gunner. "Don't be rude."

"It's okay," Will said, his voice level. "It's not an expletive."

"Certainly not," Gunner said, but he seemed a little unseated by Will's smooth response.

"Cohen," said Connell. He bounced a little on the toes of his skates and ran the back of his hand across his nose. "I don't think you've met Gunner. He came to the island after you left."

"No," said Will. His eyes were locked on Gunner, who stared right back. Neither of them turned to include Connell. "I haven't."

I realized then that the lady had stopped singing. A voice announced over the speakers, "All skaters clear the ice. After a ten-minute break for resurfacing, we will begin our next session. All skaters clear the ice."

A flood of wobbly skaters poured out of the arena and pushed forward to the benches, where they flopped down and began untying their laces and searching for their shoes.

Will turned to me and asked, "Do you want a drink before we skate?"

I nodded and finished knotting my laces. Will gave me his hand to help me up. We headed for the snack bar, leaving Connell and Gunner standing by the benches.

I felt sick. There wasn't a scenario that I could imagine in which I would have liked to see Will and Gunner face to face. But skating together, in the same packed rink, with the awful wail of a third-rate country singer over a bad sound system? Jesus.

We got a couple of sodas and stood watching the Zamboni

turn its little circles in the skating rink. By now a long line of would-be skaters had formed around the arena, laces double-knotted, waiting for the Zamboni to leave the ice and the disembodied voice on the speaker to give them the go-ahead.

I could hear Will's question—*So that's him?*—but he didn't voice it, and I didn't answer. I drank my soda way too fast, triggering hiccups. This was just getting better and better.

Finally the ice was clear and the announcer invited the crowd into the rink. The crowd shuffle stepped through the gate and did its collective best not to fall. The country singer crooned once more. And the last thing I had any desire to do was ice-skate.

I looked over at Will to see if he might possibly feel the same way, but his mouth was set in a grim line. "Come on," he said, taking my can and chucking it and his into the recycling container. "Let's go have some fun."

Somehow there was room on the crowded ice for two more of us, and Will and I joined the mob in its slow, counterclockwise turn around the rink. Up close, the country singer looked like she was having a blast, dancing along with her own music, occasionally clapping her hands and leaning into her microphone as if it was her lover.

I had to hand it to Will; he knew how to make the best of something. For even as I felt Gunner and Connell watching us, and even as I heard a few snide comments from Connell ("The Jew can't skate any better than he can kiss"), Will held my hand and rubbed his thumb against my palm in that sweetly distracting way he had, and he sang along with the country song, and he even dipped me once, managing to keep us both on our feet.

After a while I forgot to keep track of where Gunner and Connell were on the ice, and I didn't notice when it had been a while since Connell's last disparaging remark, and when the lady started singing "Sweet Baby James," I joined in, realizing only as the song reached its last poignant notes that I'd heard the song not only on the radio but in my dream, in the car where Will's mother died.

"Scarlett?" Will's voice came to me from far away. People skated by on both sides, but I was no longer moving, though it seemed the world spun around me. The woman sang, but it wasn't her voice I heard; it was the voice on the car radio, crooning, *Deep greens and blues are the colors I choose, won't you let me go down in my dreams?*

The flash of green. The sound of metal crunching. The cold hard pressure of ice beneath me.

It was the cold that brought me to my senses. I had sunk to my knees on the ice and it had soaked through my jeans. Will knelt beside me. His face was anxious, his gaze, searching.

"Scarlett," he said again, and helped me back to my feet. Together we made our way to the gate.

The singer had begun another song, and no one seemed to notice us at all. Connell and Gunner were gone. Will's arm wound around my waist, supporting my weight, and we returned to the bench where we'd left our shoes. Will lowered me to the bench and then knelt at my feet, working free the knots in my laces and pulling off my skates. After

252

we'd put our street shoes back on, Will returned the skates. It wasn't until we had walked up the street to a nearby coffee place, ordered drinks, and sat across from each other holding them that Will finally said, "So, Scarlett, what happened back there?"

I had tried to tell him once before about my dreams, but he had been distracted by his own problems, and I don't think what I had been saying had really sunk in. So I told him again, as I had told Sabine—about my visions of Will, first as a baby, then in the car, and of the day we'd met on the trail. He nodded and listened as I talked, but when I told him about my most recent dream—him running through a cityscape, leaving someone else behind, he looked confused.

"I don't know what any of this means, Scarlett," he said. "It's possible that you just have a really great imagination, I guess. Did I ever mention to you what song was playing when we got in that accident?"

I shook my head.

"Then it must be something more. But that last dream you told me about . . . I don't remember anything like that ever happening."

For now I was happy just to focus on the other dreams, to sit face to face with Will and share with him the things I'd seen as I slept. The song on the ice had brought it all back.

I sipped my drink. There was something so soothing about a cup of tea: sweet and creamy, so hot I could take only the smallest of sips.

"I wonder what my dad would say," Will said.

"I suppose we could ask him."

"We will."

I smiled. It felt better now, talking about my dreams together.

Will looked like he was about to say something else, and his hand reached out for mine, but then his head swiveled toward the window. My gaze followed; there was nothing to see, though, just a group of people walking by: two girls about my age laughing over something on one of their phones, and just behind them a father carrying his daughter—she looked about nine or ten—as she threw a tantrum.

Will stood up and started toward the door, abandoning his drink.

"Will?" I said, feeling eerily like we had traded roles in a scene we'd already run, it was so much like the way I'd zoned out and sunk down to the ice.

He pushed open the door and stepped outside. I caught up with him and grabbed his hand, squeezing it. He looked up the street, but it was empty; the people we'd seen through the window had all disappeared.

Just up ahead the door to a Chinese restaurant was swinging closed; Will strode toward it and pulled it open. At the counter, waiting for a table, were the two girls, still giggling over their phone. One of them, the blonde, grabbed the phone from her friend and typed something quickly into it.

"No way!" squealed her friend, but Will released the door, and it swung closed. I would never know what the girls had been laughing about.

Now Will walked more quickly, stopping briefly at the corner to peer to the left before pulling me to the right instead. The light was against us but no cars were coming, and as we reached the far curb Will broke into a run, weaving through the crowded street.

I could hear music from the pavilion where we'd skated; it was different now, radio music, loud and pounding through the speakers.

I ran, too, and tried once more to get his attention— "Will?"—but he didn't even turn his head. I didn't know where we were or where we were headed, but I was scared. The buildings lurched high above us, casting long stretchy shadows across the street like spiderwebs. Will turned a corner, then ran a stretch, then turned another corner. Behind us, I heard a siren's wail and chills shot up my spine.

A sharp pain bit into my side; I was having trouble keeping up. Will kept running just as quickly, dodging in and out through the crowd. I stumbled over a crack in the sidewalk.

"Will," I said again, but still he didn't turn. Instead he squeezed my fingers, and then let go.

Once he'd dropped my hand I could see how much I'd been holding him back. He shot ahead now, doubling and then tripling the distance between us, and then he turned another corner and disappeared.

I slowed and stopped, panting, the stream of pedestrians splitting around me. I massaged the cramp in my side and stood, breathing heavily, but I couldn't just let Will vanish like that, so I started walking again, then jogging.

The crowd thinned as I got farther from the pavilion and its surrounding streets. Soon there were just a few other people, and then I was alone.

The storefronts were all dark, but the windows were full of displays of dolls and strollers, monster trucks and stuffed animals.

This must be the Toy District, I thought, but knowing that didn't dispel the freaky sensation of being alone in the dark. I was starting to wonder if maybe I had missed a turn somewhere, if maybe Will had changed his mind and turned back for me, if maybe I should return to the spot he'd left me or go back to the coffee shop, even.

Then I heard a muffled cry up ahead, around the next corner, or in one of the shops off to my left. I stopped short and listened carefully, trying really hard to not make a sound.

And then I heard something else—a human voice, twisted in fury, a roar.

I knew that voice. It was Will's.

SEVENTEEN
Eye for an Eye

I stood perfectly still for one more moment. Then I went forward again, my legs shaky, my whole body, actually, trembling.

I didn't know what I would find around that next corner. Whatever it would be, I knew it wasn't good. Will had sounded vengeful, furious. Still, I couldn't turn away.

It took me a minute to make sense of what I was seeing. There were two shapes in the night-dark alley, but three voices.

There was the sound of someone—a man—begging for mercy and sniveling in pain; there was a girl's voice, crying; and there was Will, unleashing a string of curses, a tirade of anger in which the ferocious tone of his voice carried more meaning than the sum of his words.

The girl was folded into a ball against the far wall of the alley; she huddled as if she were in an earthquake drill, her head between her knees and her arms up over her head. Across from her, Will dominated the man, who was sprawled on the ground. Will's whole energy seemed to have expanded, and he rained punches down on the man's prone figure—his head, his chest—like a monster or an angered god.

I didn't recognize the man—his face was swollen and bloody—but the girl . . . I remembered her pink Windbreaker from earlier. She'd been having a tantrum in her father's arms, outside the coffee shop.

"Will!" I said, as if the recognition of the girl's jacket had shaken me from paralysis. "Will, stop!" I yelled as I tried to grab his arm, before he delivered another blow to the girl's father. But it was like he didn't even feel me, as if I were invisible. His fist made contact with the man's nose with a sickening crunch of cartilage, and fresh blood flowed in twin streams from the man's nostrils.

I was yelling, clawing at Will to get him to stop, but it wasn't until after he had stood and kicked the man twice, hard, in his gut that he turned to me.

Green fire lit his eyes. His expression—turbulent, passionate, rageful—transformed him into someone I didn't know.

I'd seen a similar expression on his face last year, on the island, when he'd attacked Andy outside of the theater. His face had borne a trace of this same fury then, though not to this degree.

"What are you *doing*, Will?" I said. "You're going to kill that girl's father!"

"He's not her father." Will's voice was steely.

I was confused. I looked at the girl, still huddled on the ground. Her crying had subsided and she seemed to be trying to disappear, as if sitting still enough would make her invisible.

And then I understood. The man wasn't her father. The girl wasn't his daughter.

"Oh, Will," I said. "You saved her."

He nodded grimly. The sirens I had heard earlier grew louder. They were searching for the girl.

Will looked around. "Get her out of here," he said. It was an order, not a request. But I didn't follow it.

"What are you going to do?" I was afraid, so afraid to hear the answer.

"Just get her out of here," he said again. He sounded desperate this time, as the siren's wail got closer.

"Are you going to . . . hurt him?" It was a ridiculous question; the man was already hurt. He lay moaning on the ground, clutching his stomach and curled up on his side.

"What do you think he was trying to do to *her?*" Will indicated the girl. She had pulled herself up to sitting and was wiping her nose on the sleeve of her jacket. Her hair was unkempt and there was a bruise forming high on her right cheek. "What do you think he'll do to the next girl he gets ahold of?"

"But you saved her, you're a hero! The cops are coming. Let's flag them down. They'll arrest him."

I felt like I was trying to talk Will down, trying to convince him not to do something terrible.

But his eyes still glowed with angry fire. "Get the girl out of here," he said again.

"No," I whispered. "I won't let you kill him."

Will didn't deny that had been his plan. "He's vermin," he spat. "You're protecting *vermin?*"

"Will!"

"The world would be better without him, without people like him. I'd be doing everyone a favor."

Maybe that was true; maybe the world would be a cleaner, better place if Will snuffed out this man's life here, tonight. The thought sickened me. "But, Will, that's not your call to make."

"Maybe it is. Maybe it should be."

I shook my head. "No. Don't you see? If you kill him, then you're a criminal, too."

"An eye for an eye," he said grimly.

"You don't mean that."

"Don't I?"

We stared at each other, our gazes locked, neither of us willing to back down. I don't know what would have happened next, if we'd stayed like that, just the two of us with the poor girl as our witness. But then the alley was flooded with the blinding lights of the police cruiser, and two cops got out, guns drawn, and the girl cried with relief as she stumbled toward them.

Will looked at me still as the officer yelled at us to put our hands behind our heads, and his eyes told me I had failed him.

• • •

The next hours were a blur. It didn't take the officers long to sort out who was the good guy and who was the bad guy, and they led the girl's assailant off in handcuffs. He didn't fight them, and his eyes were so swollen that he had to be guided to the cruiser.

The girl explained that Will had shown up in the alley, that he had torn her from the man's arms. After the cruiser had pulled away with the man in the back, the girl calmed down measurably.

"I tried to fight," she said to the cop who'd stayed behind. "I kicked and yelled, but no one did anything. Until *he* came. He saved me." She smiled at Will, a broad bright smile.

I had seen her through the window. I had thought nothing of it.

Does that happen often? I wondered. How many cries for help go unnoticed?

"You roughed him up pretty bad," said the cop, a young guy with cropped dark hair and a mustache. I thought at first that he was going to reprimand Will, maybe even charge him with assault, but then he held his fist up in the air for Will to bump.

Will looked at it for a second, then tapped it with his own fist. Dried blood crusted his knuckles.

Two more cop cars arrived, one of them carrying the girl's parents. The woman pushed out of the cruiser almost before it had stopped, and the sight of her mother crumbled the girl again and she collapsed, sobbing, in her arms. The girl and her parents left in one of the cars, for the hospital or the police station, I didn't know.

"We're going to need your statement," the young cop said to Will. He sounded apologetic, like he felt bad about inconveniencing him after all he'd already done.

"Sure, sure," said Will.

"Yours too," the policeman said to me. "Are you his girlfriend?"

Mutely, I nodded.

"Lucky girl to have such a brave guy," he said. "*You'll* never have anything to worry about, huh?"

The cop with the mustache drove us himself. Will told him where we'd left our car, and he took us to it. "It must be your lucky night," he said, nodding to the broken meter. We climbed into the car and followed the cruiser to the station. He even turned on his whirling lights, which fractured and blurred, magnified by my unspilled tears.

Of course they called my mother. I was still seventeen—a minor. It was like a weird repeat of last spring, when my parents had come for me after the Long Beach fire.

But everything had changed since then. My mom came alone and was wearing heels and a frilly shirt. Date clothes.

And Martin wasn't here, as he had been in the spring. Will, nearly nineteen, didn't need a guardian.

Mom hugged me quickly, leaving a cloud of sweet perfume around me. "Scarlett, what happened?"

I wasn't sure what to say. I didn't fully know what had happened in that alley—to Will, to me.

"She's okay, Mrs. Wenderoth," Will said. "Scarlett's not hurt."

The mustachioed cop chimed in, "I'll say! As long as she's got that boyfriend, she won't be, either."

He seemed to have one line.

Will gave my mom the abbreviated version of the night's events. She gasped and shook her head in all the right places. But I couldn't get past wondering who she was so dressed up for. Where had she been when she'd gotten the call from the police station? Whom had she been with?

The officers interviewed each of us, and then we were free to leave. But not before each cop stood up to individually shake Will's hand. Then one of them got the idea to take a group picture with the hero. No one seemed to notice when I opted out, heading toward the door.

No one but Will. He noticed, but said nothing.

My mom offered to take me home with her, to the apartment. Part of me wanted to go, to avoid being alone with Will, but then I wouldn't get another chance to talk with him before his flight in the morning. And though she acted disappointed when I refused, she kissed me rather distractedly before hurrying off to her car.

I wondered if maybe she planned to resume her date.

Will and I didn't talk much as we drove back to Sabine's house. He asked me once if I was okay, and I nodded. I watched out the window as the stream of lights flashed by.

When we got back to Linnie Canal, Will hit the button on the garage door opener and we pulled into the garage. He cut the engine and the door closed behind us, but neither of us moved to leave the car. Any minute someone might come out to the garage. I had to ask the question that had been preying on me since the alley. I had to ask it now, while we were still alone.

"Have you ever killed anyone?"

Will's jaw tensed. He stared straight ahead, hands gripping the wheel as if he was still driving. Finally he shook his head.

I let out a breath I hadn't realized I'd been holding.

"No," he said. "But I should have. The only reason I haven't yet is because I'm weak."

"That's insane, Will," I said. "You haven't killed anyone because you're not like that."

"I'm not so sure," he answered. "I think I'd *like* to be like that."

"No, you wouldn't."

He laughed a little, probably at how certain I sounded. "You can never really know what's going on in someone else's heart," he said. "But I know what I've seen. And some of the things I've seen . . . the people who were doing them, those people don't deserve to live."

The door into the house opened and a square of light illuminated the dark garage. Martin's shape filled the doorway.

"Son?" he called.

Martin started the teakettle. Slumping into a kitchen chair, I thought about how different everything had been when I'd had my last cup of tea. Then, I had felt that I knew Will better than anyone. Since then, I'd seen parts of him I didn't understand. Things I wish I could unsee. And since then, he'd warned me that I could never really know what was in his heart. Maybe he was right.

Of course Martin had known as soon as Will had gotten out of the car that something had happened; though Will had definitely dominated the fight with the man in the alley, he hadn't escaped entirely unscathed. Aside from his bloodied knuckles, Will had an eye that was growing more purplish black by the minute. There were dark stains on his sweater, and the knees of his pants had been blackened by the asphalt. One was torn.

"Take a shower, son," said Martin. "I'll keep the kettle warm for you. Then we'll talk."

The rest of the household must have been asleep. That particular kind of quiet permeated the house, the quiet of peace and night. Martin was wearing his pajamas—striped flannel—and a plaid robe. On his feet were corduroy slippers. It didn't look like he'd been woken by the sound of the garage door opening; a lamp was lit next to the kitchen, illuminating a stack of books and papers.

"I was planning for the new semester," Martin said, following my gaze to the table. "We all try, don't we, to plan the best we know how?"

In English this year, we were reading Steinbeck and the poetry of Robert Burns. " 'The best-laid schemes of mice and men . . . ,'" I murmured.

"'Often go awry,'" finished Martin. "So you know just what I mean."

The kettle boiled. Martin placed tea bags in two cups and

poured water over them. "Why don't you tell me what happened, Scarlett?"

Then the tears came. I sniffed and sobbed and spilled out the story to Martin, telling him much more than I intended to share. I told him about watching Will beat the holy hell out of the man in the alley; I told him about the song that played at the ice rink, and the dream it recalled; I told him about how my most recent dream had seemed to herald tonight's terrible string of events. I even told him about Gunner, and my father and Alice, and how pretty my mom had looked at the station, all dressed up.

And Martin listened. Honestly, he was probably the best listener I had ever met in my entire life. He listened and refreshed my tea and spooned sugar into my cup. At last I had emptied myself of all the weight of my worries, the burden of my secrets. And my tears were spent, too. In my hands I held my cup of tea, my head bent over it as if in prayer.

Martin said nothing for a good while after I'd finished speaking. There was no way Will was still in the shower, after all this time. Most likely he was giving me some space, which I appreciated. Really, I wasn't ready to see him. Not right now.

Finally, Martin spoke. "Scarlett, I have known from the first that you are a remarkable young woman."

"I don't see what's so remarkable," I said. "I'm angry at my parents and ridiculously emotional and confused about just about everything."

"And do you think your visions are run-of-the-mill as well?"

He had me there. "Probably not," I said. "But it's not like I can control them."

"No. Not yet."

"Wait. You think I could *learn* to control them?"

"Most probably yes. If you would like to."

I considered. "I don't even know what they mean."

"I think *I* might," said Martin. "What you've told me lends credence to a theory I've had for some time."

"A theory?"

He nodded. "Would you like to hear it?"

"Of course!"

"In all your reading, Scarlett, the research you have undertaken in your Kabbalah studies, have you come across the term *yehidah*?"

I shook my head.

"Kabbalah teaches that there is more than one dimension to the human soul. In fact, there are five. Each of these five soul levels allows us to interact in a different way with the world around us. Some of the dimensions of our soul are grounded in the physical; others relate intimately to less tangible aspects of our world. And I think that each of us has developed these different soul dimensions to various degrees. What you or I might call the *highest* level of the soul—that which is most closely connected to the divine—is *yehidah*."

"Okay," I said. "So where do I come in?"

"*Yehidah* is a part of us that most people never tap into. Have you ever heard the old saying that we only use ten percent of our brain?"

I nodded.

"Maybe a Kabbalistic equivalent of that belief would be to say that we all have *yehidah*, but very few of us can access it."

"I'm confused. What is *it*, exactly?"

"*Yehidah* is that which unifies. That which connects us to each other, to the God within us all. Maybe when you have one of your dreams, you are connecting that which is God in you to that which is God in Will."

I didn't know what to say to this.

"Incidentally," Martin said, smiling now, "many call *yehidah* the 'world of will.'"

My head was spinning. Here was Martin handing me a far-fetched explanation that used terms like "God in you" and "soul dimensions" to explain my impossible dreams. And he was talking about it as calmly as whether or not it might rain tomorrow. "How can you be so mellow right now?" I said. "I mean, after what happened tonight with Will?"

Martin sighed, and his expression changed, growing weary. "I have many teachers, Scarlett, many scholars and philosophers whose advice I turn to when I feel lost. One of them once said, 'The saddest thing in life and the hardest to live through is the knowledge that there is someone you love very much whom you cannot save from suffering.'"

I considered his words. "It's not fair, is it?"

"No, it is not. Not at all."

"Who said that, by the way?" I was thinking he'd answer with the name of some professor or rabbi.

"Agatha Christie," he said. "Something of an anti-Semite, but she can write a hell of a good mystery."

268

I laughed. Martin did, too. It felt good to laugh for a moment, after everything that had happened. Then I asked him, "Martin, if it's true—about my soul—why would *I* be tapping into the *yehidah* part of it? Why me?"

"Ah, yes. The age-old question. Perhaps, though, Scarlett, the question should not be 'why you?' but rather 'why not the rest of us?' We all have *yehidah*, but so few of us can access it. Think of it this way: each of us has the door within us that leads to that place. But few of us possess the key that can open it. You have the key, Scarlett, whether it was something born to you or something you have developed, we cannot truly know. Only that you have it. There is something brilliant in that truth, Scarlett. Something full of splendor."

My cup was empty. I was so tired. Will had not come back downstairs; I was beginning to doubt whether he planned to. Finally I stood. "Well, Martin, thank you."

"What for?"

"For the tea. For listening. For being great."

"Ah, yes. My specialties, all three. I have one more specialty—giving unsolicited advice. Might you take some?"

I shrugged. "Why not?"

Though his tone had just been light, he grew more serious before he spoke. He stood too, as if to indicate the importance of what he was about to say. "It can be tempting, Scarlett, to lose yourself in the search for truth, the search for beauty. Actually, one can become lost in the search for anything at all, no matter how significant or insignificant. But remember—to get lost is a choice. To lose yourself is a choice. We all make choices. And those choices lead to consequences."

Martin was speaking to me, but I got the feeling that he was thinking of Will as well. And then he said, "The older I get, the more I find importance in balance. Lean too far in one direction, there is no balance. Lean too far in the opposite direction, and balance is lost as well. Try to remember, Scarlett, that too much of anything—even something good—results in instability. And without balance, all is lost."

But I think by this point I was too tired to fully hear what he was saying. Suddenly I needed to lie down, to pull a blanket up over my shoulders and shut my eyes. So I said, "Okay, Martin, thanks for the advice," and I set my cup in the sink, and I walked to my little room, weary to the bone. Too tired even to change, I stripped off my jeans and crawled into bed.

And then I slept, undisturbed by dreams, unvisited by Will.

EIGHTEEN
Witch's Brew

I had one day of peaceful solitude on the island. Dad was working in the garden, raking up the last of the late-falling leaves, and Lily was still making her way home from Australia. She'd sent me a text (*Australian boys are rad*), and we'd made plans to hang out at her place as soon as she landed.

I spent the day hand-walking Delilah on the trail. She seemed to enjoy the company. We stuck to the flat, easy trails just around the stable. Alice was in her office, but other than poking her head out the door to wave at me, she kept to herself. Maybe she could feel my vibe—not social—or maybe she had an idea that I knew what was going on between her and Dad. Or maybe she just didn't feel like talking, either. Whatever.

Just seeing her face, the smooth winglike waves of her hair, her neatly rolled sleeves, made my insides roil. She had a husband! She had sons! Not to mention my mom, who was her close friend—sure, Mom had left Dad, but even still. . . .

Looking back, maybe I shouldn't have been surprised to find out that Alice wasn't entirely who I'd thought she was. What was it she had said, the day of the Undersea Ball last year?

"I love Howard," she'd said. "But there's something about the first date . . . if it's with the right guy, it can be magic."

Was it magic she felt in the arms of my father? Did *he* feel the magic, too?

And *could* it be magical—this thing they were doing, this illicit affair? How could it be, when it stood to ruin Alice's marriage, to disappoint and hurt her children?

Can one person's magic be another's horror show?

Apparently.

And of course this brought me back to Will, in the alley, smiting that little girl's assailant. The look on his face, in his eyes . . . I couldn't get it out of my mind. He'd been vengeance personified.

No matter what the circumstances, no matter how much the guy deserved it, there was something *wrong* about Will enjoying it so much.

By now Will was back at college. Maybe he would go out again, tonight. Maybe he would look for someone who deserved to be punished. Maybe tonight would be the night when Will would cross the line I felt so certain he should never cross.

Would I feel it, if he did? Would I know in my heart, through our connection, that Will had made a choice like that? If he chose to end a life?

Was there no one I could count on to remain the same? It didn't seem like it. Mom, Dad, Alice, Will, Lily . . . all of them seemed to be changing, slipping away from me. Only Ronny remained the same—consistently, persistently dead.

Delilah was certainly changing. Just in the couple of days I'd been away from the island, she seemed to have grown. I wondered glumly if she would transfer all her affection to her foal when it was born, if she'd even nicker anymore when she saw me coming.

"Enough!" I said, sick to death of my own petulance. Delilah snorted into the grass she was chewing, as if agreeing with me.

When I left the stable, I honked two sharp blasts instead of saying goodbye, not even looking to see if Alice responded.

Lily got home on Friday, late; school would start back up on Monday. That Saturday night, some of the guys had decided to have a bonfire. I didn't really feel like going, but there was no way Lily was missing a party, and moping around my place all alone didn't sound like a lot of fun.

It was just past noon when Lily texted me. *Come over! Bring chocolate.*

Luckily I'd spent the morning making brownies. Normally I'd leave a few for my dad, but I guess my passive-aggressive dark side kicked in, because I packed them all to take with me. The twins, I knew, could scarf down three each, minimum.

Laura answered the door. She smiled and hugged me. "Boy, will Lily be glad to see you," she said. "Come on in."

Lily was taking a shower, so I followed Laura to the kitchen. The house was strangely quiet. Jet lag, I figured, just one of the many drawbacks of being globe-trotting millionaires. Jack was sacked out on the couch in front of a football game, his head back and his mouth open. The twins curled on the oversized beanbags; it looked like they'd been in the middle of some building project when they'd passed out. A half-completed structure sat between them, and Henry still clutched a little plastic block in his sweaty palm.

Laura unwrapped my brownies and bit into one. "Mmm, still warm."

"So how was Australia?"

"Hot. Dry. Beautiful. Want to see the pictures?" She tossed me her phone and I scrolled through about a hundred snapshots: the twins snorkeling; the twins kayaking; the twins sharing a gigantic platter of shrimp; the twins grinning hugely, flanking a kangaroo . . . in boxing gloves.

"Look at that!" I said. "They boys got their wish."

"I know. Isn't it great?" Laura had that particular look of satisfaction she wore when her children got their way.

"Not a lot of pictures of Lily," I noted.

Laura's expression went flat. "No," she said. "Lily wasn't feeling very photogenic, I guess."

I have to admit, I felt bad for Laura. It seemed like all her everything was wound up in making sure things went just right for her kids. She and Jack were probably the most devoted parents I'd ever known; everything for them was about *family.*

Why couldn't Lily just enjoy what she had? Would it be

that hard to pose for a few family pictures while on vacation in *Australia?*

"Scarlett," said Laura, "maybe you can fill me in. Do you have any idea what's going on with Lily? Do you think it has anything to do with this new boy she's been seeing?" Her face wrinkled up. "I never thought the day would come when I'd have to ask anyone else what was going on with my own daughter."

I squirmed a little. I loved Laura, and I wanted to help her out, but my first loyalty, whether or not she irritated me, was to Lily. Besides, I didn't have any special insight into her inner workings. Lily was Lily.

"I guess it's pretty normal, right?" I said. "Teenage rebellion?"

"For *other* people's kids, maybe. Not *mine*. Honestly, what on earth could Lily feel the need to rebel *against?*" Laura spread her arms wide, indicating their beautiful kitchen, the homey stack of books and games on the table, and even, I thought, herself.

"I don't know, Laura. Maybe it's just a phase."

She sighed. "A phase. I'm sure you're right." Then she brightened a little. "Well, in any case, it can't last too much longer. None of Lily's phases do. Remember when she decided in the seventh grade to be a vegan? That lasted only about three hours." She put a half-dozen brownies on a pink plate and handed it to me.

"Sure, Laura," I said. But as I headed up the wide blue staircase to Lily's room, it occurred to me that maybe Laura should try to stop thinking of her daughter as the preteen she used to be. That was bound to lead only to disappointment.

"You are an *angel*," Lily moaned as I entered her room with the plate of brownies. Droplets of water clung to the ends of her curls and dripped onto her bare shoulders. She was wrapped in a cloud-soft white towel. From her attached bathroom, steam seeped slowly into the room.

"Welcome home." I held out the plate and Lily chose a brownie.

"*Divine*," she said. She took a bite and walked over to her dresser. Setting the brownie on top of it, she pulled open a few drawers and assembled an outfit: underwear and a bra, a black turtleneck sweater, a pair of charcoal jeans.

"*That's* what you're wearing?" The outfit she'd chosen was perfect for a bonfire, and it wasn't all that different from my own jeans-and-sweater ensemble (though I couldn't stand turtlenecks). But it was just so . . . sensible.

"You think I'll be warm enough?"

"Uh-huh. But will you be *fashionable* enough?"

"I look great in sweaters, Scar. You know that. And besides, Gunner texted especially to remind me to dress warm. Isn't that sweet, how he looks out for me?"

"Mm-hmm," was all I said. I watched her shimmy into the jeans and smiled a little as she fastened a silver chain around her hips, almost like it would have pained her to forgo a little something fun.

"Shut up," Lily laughed, catching my smile in the mirror above her dresser. She spritzed some stuff in her hair and leaned her head to the side, lightly tousling her curls. Then she retrieved her brownie and took another bite. "So," she said, "spill it."

I knew she wanted to hear all about my time with Will. But I didn't know what to say. I could tell her about how we'd lain together in my bed, how he'd kissed my breasts, flicked his tongue into my belly button, how I'd worked up the nerve at last to stretch my hand down between his thighs, how the sound he'd made at my touch did as much to turn me on as any of his kisses.

Or I could tell her how we'd roamed the island together, sometimes sitting quietly, facing toward the mainland, and other days from other vantage points looking out at the open sea, the only boundary the straight line of the horizon, far away.

I could tell her about the look in Will's eyes as he implored me to leave him alone in the alley, the look of desperation as he realized the sirens were drawing closer.

I could tell her how we said goodbye—awkwardly, Sabine and her family trying to look away to give us some privacy, David behind the wheel of the car waiting to take Will and Martin to the airport.

I could tell her that four days had passed since we had spoken. That I knew Will was waiting for me to call him. That I didn't know what to say.

"I think Will and I might break up."

"What?" Lily's dark eyes were huge. "What happened?"

I shrugged, miserable. "I don't know. Maybe things are just different, you know, after someone goes away to college."

"Is there another girl?"

I remembered the girl who went to school "in Cambridge." "No," I said. "Maybe. I don't know."

I sat on Lily's bed. She shook her head, thinking for a minute, and then she sank down next to me. "Here," she said, holding out what was left of her brownie. "Have mine."

There was a plate of half a dozen brownies resting on her desk where I'd set it. And Lily was offering me this one—half-eaten, the depressions of her front teeth carved clearly into its side.

That was why I loved Lily. That was why she was my best friend. Because she would always, always give me half her brownie.

I took the brownie. I bit into it. There was still a hint of warmth, just enough that the little chocolate chips burst open as I bit down. It was the sweetest thing, maybe, that I had ever tasted.

"Hey, Scar," said Lily.

"What?"

"Let's have fun tonight."

The party was at the same hidden cove that Lily and I had gone to last year, the day we'd ditched school. The only way to access it was down a cliff, hard enough to manage in daylight but far more difficult on a moonless night like this one. Lily and I managed it fairly well; she scraped her hand on a rock and swore viciously, but other than that we arrived on the sand unscathed.

Down the beach a ways, the bonfire was already glowing, its orange and red flames a welcome beacon.

"Imagine having to carry firewood down that cliff," Lily said, sucking on her hand where she'd scraped it. "I am so glad I'm not a guy."

"Why? Because you don't like carrying things?"

"Sure. Among other things. Come on."

As we got closer to the fire, the silhouettes of my classmates began to come into focus. But even before the forms grew faces, I could tell who the main players were, just from the way they held their bodies.

There was Kaitlyn Meyers, perched predictably on a boy's lap—was it Josh Riddell's?—her legs crossed, her head thrown back in laughter. Andy was nowhere to be seen.

There was Connell, brutish, broad, stacking logs near the fire.

And Gunner. True to form, he stood apart from the rest of the people, who were all huddled pretty close to the fire—it *was* January, after all. But maybe he was kept warm by the tiny glow of the cigarette drooping from his mouth.

He turned toward us as we walked up the beach, though our feet were silent against the sand. Like he could sense us coming, or smell us.

"Ladies," he said when we met halfway. He inserted himself between Lily and me and took Lily's hand in his left, mine in his right. "Now the party can begin."

Debauchery. That about summed it up. Alcohol was a given. So was pot. The thrumming music, the flickering fire, the briny ocean smell . . . it all combined into a witch's brew, a concoction designed to stoke the smoldering fire.

After the Halloween party at Andy's house junior year,

I'd resolved never to get drunk again. So as the beers got passed around, lubricating the conversation and the dancing and the kissing, too, I staunchly shook my head.

Not Lily, though. It was like she was a special kind of alive; everything about her seemed a little bit sharper, brighter, and more beautiful than usual. Always there had been something magnetic about her. As long as we'd been friends—all our lives—others had looked to Lily as their measuring stick.

What to wear? After Lily showed up to school last fall in a buttery leather suit from Italy rocking a pair of shoulder pads, other girls started working shoulder pads into *their* wardrobes. In the eighth grade, when Lily had triumphantly appeared on the first day of school with her curls—which she'd always worn long—trimmed into an ear-length bob, it wasn't long before more than a few of the other girls cut their hair off, too.

And when Lily started dancing at a party—like she was doing now, swinging loose from her hips, her arms up over her head as if she wanted to fill as much space as possible with her wonderful Lily-ness, her eyes closed because she didn't care whether or not people were looking at her— invariably, that was when others joined in.

And that was how I would remember her. In motion. So beautiful. Alive.

I guess I was shivering, watching Lily dance, because Gunner came over to me and offered his flask.

"Just a little nip," he said. "To warm you up."

"Alcohol doesn't actually make you warmer," I said. "It only makes you *feel* warmer."

"Isn't that just as good?" Gunner smiled and wagged the flask in front of me. It caught the light of the fire and shimmered.

Was it? Is illusion as good as reality, as long as you can't tell the difference?

I accepted the flask, unscrewed it, and took a sip. I didn't know what kind of liquor it was; it was cool in my mouth but burned as I swallowed, and it tasted sweet and bitter all at once, like licorice.

"What is this?"

"Absinthe," Gunner said. "Do you like it?"

I shrugged. Not really, but I took another sip anyway. And then a third. My year-old promise to myself to avoid drunkenness seemed less important with each sip.

Eventually, Lily danced over to us. She looked like she'd maybe been doing more than drinking. Her eyes were shining ebony, like her pupils had taken over, and a high spot of red colored each of her cheeks. "Two of my favorite people," she said, and held a hand out to each of us.

Gunner tucked his flask back into his jacket—shaking it first, to determine how much I had drunk and then smiling at me with approval—and took one of her hands. I took her other. The absinthe was doing its job admirably; I wasn't so cold anymore, and the music seemed to have seeped into my muscles, moving my limbs almost without my deciding to do so.

With his free hand, Gunner entrapped mine. We formed a little circle, the three of us by the fire, and though all around us Connell and Kaitlyn and everyone else laughed and flirted and moved along with us, it was like they were just background noise. Even Will seemed not so important as the absinthe moved through my system. There was just the three of us—me, and Lily, and Gunner, a closed circuit—and as the music thrummed, we closed the circle more and more until all the empty space between our bodies was gone and we fit together like three parts of one single creature.

Lily laughed, even though no one had said anything funny, and I laughed too. Gunner smiled and slipped his hands free of ours, winding his arms around our waists.

"My two people," Lily said, and it seemed to me that maybe her voice was slurred a little. Then she leaned over and kissed me, her lips colder than they should have been considering how hot her cheek felt, pressed against my face. Then she kissed Gunner, this time longer and harder, and I couldn't look away from it.

"Now the two of you kiss," Lily demanded. I looked at Gunner. He smiled and shrugged, as if it wasn't up to him, like he was just following orders. With one arm still around Lily's waist, he leaned into me, and almost hypnotized by the marble of his eye, the slant of his mouth, the beat of the music, and the blaze of the fire, bewitched by the absinthe and the night, I kissed him back.

His tongue tasted of smoke and spice and the sweetness of the same absinthe I'd drunk. He pushed into me, and I pushed back, and our kiss was like a challenge or a fight, almost bruising in its force.

Finally we broke apart. I looked at Lily, worried what her reaction would be. But she was smiling. "See?" she said. "Isn't that better?"

Time grew liquid. We danced, and danced, and danced. I drank some, but not a lot, from Gunner's flask. I was starting to like the taste of absinthe. A couple of times other people tried to interrupt our threesome—Connell, once, and later Jane—but it was as if their voices didn't come in on the same frequency as Lily's and Gunner's and my own. As if they couldn't penetrate the private circle we'd created, our hearts toward a shared center, our backs turned to everything else.

I didn't feel drunk like I had at Andy's party; I didn't feel spinny or sick at all. Instead I felt brilliantly clear, like a film had been wiped away from things I'd thought I'd seen clearly before, but now realized had been corrupted, blurred. Each grain of sand at my feet seemed to glow; I could feel the splash of the water as it crawled up the shore.

Maybe it was the absinthe that colored my vision of Lily. Maybe it was Gunner's fault, since he had given it to me. But I had taken it. Either way, it was because of the absinthe that it took me so long to realize that something was wrong.

I couldn't have told anyone if it had been minutes or hours or days that we'd been at the party. Maybe the others had told us they were leaving; maybe they hadn't. I couldn't remember later, when Lily's parents demanded answers, when the doctors and the police wanted to know what had happened, in what order, when and where and how.

But one way or another the crowd thinned and the firelight dimmed.

I had been cold all night, in spite of our fierce dancing, but Lily's hand in mine remained warm.

Here is an interesting fact: if you put a frog in cool water and then slowly, very slowly, heat the water until it boils, the frog will not notice that anything has changed. As long as the changes are incremental—as long as there is no sudden increase in temperature—the frog will sit, perfectly content, as the water around him warms, then simmers, then boils his blood inside his veins and he dies, cooked.

I tried to comfort myself with that later. I did not notice that Lily's hand had grown so hot. I was like the frog.

It was only when Lily collapsed on the sand, her eyes wide open, her body convulsing in jerks, and when her brand-hot hand slipped from my fingers that I noticed how hot it had been.

Someone screamed; it was me. Someone went for help— Gunner. I fell to my knees in the sand and I think I said her name. I touched her cheek and drew my hand away, shocked by how hot it was. How could I not have noticed? How could I have failed her so?

"Lily," I said again, and turned her face toward me. Vomit streaked her cheek; she convulsed in my arms.

And then she died.

NINETEEN

Dark Places and Light

*H*ow could it be that another day could break? How could it be that my own breaths still came, one after the other, in and out and in again?

It seemed too much to bear. But still they came—the breaths, the days.

The first thing that happened following Lily's death— Sunday morning—was that Gunner Montgomery-Valentine left our island. Connell's parents put him on the ferry and he took a taxi from there to the airport and he went home.

Probably his desire to leave quickly could be explained by the coroner's report, delivered a few days later. Officially, Lily's death was caused by Ecstasy-induced hyperthermia and dehydration. Connell, a blubbering mess, told the cops that Gunner had given Lily the Ecstasy, but it wasn't like he'd slipped it in her drink. She had asked him to get some for her. She'd wanted to try it. Connell showed them the texts on his phone that confirmed his story; he'd been with Gunner in LA, and Lily had communicated with both of them while still in Australia with her family. There had been a guy, Connell said, a guy whom his cousin hooked him up with, who sold Gunner the X. He didn't remember his name; he didn't have his number.

Neither Gunner's departure, nor Connell's blubbering confession, nor the toxicology report made any real impact on me.

I was already destroyed by having held my best friend's body in my arms as she died—by Laura's reaction upon hearing that there would be an autopsy.

Her face was swollen from crying. There were lines that I'd never seen before, and the shape of her face, its whole structure, seemed different in grief.

"They can't cut into my baby!" she half choked, half screamed, her hands gripping and twisting Jack's shirtfront. "They can't cut her apart! My baby girl! Don't let them, Jack. Don't let them cut our little girl!"

Jack was sobbing, too, his nose running and his shoulders sloped with grief and shock. He tried to wrap his arms around Laura's shoulders, wanting to comfort her, but she screamed, rageful like a feral animal, and shook him, clawed at his shirt, at his arms.

"Don't let them cut our baby!" she wailed, over and over again, until finally the doctor came to the house and gave her a shot of something. Then the lines of her grief softened and her talonlike grip loosened and her eyes closed.

But I wasn't fooled. I knew her grief raged on inside her.

I knew she was burning up from the inside, that she was *ruined* inside. It was just that we couldn't see it, or hear it, anymore.

Jasper and Henry were shipped off to stay with their grandparents in Santa Barbara for a few days. I didn't say goodbye to them before they left the island, though I did see the helicopter that took them away, cutting across the sky.

Someone, maybe my dad, must have contacted Martin, because Will called me. His name lit up the display on my phone, but I just watched the phone glow and listened to its ring. He called three times without leaving a message, and then finally sent a text.

I'm coming, it read.

Even this could not make me feel.

School was canceled Monday and Tuesday. In a community as small as Avalon, Lily's death touched us all. Grief counselors were available at the school all week, including the days that school was closed, and maybe some of the other kids visited the counselors.

I didn't. I knew they would not comfort me. I knew this pain. It was my old companion, come home again.

But Wednesday the school bells rang once more, and though Dad encouraged me not to go ("Take as much time as you need, honey"), I found myself in the hallways of Avalon High.

There was Lily's locker, next to mine. There were the doors she'd burst through so many times, her broad grin lighting up the hallway. There was her empty desk in each of the classes we'd shared. So much Lily all around me, but no Lily.

I guess people said things to me—teachers and students, the vice principal, Mr. Steiner. I nodded and walked on, not hearing their words, not feeling the touch of their hands on my arm, their embraces.

At lunchtime, I found myself wandering into Mr. McCormack's classroom. I don't know why. Maybe because I wasn't hungry.

"Scarlett," Mr. McCormack said, surprised. "What can I do for you?"

"Hi," I said. "Nothing. I just wanted to see my pig."

His brow furrowed. "I don't think that's really a great idea, Scar," he said. "I thought we'd skip the last few days of the lab and just move on to the next unit a little early."

I looked over to the rack where the piglets were kept. It was empty.

"Where is she?"

"Who?"

"My piglet," I said. "What did you do with her?"

"I packed all of them up. I thought it would be . . . easier that way."

I shook my head hard. "You can't do that," I said. "I want to see her again."

Mr. McCormack looked at me like I was crazy. He stood up from behind his desk and came around to the front of it. I realized my arms were folded across my chest and I was shaking.

He put his hand on my arm. "Scarlett," he said. "I'm so sorry."

Tears flooded my eyes. *Not yet,* I seethed to myself. "Where's the piglet?"

I guess he figured I was already as unstable as I could get, because he pointed to a large cardboard box near the back door. "They're all in there," he said.

I pulled open the flaps of the box and the strong fumes of formaldehyde hit me hard. There they were—all ten of the piglets. Mine was right on top, the plastic shroud labeled in black Sharpie. *Wenderoth/Montgomery-Valentine.*

Carefully, I lifted it out of the box. I didn't unwrap it. "Thanks, Mr. McCormack."

As I pushed open the back door, he called after me, "That's medical waste, Scarlett! I'm supposed to dispose of it properly!"

But he didn't come after me, and I didn't turn around.

Dad was in the kitchen with a cup of coffee and the paper when I came home. "You're home early," was all he said.

I didn't answer and headed into my room. I didn't mean to slam the door.

Of course I knew Lily wasn't the piglet. The piglet wasn't Lily. I wasn't *insane*. But even so . . .

Even so, sending the piglet to a mass grave, or even more likely, an incinerator, didn't work for me.

I found a shoe box in my closet and dumped the sandals inside onto the floor. Then I looked at the plastic wrapping that shrouded the piglet.

Wenderoth/Montgomery-Valentine. It read like an accusation, a guilty verdict. What percentage of Lily's death was my fault? What percentage was Gunner's?

It would be easy to blame Gunner. He had bought the drug in LA; he had brought it to Lily on the beach.

And worse than that . . . it seemed that Gunner was to blame in less palpable ways, as well. There was something about him, something that both attracted and repelled, some quality he radiated that was like poisoned honey to a girl like Lily.

Suddenly, out of nowhere, I remembered Amanda. Now twenty-four, she had left Avalon High while Lily and I were still in grade school. But we all knew the story—how the football coach had gotten fired for having sex with three cheerleaders. Amanda was one of them.

And though the coach was long gone, Amanda wasn't going anywhere. Since leaving school at the end of her junior year, she'd given birth to two kids, each fathered by a different guy. She lived on and off with her parents, and whenever I saw her around town she had this hollowed-out look, like life had failed to live up to her expectations.

Some people might argue that it wasn't the *coach's* fault things were the way they were for Amanda; *he* hadn't knocked her up.

But he had knocked her *down*.

There are people like that. They use people; they suck them dry. The coach was one of those people. Maybe Gunner was, too.

Mazzikim. That was the word Sabine had used. Demons.

I left the piglet and went over to my desk, searching for a book I'd taken from Martin's house, *Kabbalah Magic*. Flipping to the index, I ran my finger down the list of words until I found *mazzikim*.

I read what the author had written:

Mazzikim, meaning "demons of destruction," are misplaced, rootless forces. They carry with them a sense of exile and displacement and may look for homes to occupy or colonize, to make their own. Like parasites, the mazzikim may infiltrate a host and sap it of its strength before moving on. Mazzikim, like all demons, can occlude the mind; they can bring sickness and even death. Nighttime is their realm. Beware especially the nights of Wednesday and Saturday, during which demons may have additional strength. The Talmud teaches us never to open our mouths to the demon.

Sabine had warned me. . . . "Be careful which doors you open, Scarlett. And be careful of what you invite inside."

I had been the first to let him in; it had been Lily's door I'd opened. And both of us had opened our mouths to Gunner Montgomery-Valentine.

A chill pricked my flesh. The hair at the nape of my neck tingled. I thought of how trouble had brewed between us after Gunner appeared on the island. At school, too, Gunner had upset the social order, displacing Andy.

For one long, satisfying moment, I allowed myself the luxury of pinning Lily's death entirely on Gunner

Montgomery-Valentine, of casting him in the role of demon. It certainly fit him as well as any of his finely tailored clothes.

The book told me that demons ate fire for sustenance and liked the smell of spices; it had certainly seemed to me that Gunner's clove cigarettes had fueled him, had given him pleasure, maybe even strength. The more I read, the better it fit—the left is the side of evil, and Gunner was left-handed. Demons dwell in the shade; the first time I had seen Gunner, he was stepping from the shadow of Lily's palm tree, the night of her Halloween party. And he had not come in costume; perhaps he hadn't needed to. Maybe he truly was a Creature of the Night, a *mazzik*.

Oh! It felt so good, so satisfying, such a relief, to lay the burden at his feet, to imagine that Gunner was solely to blame, that he alone had killed my friend.

And it felt good, too, to let rage percolate in my chest, to imagine myself chasing him across the ocean to his home, finding him and screaming in his face, slicing his skin with my nails, punishing him, pummeling him, smiting him.

I tasted those sensations, and I knew for a moment how it must feel to Will—to see a person, a bad person, a horrible, twisted, demented, harmful person, and to know he had the power, and perhaps the reason, to end him.

Maybe if Gunner had appeared in front of me I would have exacted my revenge, in Lily's name.

But time passed, and with it my first sharp hate. For I knew I couldn't pin all the blame on Gunner.

I was culpable as well. Lily was *my* best friend; *I* should have acted as her first line of defense, as she had acted for

292

me all last year, each morning bringing me a gift of food when I hadn't wanted to eat, watching over me as I chewed and swallowed, waiting for me as I healed and returned to her—sometimes patiently, sometimes not so patiently, but waiting, just the same.

I should have been a better friend. I should have been more present, instead of getting so wrapped up in Will and Kabbalah and Sabine. I had failed her. And I would never be able to repair that failure.

Because she was dead.

As was the piglet on my bedroom floor. Slowly I peeled back the plastic and looked at its body. I didn't want to, but I forced myself to really *look*—at the lines of incision, at the little organs, which Gunner and I had disembodied and then replaced, at the loosely jointed hips that Gunner had snapped as I calmly stood by and took notes.

And I thought of Lily, whose body had been zipped inside of plastic, whose eyes had been closed by gloved fingers, who had been placed on a hard cold table and sliced open.

Someone had opened her stomach to see what she had last eaten. Would the remnants of the brownie we'd shared still have been inside? Someone had used an electric saw to open her skull, then peered into her brain. Someone had turned Lily's sacred body into a science project.

Lots of "somebodies" had, least of all the doctors who performed the autopsy.

Lily's death was nothing like one of the satisfying murders in Agatha Christie's books; there was no single villain. Real life isn't like that. There isn't always someone to prosecute for a failed marriage, or a death, or a broken friendship. Real life is messy, and sometimes—very often—terrible. Fiction lies.

The truth was ugly, and complicated. I wanted to blame Gunner. And he *was* guilty . . . but so was I. And so were her parents, who indulged their children's whims beyond reason, giving them so much that their kids felt the whole world was theirs for the taking.

And Lily was to blame, too.

Lily had failed Lily. Maybe she'd been in self-destruct mode. Maybe if Gunner and his Ecstasy hadn't happened along, something else would have, sooner or later.

I thought of a poem I'd once read. It was about a man everyone admired. One line said he "glittered when he walked."

Lily had glittered when she'd walked.

But at the end of the poem, when the man everyone looked up to went home, he put a bullet in his head.

Maybe Lily was like that guy. Maybe she was looking for a way out.

I didn't know.

But I *did* know one thing, right then.

I found my long silk scarf, the one Lily had brought me from San Francisco, and gently I wrapped it around the piglet, covering all the places it had been sliced, all the ways it had been broken. Then I laid the piglet in the shoe box and replaced the lid.

I stayed in my room for a long time. When I emerged, holding the box, my dad was still sitting at the table in the kitchen. He'd been waiting for me.

"I need to bury my piglet from Anatomy in the garden," I said. "Near the koi pond."

He didn't ask me any questions. He just stood, folded his newspaper, and said, "I'll find the shovel."

I thought about arguing with him, insisting on doing this alone. But he was my father, after all. And he wanted to help me.

So I nodded mutely and headed down the stairs, the echo of his footsteps behind me. And I stood holding the box as he dug the grave, and he watched me lay it in the ground, and then together we covered it with dirt.

Then my father held me in his arms, and I cried, and cried, and cried.

Lily had been dead a week when Will returned to the island. I hadn't gone back to school the day after I kidnapped my pig corpse and had basically spent the past three days in bed.

There should have been a funeral by now. It had been seven whole days. But when my dad had called Lily's house, he'd hung up after just a few minutes, saying, "Oh. I see," and looking disturbed.

"What is it?"

"They've decided not to have a service," he said. "Jack said it would be too much for Laura to handle right now."

"But . . . can they *do* that?"

"I don't know, honey. Everyone grieves in their own way." He looked like he could tell this wasn't a satisfactory answer.

"But what will they do with . . . Lily? With her body?"

"They didn't say."

I've always thought the whole idea of closure was lame.

No way can a ceremony make everything okay. Ronny's service at our island cemetery certainly hadn't brought me any solace. But the thought of *nothing*—no gathering at all—seemed wrong.

I guess Dad was starting to worry that I was looking way too much like Mom last year, because Saturday afternoon he kicked me out of the house and told me not to come home until dinnertime.

I wandered in and out of the little shops for a while, looking at refrigerator magnets and water bottles that said Catalina Island on the front and Made in China on the back. But pretty soon I realized that I was running into way too many people I didn't want to see and I headed away from the storefronts.

Briefly, I considered visiting Lily's parents, but the thought of being in the same room as Laura's pain right now felt too scary. And though they'd said they didn't blame me, it was hard to believe that could really be true.

I didn't even want to go out to the stable.

Even the knowledge that Will's plane had landed and that by now he must be making his way to the island didn't elicit any real response in me. We still hadn't talked since we'd parted at Sabine's. The idea of seeking comfort from him, after the way I'd seen him in the alley that night . . . I didn't know if it was possible anymore.

I was indifferent. Apathetic. Will could come to the island if he wanted to, though it seemed like a lot of money and time to spend when maybe we weren't even really a couple anymore.

And though it was insignificant now, up against the hugeness of Lily's death, the fact of my kiss with Gunner still existed.

A part of me was anxious for Will's arrival, anyway. As I'd been thinking, my feet had taken me to the dock.

There was a while before his ferry would arrive. I bought a soda from the vending machine and found a place against a wall where I felt unobtrusive. I slid to sitting, my back against the wall, and drank my soda.

Almost automatically, I fell into the breathing that I'd practiced with Sabine, stretching my neck up, back to center, then left, center, right, center, down, center. And then I began to chant, looping together the sounds I had learned. I felt myself starting to leave my body in that way that had felt so good, so promising before.

I don't know why. I don't know what changed or snapped inside of me. But all of a sudden, mid-chant, on the edge of letting go, I was hit with a wave of panic. I didn't *want* to go! I didn't *want* to leave my body! I wanted to be grounded, right here, in this flesh, on this concrete dock, on this island, in this world.

I jumped up fast, knocking over my can of soda, and I stared ahead, wild-eyed, at nothing in particular, breathing deeply, not methodically or purposefully, but like I'd been underwater for a long time, and I rolled my head and stretched my arms, not in a prescribed pattern, but in a way that felt natural, and good, and *free*.

I didn't want to dull my senses, or sharpen my senses, or tune in or tune out to anything. I didn't want to escape my pain. I didn't want to avoid my truths. Some of them were painful; some of them were awful.

But they were *mine*.

And then I could see Will's ferry coming toward me, traveling much too slowly toward shore, and I knew then that I wanted Will, too. I wasn't ambivalent at all. I was grateful that he was coming to the island.

Will was flawed. He was broken in some ways I couldn't mend. But wasn't everyone?

Lily hadn't given up on me, that long winter of my mourning Ronny. Lily would never have given up on me, not ever, because she was my friend. No matter what.

I ran to the edge of the dock. I held my hand up to shade my eyes. I scanned the crowd, and though I couldn't make out Will from this distance, I felt as though I could sense him reaching out to me across the sea.

A cold wind blew; clouds darkened the sky, and yet the sun still shined in its last brilliance before sunset. It was awful and miraculous how two things in direct opposition could exist in the same moment—the sun and the clouds; my anguish over Lily's death and my sudden, searing joy in knowing that, once more, when I needed him, Will had come for me.

TWENTY

Homecoming

*I*t wasn't as if nothing bad had happened; it wasn't as if things were just as they were before. But when Will stepped off the boat and embraced me, when I rested my forehead against his chest and breathed in the clean warm scent of him, I had a sensation of peace, of safety, of coming home.

We didn't need to talk to know where we would go. We walked hand in hand to my house, but we didn't go inside. Instead we climbed into the beat-up Volvo and headed out across the island, toward Two Harbors.

While we drove, the clouds overhead began to look more menacing, and by the time we'd reached Will's cottage, the rain had come.

The front garden beyond the gate was covered with fallen leaves; the windows were shuttered. In the misty rain and half-dark of coming night, Will's house looked abandoned, or maybe enchanted.

Will grabbed his duffel bag from the backseat. We hurried through the rain, bowing our heads as we ran toward the front door. But when we got to the porch Will stopped short.

"Uh-oh," he said. "I didn't bring my key."

He began scanning the front of the house, looking for an open window, but I held up my key. "Remember?" I said. "I've got one."

I pushed the key into the lock and turned it. The door swung open. We crossed the threshold and went inside.

The front room was cold and dark. Will set to building a fire, piling logs from the hearth and adding yellowed newspapers to help it catch more quickly. I turned on a couple of lights and then went into the kitchen to make a pot of tea.

After I'd filled the kettle and lit the flame beneath it, I searched in the cabinets for snacks.

There was an unopened tin of cookies, so I peeled back the foil and arranged some of them on a plate. Soon the water was boiling and I poured it into a teapot over the loose-leaf tea I'd found on a shelf near the kitchen sink.

Will had built a beautiful fire. We spread a blanket on the floor and sat together, drinking tea and watching the flames.

More than once the thought of the last fire I'd seen—the bonfire down at the beach—came to me. More than once I pushed it aside.

"Do you want to talk about it?"

I shook my head. "I think I want to talk about the alley, though."

Will took a sip of his tea, said nothing.

"Is that okay with you?"

"We can talk about anything you want." He turned and smiled at me, but his eyes were sad.

"Okay." But it was a long time before I said anything else. My tea had cooled to lukewarm when I finally said, "Will, do you know that I love you?"

He nodded.

He was going to say something, but I stopped him. "I'm not going to tell you what to do. I couldn't, anyway. I know that. Just like no one could tell me what to do last winter, when you tried to save me but couldn't. Only I could do that."

Will was sitting very still, his green eyes watching me closely. The fire behind him crackled like a warning.

"But, Will, I know who I am. And I know this—I can't love a killer. I *won't* love a killer. That's my truth."

He looked troubled, and he didn't hurry to speak. At last he said, "I'm not a killer, Scarlett. I don't want to be."

My shoulders were twisted in tension. I relaxed them. "I know you're not, Will. But sometimes people do things they don't mean to do. Things that aren't *them*, really. But some things, once you've done them . . . make you into something else. Something you can't unbecome."

His expression was inscrutable. "You kissed that guy, didn't you?"

I didn't know what to say. So I didn't say anything.

"You're not changed, Scarlett. You're not corrupted or bad. You're still Scarlett. The girl I love."

My lip started to tremble. My vision blurred. "I should

have been better." My voice came out in a broken whisper. "I should have been there for her."

"You can't save everyone."

I half choked on a bitter laugh. "That's funny, coming from you." Except, of course, that it wasn't funny. Not really.

"Let's do something, Scarlett," Will said. He put down his cup and slid closer to me until our folded knees were touching. He took my cup away and set it down. Then he entwined his fingers with mine, both hands, and held them up between us. "Let's be here together," he said. "Let's save each other."

We kissed then, the fire warming one side of our faces, the other sides pressed against the coming dark.

For the dark is always there—whether we feel it or not. It's there, just to the other side of light. And fire can keep it away for only so long.

But lighting a fire is an act of hope. An act of defiance against the dark.

And so was what we did together that night, our bodies naked and wound together. I don't think we saved each other; but we pushed away the darkness in the brilliant light of our fierce connection. We pushed it away and grabbed on tight to life, to each other.

Will stayed three days. He offered to stay longer, but I shook my head. He needed to get back to his life.

He twisted up his mouth kind of funny when I told him that, but he didn't declare, sappily, that *I* was his life.

Because I wasn't.

I was part of it, sure, and he was part of mine. But not all of it. And it was better that way.

We didn't make any promises, though they floated between us, unsaid. But we kissed long, and deeply, and I think we told each other some of what we wished we could promise out loud with that kiss.

When his boat had dipped beyond the horizon—one instant still visible, and the next disappeared, as if by magic—I blinked hard and tried to recapture the image of it for one more moment.

But it was gone.

I had learned the year before that time passes. A stupid thing to say, but a deep and important truth.

It passes; it really does. In a way, I was glad in those first few weeks that I had already mourned Ronny; it prepared me for the painful disengagement I was now forced to go through with Lily.

I knew from experience that some part of my brain would still expect her to be alive, would respond to normal cues that had usually precipitated Lily—like the ring of my phone, the slamming of a locker door—as if Lily would really be there. Of course, she wasn't.

It was like the phenomenon of ghost limbs, when an amputee feels emphatically and certainly that the foot no longer connected to his leg needs to be scratched.

The things we've depended on, the things that are part of us, they don't go away easily. But I remembered this from before, with Ronny, so these moments at least didn't catch me entirely unprepared.

My desires to push food, conversation, connections away were my ingrained responses to dealing with tragedy, so they came back. I couldn't stop them from coming back, but I could observe them coolly and choose to refuse them.

In March, Sabine called me. Actually, she called me more than once between Lily's death and the day I finally answered.

"Scarlett." Her voice was full of empathy that I didn't want to hear.

"Hey, Sabine. I'm sorry I haven't returned your calls." I didn't lie and say I'd been busy.

"All of us are so sorry for your loss," she said, "the whole family."

"Thank you."

"Scarlett," she went on, "do you think you'd like to visit us again? I really think that focusing on your practice could help you heal."

I cleared my throat. "Thanks, Sabine, but I think I'm going to take a break from all that."

Her silence was intense. "A break?"

"Yeah. I think right now I'm going to be staying close to home."

"I see. But, Scarlett, I really think you have a particular talent. A gift. With the right guidance—"

"Thanks, but I'm not so sure I want to develop that particular gift."

She was baffled. "Why on earth not?"

Sabine had been good to me. She'd invited me into her home; she'd fed me and taught me things and bought me chai tea. So maybe I did owe her an explanation. "Sabine," I said, "maybe I'll come back to it later. But right now I want to finish high school. I want to watch my mare foal. I think I might want to learn to garden."

"You know," she said, trying once more, "an ecstatic practice can be part of all of those things. It can enrich those experiences, deepen them."

"Maybe," I said. "For now, though, I'm staying on the island. But thank you, Sabine, really. Thank you for helping me. I just need to stay here. Okay?"

She sighed. "Okay."

Even though I didn't want to follow Sabine in her ecstatic practice, I turned once more to Martin's book. I returned to the Sefirot.

Slowly, carefully, I ran my finger along the spiderweb outline of the Tree of Life. Over and over again, I read the words. *Malchut. Yesod. Hod. Netzach. Gevurah. Chesed. Tiferet. Binah. Chochmah. Keter.*

Kingdom. Foundation. Awe. Victory. Judgment. Lovingkindness. Balance. Knowledge. Wisdom. Crown.

I had built a foundation last year, a foundation of self-care born out of darkness, and it was to that foundation I turned now, in the wake of Lily's death. Awe . . . I had experienced that sensation many times—more often in the past year or two than ever before. Victory I had tasted too, each time I earned an A, or nailed my lines for a play, and most recently, just a few weeks ago, when I had finally coaxed Traveler over the dreaded trot poles.

Judgment. I was good at that. I had judged myself, not kindly. I had judged my father, my mother, and Alice. I hadn't spoken with them about my secret knowledge of Dad and Alice's kiss—my judgment of it—which had become like a wedge between me and these people I loved, these people who loved me. That would have to stop.

Loving-kindness? Balance? Knowledge, wisdom, kingdom, and crown? Yes. I wanted to feel these things. I wanted to embody them.

I had read something at Martin's house; it was in needlepoint and framed, hanging in his office.

A person without knowledge of his soul is not good.
One who moves hurriedly misses the mark.
Proverbs 19:2

Maybe I'd been doing that by rushing my study of Kabbalah, by downing Sabine's mystic egg and traveling away from my own home in my desire to learn, to change, to widen myself.

I wanted to return to basics. I didn't want to be a mystic, or an oneiromancer, or a prodigy. I just wanted to be whole, as whole as I could be.

The rest of it would still be out there, if I wanted it later. For now, it could wait.

• • •

After March came April, and with it my eighteenth birthday and college acceptance—and rejection—letters. UCLA said yes; so did UC Davis and UC Santa Barbara. Berkeley said no thank you.

Dad insisted on taking me out to celebrate. I didn't want to, but I could tell how much it meant to him, so we both got kind of dressed up (I wore my best jeans, he wore a collared shirt) and walked to the fancy seafood place on the waterfront.

He ordered shrimp scampi. I did too.

Our food came and we dug in.

Suddenly he said, "Remember what Ronny used to say about shrimp?"

I was mid-bite and I half coughed, half choked. We weren't in the habit of bringing up Ronny. We tiptoed around the whole subject, each of us afraid of pulling off the other's still-tender scabs of grief.

"Yeah." My voice sounded normal. "He said they were glorified pill bugs."

Dad laughed. "And he'd always say it just when someone was about to bite into one." He waggled his eyebrows at me and then took a healthy bite of one of his shrimp.

I ate one of mine. "Ronny loved to ruin people's dinners," I said.

"Anything for a laugh," Dad agreed. "Totally unscrupulous."

"At least he was consistent."

Dad nodded. "Consistently unscrupulous."

"People loved him for it. He was the life of the party."

"Like Lily," Dad said. "She was like that, too."

It was as if he had thrown down the gauntlet. And now it was my turn.

It hurt to say her name. It hurt so much, and I couldn't keep back the tears. But I spoke it anyway. "Lily was the brightest, shiniest person I've ever known."

Dad nodded. There were tears in his eyes, too, but he smiled. "Those costumes she'd put together every Halloween . . ." He shook his head and whistled. "Boy oh boy, did that girl like an audience!"

I laughed. Tears ran down my cheeks, but I ignored them. "Yeah," I said. "It never bothered Lily to be looked at. One time she said"—and I laughed again at the memory—"she said she *liked* being objectified."

Dad snorted a little. "Not a statement the feminists would be real proud of."

"But she *was* a feminist!" I said. "She was all for girl power. For strength. She just didn't mind if people liked to look at her boobs while she was conquering the world."

Suddenly I felt hungrier than I had in a long while, and I stabbed another glorified pill bug, dragging it through the garlic sauce before popping it into my mouth.

"So," Dad said, "where do you think Lily would want you to go to school?"

"Probably LA," I said. "Santa Barbara *is* known for being a party school, but it's not as cosmopolitan as LA."

"What about Davis?"

"Oh, Lily *definitely* wouldn't approve," I said. "A small-town farm school? No way."

"Well, no matter what you choose," Dad said, "I know Lily would be proud of you. So would Ronny. And *we're* proud of you—your mother and I."

He smiled at me in that sweet sad way of his. I thought about what I'd seen in the winter—him and Alice kissing. I thought about Will's assertion that you can never see inside another's heart. And I thought about the Sefirot, how loving-kindness was juxtaposed with judgment.

The point was to strike a balance. To not lean too far to one side or the other. I looked into my father's eyes, and I saw love there, reflected back at me. And I knew I wasn't going to bust my dad and Alice. I couldn't know what was in his heart, or hers. Or my mother's or Alice's husband's, for that matter. I couldn't understand all the nuances of what had transpired between them. I couldn't ferret out all their reasons and all the stories that might have led my dad and Alice to that kiss by the koi pond.

What was more, I didn't *want* to know all those things. It wasn't my business. And I didn't want to judge Dad and Alice. I just wanted to love them.

So it was with a wonderful feeling of openness that I reached across the table and touched his hand. "I'm proud of you too, Daddy," I said. "Really proud."

For my eighteenth birthday, I was showered with gifts. My mom insisted that I spend the weekend with her in LA, shopping. It was actually not terrible. Her new, purple-wall-embracing self actually had pretty good taste. Not as great as Lily's, but still. Better than nothing.

My dad gave me an IOU for transporting Delilah and her foal off the island. It would be a while before she and her baby—who would be born in less than a month, the bolero-wearing vet said Delilah was "almost ripe"—would be ready to go anywhere with me.

I'd already settled on UC Davis; it had a good premed program, and farmland all around meant that I'd be able to find a place to board Delilah and her foal for a reasonable price. There was no way I'd be able to afford to keep them in LA or Santa Barbara.

Alice gave me a new pair of riding chaps—I'd had mine since freshman year, and they were way too short. These were beautiful—dark brown, soft, supple, so great.

Martin sent me a bouquet of eighteen roses, all different colors, with a note—

Scarlett,

Eighteen is as magic a number as exists. It represents chai—life itself. May life be full of beauty and bounty for you in the coming year. Did you know that in Hebrew thought, the names we give our children are more than just something to call them by? A name is part of the defining essence of a person. Therefore, one's name can be a source of great power. It can even influence who that person may become. Your name, my dear, is Scarlett—Red. And for us, red is the color of life. The color of power. You were well named. Mazel tov, and happy, happy birthday.

—Martin

I read the note three times, each time feeling as if a portion of weight was lifted from me. I liked what Martin said, very much. Gunner had said that he and I were linked—Gunn and Scar, both related to pain, to injury, maybe even to death.

I could see it his way, if I wanted to. But I didn't. I was scarred; who wasn't? But I didn't need to be *defined* by those scars. I was more than the sum of the pain I had suffered. Scarlett.

For the first time, I loved my name. The flowers were lovely, but the real gift was Martin's words.

The last present was from Will. It came wrapped in a flat package, plain brown paper tied around with twine. He'd addressed the package in his careful script. I pulled back the paper and set it aside.

Inside was a thin cardboard box. I opened it and gently shook out its contents. There was a painting, and with it a folded note.

I would have read the note first, but the picture arrested me. Will had painted me astride Delilah. Her face was in the foreground, broad and red with round dark eyes. He'd drawn me with my hair down, the way he liked it. I was smiling and bright-eyed; the sun exploded in light behind me. In the far distance was a line of blue-green—the ocean.

His note read, *No matter what, Scarlett, I love you.* That was all.

The day after my birthday, I visited Lily's house. It had been too long since I'd been there. I had checked in with her brothers a few times, when I saw them in the grade school yard adjacent to the high school's. They seemed okay; I watched them laughing and playing with their friends, and they didn't seem all that different from before.

Henry had developed this habit, though, where he sort of tapped his hand against his thigh, quick short slaps, three in a row. I watched him for a while and saw him do it four different times.

And I'd seen Jack around town a bit—taking the boys to get ice cream, picking up milk at the store, things like that. He had seemed glad to see me, hugging me each time we met. Maybe he was a little thinner than before; I couldn't be sure.

But I hadn't really seen Laura. She called me on my birthday and asked me to come by the house sometime soon. She had something to give me, she said.

I went over after school on the last day of April. It was a glorious day, over eighty degrees, the kind of weather that makes you happy in spite of yourself. When I got to the house, I wasn't really sure what to do; usually I'd go in through the kitchen door, in the back, just sort of knocking and calling "hello" as I opened it.

But now that Lily wouldn't be there to answer, this felt weird. Standing formally on the front porch and ringing the bell would be equally awkward, so I settled for knocking on the kitchen door and waiting for someone to answer it.

Laura did.

Everyone grieves in their own way. There's no right or wrong way to mourn. That's what the books and the websites say. But I think they're wrong.

Her eyes had the same shadow of pain that had been in my mother's and my father's and my own eyes, too. Maybe there's some part in all of us, some connected part of us, maybe that thing that Martin would name God, or that Carl Jung, this guy we learned about in psychology class, called the collective unconscious. Maybe that's the part that recognizes grief in others, because that part in all of us knows its story, knows its sting.

After Ronny died, I'd thought that people looked at me differently because my brother's death meant that their sons, brothers, and husbands had an additional level of protection from harm. Like tragedy could strike in only so many places at once. But now I wondered if maybe they had been looking at me with wordless empathy, coming from a place of infinite connection rather than separation. Maybe if I had turned toward them rather than away, and inward, I could have found comfort in that connection to other people.

I thought this now as Laura let me into the kitchen, as I looked at the dividing line in her hair: below a certain point, her curls were caramel-colored; above that line, and to the root, they were laced with gray.

That line marked Lily's death.

I thought these things, but I didn't say them. "Hi, Laura," I said. "It's good to see you. I'm so sorry I haven't visited more."

"It's okay, honey, I understand." We hugged for a long time, and with my eyes closed, I could almost imagine that the curls that touched my cheek were Lily's.

When we parted, I noticed a necklace she was wearing,

one I'd never seen before. It was a colored stone, dark reddish pink, set simply in a four-pronged bracket, on a chain.

"That's pretty," I said.

Laura's hand came up to the stone in a gesture that seemed well practiced, as if it were a habit of hers to touch the pendant.

"Don't think I'm crazy," she said. "Jack does."

"What?"

She sat at the kitchen table. Her hand stayed on the stone. "I couldn't stand the thought of letting her go."

I knew how she felt; I didn't want to let Lily go, either. But what choice did we have? She was gone. We were here.

"This necklace is made from Lily," Laura said. Her expression was raw, open, and defiant, too, as if daring me to say anything negative.

But I didn't even understand what she meant.

My confusion must have showed because Laura clarified. "We had Lily cremated," she said. "And I chose to have some of her remains made into this stone."

I'd never heard of anything like this. But I thought for a minute—diamonds come from carbon. People are made of carbon.

"There's a business that does that?" I asked. "Makes gemstones out of people?"

Laura smiled grimly. "Honey, if you have the money, there's a business for everything."

"Can I touch it?"

Laura nodded, but she didn't unclasp the necklace. Instead she leaned across so I could reach it. The stone felt smooth, hard, cool. Just like it looked. Lily had been none of those things, in life. She had been soft. She had been warm. She had been uneven and mercurial and brightly alive.

"I had one made for Jasper and Henry, and Jack, too. The boys keep theirs in their room. Probably mixed in with their building toys." She smiled, a little. "Jack doesn't carry his, but I've caught him looking at it a few times. And . . ." She stood up and opened a drawer in the little built-in desk in the corner, pulling out a box. "I had this made for you."

I opened the box. It was latched with a tiny lever that swung open easily. Inside was a ring, yellow gold, with the same reddish-pink stone that Laura wore, only slightly smaller.

I lifted it from the box and slid it onto the ring finger of my right hand. It fit perfectly.

Laura smiled. "That would make Lily so happy," she said, "knowing that she can go everywhere with you."

"Thank you, Laura."

"You're welcome."

"Laura?" I asked. "Can I ask you something?"

She nodded.

"Are you going to be all right?"

She laughed, humorless. "I'll *live*, if that's what you mean."

I shook my head. It wasn't. "Because, Laura, my mom wasn't okay after Ronny. Not for a long time. And even though I needed her, she couldn't see it. I don't want that for the boys. Or for you, either."

She was listening, and I grew bolder, telling her what I wish someone had said to my mother, speaking for Lily's brothers in the way I wish someone had spoken for me. "Henry's doing this weird tapping thing on his leg, Laura. Have you noticed?"

Slowly, she shook her head.

"I think the ring is beautiful, and your necklace, too. But so are your boys. Don't go away, okay, Laura? Your boys need you."

Laura looked down at the table, the crown of her head exposed to me fully, the demarcation in her hair color so obvious from where I was sitting.

Finally she looked up. There was something in her eyes, something I had seen in Lily's. "I'm not going anywhere," she said.

TWENTY-ONE
A Beginning

By early May, Delilah's belly was as round and hard as a huge, ripe apple. She moved slowly now, like her hips were loose in their sockets. Her coat shimmered golden red and her eyes were brightly peaceful.

On the seventh of May, I spent the afternoon switching out the wood shavings in her stall with straw. Shavings could irritate her or the foal after birth; straw was less dusty, Alice told me, and the traditional bedding for a foaling mare.

Delilah wandered loose in the arena while I worked, hauling wheelbarrows of shavings from the barn and over to the far end of the field. She watched me disinterestedly, her long tail flicking the occasional fly.

When the stall was finally empty, I sprayed down the thick black rubber mats that lined it and left it open to dry out.

It was a fine day. I didn't mind just waiting around for the sun to dry Delilah's stall; I was in no hurry to go anywhere. So I sat on the arena's railing and watched my mare enjoy the sun.

She didn't do much of anything, just wandered around a little, sometimes closing her eyes as if to feel the sun's rays more fully. A couple of times she came over to me, as if she was just checking in, saying hi.

Dr. Rhonda had been out to the island just before my birthday to do one final checkup. She gave Delilah a tetanus booster, a routine procedure for mares about to foal.

She had been just as intense as always, with that single-minded focus that I admired about her. And her hands were gentle with my mare. I watched her examining Delilah, the way she listened with her stethoscope to Delilah's belly, the way she moved around the horse, exuding an air of confidence.

That was how I wanted to be, I decided, around my patients, one day. Of course, mine would have two legs rather than four.

"So, off to UC Davis, eh?" Dr. Rhonda seemed pleased by my decision. She told me she'd loved living up there while she was in vet school, though it had taken her a while to get used to the heat. "You're sure you wouldn't be happier as a vet, though?"

"I want to work in neuroscience."

"Horses have brains too, you know." She was reaching under Delilah, checking behind the swell of her belly. "Your mare's starting to udder up," she said. "I think she'll be delivering sooner rather than later."

"Really?"

"Mm-hmm." Dr. Rhonda didn't look at me, or Delilah. She stared off into the distance as if not to distract herself from what she was feeling. "Right around the middle of May, I'd guess."

And here we were, edging closer to her predicted date of delivery. I'd taken to almost obsessively watching Delilah for signs of impending labor. But as far as I could tell, she looked pretty much the same. Except bigger.

Alice came out of the office and wandered over to the arena, resting her arms on the rail where I sat. For a few minutes we just watched Delilah together.

"That's a beautiful mare, Scarlett," she said.

"Yeah," I answered. "I'm really going to miss her in the fall."

UC Davis wasn't all that far from home, not compared with some schools, but it was far enough to prohibit regular weekend visits.

"It won't be forever," Alice said.

"I know. And when I go back my sophomore year, I'll take Delilah and the baby with me."

She nodded. "I'll keep an eye on her when you go away. The foal, too. I'll make sure everyone here is taken care of."

"My father, too."

Alice looked up at me sharply, but I didn't let my face reveal anything.

"Take care of him, will you, Alice? I don't like to think of him all alone."

Slowly, she nodded. Alice was more perceptive than Dad, but she didn't push me. "I'll take care of him," she promised.

Delilah came back around and rested her chin on my knee. I stroked her sun-warmed cheek.

Alice's keen eye roamed over Delilah. She looked at her udder. "You know, I wouldn't be surprised if your foal came in the next few days. You see this?" She ducked into the arena and reached behind Delilah's belly. I looked where she was pointing. The tips of Delilah's teats looked waxy.

"She's getting ready to feed a foal."

I started to get excited. "Did you hear that, Delilah?" I said. "You're going to be a mama soon!"

She snorted at me, like I wasn't telling her anything she didn't already know.

When Delilah's stall was dry, Alice helped me haul in four bales of straw. I clipped the twine with wire cutters and the bales burst open, their sweet fragrance filling the air. Using a pitchfork, I spread the straw evenly in the stall, and by the time I was done my whole body itched from the work. Little pieces of straw floated from my hair; I fished more than a few others from the back of my shirt. I sneezed.

The next day when I went out to the stable, I took my sleeping bag with me. I got there in the late afternoon. I'd read that mares—especially maiden mares, those that hadn't foaled before—are most likely to give birth between eleven at night and four in the morning. And I didn't want Delilah to be alone when her time came.

Alice just smiled and shook her head when she saw me unloading the back of the Volvo. But she didn't try to dissuade me. "You're just like I was, when I was your age," is all she said.

I spent that night in front of Delilah's stall. It was cold, but the stars were bright above my head. A few times I heard Delilah rustling around, but nothing happened. Mostly I just lay on the ground and stared up into the sky.

One good thing about living on an island is that the sky gets really, really dark at night. And you can see the stars.

The night was perfectly clear and there were so many bright pinpoints of light above me, too many to count. I made myself dizzy trying.

The next day was a Monday, but after school I headed out to the stable again. I'd left my sleeping bag in the tack room, so I didn't even have to go home. Dad brought me some tacos from a little place in town, and he stuck around long enough to eat with me. Then it was just me and my mare, and the stars, for another night.

Again I rested just outside Delilah's stall door. My gaze returned to the sky; the stars were still there. Because it wasn't like they disappeared during the day. We just couldn't see them.

Ronny had told me something once. He'd been all amped up about space during his freshman year of high school; he even had a telescope. "Did you know," he said, "that we're all made of stardust?"

I was about twelve years old. We'd been sitting in the gazebo in our backyard, sharing a bowl of grapes. There was no koi pond yet. There was no death in my life, no great sadness. My mare was herself just a foal.

"What are you talking about?" I answered. It was irritating, how Ronny was always trying to educate me.

"It's true. When the universe first came into being after the big bang, the only elements that existed were hydrogen, helium, and a little bit of lithium. That's all there was! Those elements just floating around, and gravity started pulling them together into lumps and balls of matter."

"Is this going to take long?" The grapes were gone. I was getting hot.

He ignored me. "So those lumps and balls, when they were big enough and dense enough, and there was enough pressure from gravity smushing the hydrogen and helium atoms together, the atoms actually bonded into heavier elements."

"Smushing?" I interrupted. "Is that a technical term?"

"Shut up. So while the stuff is bonding, energy gets released. And a star is born."

"Uh-huh."

I guess I didn't sound as impressed by his wealth of knowledge as Ronny would have liked, but he went on anyway. "Eventually," he said, "the star uses up all its fuel."

"How long does that take?" I was getting sort of interested, in spite of myself.

"A really long time. Like millions or even billions of years."

"Then what?"

"Then it collapses inward." Ronny demonstrated with his

hands, forming a ball and tucking his fingers into the middle. "So when the star dies, it scatters its material in a huge explosion." He threw his hands out wide, fingers spread. "And all the elements that created the star are released, and the whole thing happens all over again. Only this time *our* star is formed—the sun. And our solar system. And all of life, everything you see, everyone you know, all of it, all of *everything* is formed from the matter that once made up those stars. Do you know what that means?"

I shook my head.

He reached out and touched my nose. "It means you're made of star," he said. "And *I'm* made of star. Really, truly, we're all freaking stardust. Isn't that cool?"

I shrugged. "I guess."

He snorted. "You *guess?* You *know.*" He got up, grabbed the bowl from the table, and carried it inside. Just before the back door slammed shut he turned and grinned at me. "Stardust," he said. "It doesn't get any cooler than that."

It was way past midnight, close to three in the morning, when I was woken by sounds from inside Delilah's stall. I unzipped my bag and blinked, waiting for my eyes to adjust to the dark. In a moment I could see vague shapes, shadows and outlines, so I stood up and peered into the stall.

Delilah was pacing in her small space, swishing her tail. She'd take a few steps, then stop and look back at her flanks. Then she'd walk some more. Once she bit at her side.

This was it. "Easy, girl," I soothed, but Delilah didn't seem to notice me. I watched for twenty minutes as she paced and stopped, checked her flank and walked again. Even though it was cold outside the stall, she breathed hot steamy breaths and a fine coat of sweat began to break across her pelt.

Suddenly I knew who I wanted here with me tonight, who I wanted to share this with.

Their car pulled into the stable yard before four o'clock. Four doors opened and slammed closed. And then the twins came running at me, their father whispering, "Keep it down!"

There they were—Jack and Laura, Jasper and Henry.

I walked out to meet them. "Hey, guys. I'm so glad you came."

"Not a big fan of the middle-of-the-night phone call," Jack said. "But here we are."

"Where's Delilah?" Jasper asked.

I pointed to her stall. "She's in there. But we've got to be really quiet, and we can't crowd her, or she might not stay in labor."

"You mean she has a *choice?*" Henry sounded surprised.

I nodded. "If a mare doesn't feel safe, her labor stalls until she feels more secure."

"Cool," said Henry. I noticed him tapping his hand against his leg, but then he stopped and shot a look at his mom.

She smiled at him gently and put her hand on his shoulder. In the night's blue darkness, her red gemstone looked black.

I led them over to Delilah's stall. I peered inside; she was lying down.

We all watched her silently for a minute, but then she stood up. It looked uncomfortable and awkward, getting that big body back up on her four slim legs, but she did it and then she resumed her pacing, her tail swishing. She turned straight toward us once and looked into my eyes, curling back her upper lip in a way I'd never seen her do before.

"What's she doing?" whispered Jasper.

"I don't know," I whispered back, and for a moment I was shot through with panic. What if this didn't go right? What if Delilah had trouble in labor? What if she didn't live through it?

For a second I considered telling Jack and Laura to leave, but then Delilah lay back down and rested her head in the straw, and I forgot about the cluster of people around me; I only saw Delilah.

"What's that?" Henry asked, pointing. I looked down between Delilah's hind legs and saw the white membrane of the amnion pushing out, and then her water broke and it came out in a rush, soaking the straw beneath her.

"Gross!" said Jasper, and if I hadn't been so focused on Delilah I would have told him to keep it down, but now I saw something amazing—a tiny hoof emerging from my mare, glistening wet and tiny. A second hoof followed the first and Delilah groaned, just like a person, as the foal's muzzle pushed out. There was a moment of rest between contractions, and then with the next one the foal's head came out quickly.

I could see from where I stood, leaning over the stall door, that his eyes were closed tight, pressed and wrinkled. His face was shiny with amniotic fluid, dark the way Delilah looked sometimes after a hard run when she was coated with sweat. But even though he was wet and in the dark, I could see a tinge of copper in his coat.

His ears were folded back against his head like fragile wings, and at first they looked too long for his head, but then his neck emerged and then his head looked too heavy to be supported by it.

I watched the contractions ripple over Delilah like waves, one after another, as her foal emerged, and I felt within myself as if waves were crashing, too, and I felt lighter and freer, more and more full of joy as each inch of her foal was born.

"Will you look at that," Jack said, full of wonder. The boys were quiet, openmouthed, at a loss for words. Laura had a hand on each of their backs, and she looked at Delilah as if hypnotized, eyes gleaming.

After the foal's shoulders came through, the rest of his body slipped out, effortlessly, and I could see Delilah's muscles relax. Her head, which she'd lifted during the strain of her labor, relaxed into the straw. She didn't even look at the baby she'd birthed.

I wanted to climb into the stall but contented myself with looking from where I stood. I could see the foal's chest rising and falling. He looked healthy but tired, as if his journey to life had exhausted him as much as it had his mother.

His short tail fanned across the straw. He wrinkled his muzzle and snorted, a soft sound, but strong.

"Wow," said Jack, and I turned around and smiled at him, at all of them, as if I'd had something to do with what had just happened.

The sun hadn't yet risen, but the glow that precedes a sunrise was just touching the sky. In that light I noticed that Laura's caramel hair had no more hints of gray. And though her hands came up to touch her necklace, they didn't rest there for long; they returned to the shoulders of her sons, and she smiled at them.

"That was cool, Scar," said Jasper. "When can we ride him?"

I laughed as I walked them back to their car. "Not for a long while. He's got to get big first. But I wanted to ask you guys for a favor."

Both Jasper and Henry looked at me. They were like miniature versions of their father, but the excitement in their eyes reminded me of Lily.

"I'm going to need help in the fall when I go away to school," I told them. "I'm going to need someone to come out here a lot and play with the colt to make sure he gets used to people. Do you guys think you could help me out?"

They nodded, grinning.

"Good," I said. "And between now and then, maybe I could bring you with me to the stable and teach you how stuff is done?"

"Like when you gave us the lesson before?"

God help me. "Uh-huh."

"Yeah!" they said. "That sounds like fun." They climbed into the backseat of the car. I could hear them fighting already over which of them the foal would like better. But then, mercifully, they slammed their doors and I couldn't hear them anymore.

"Thanks for hauling us out here, Scarlett," Jack said,

giving me a quick hug. "Don't be a stranger, okay? We always have enough dinner for one more mouth."

"Okay, Jack," I promised. "I'll visit soon."

Then Laura embraced me. "That was beautiful," she said. "And what a special day for it."

I must have looked confused, because Laura said, "It's May tenth."

She squeezed my hand and slid into the passenger seat. I waved as their car pulled away.

May tenth, I mused as I headed back toward Delilah's stall. Two years to the day since Ronny had died.

In the stall, Delilah and her foal were starting to wake up to each other. They nickered back and forth, and Delilah shifted around to reach the foal with her tongue. She licked him with thick warm strokes, and he nickered again and again.

Around us, the sun began to fill the sky. Delilah pulled herself to standing, and she bowed her head to the foal, nudging him, nipping him lightly, urging him to rise.

He folded his legs beneath his body, struggling to keep all four of them under his control, and finally, after two false starts, he managed to coordinate himself enough to rise up from the straw.

I swear, Delilah looked proud of him. She looked over to me, as if to say, *Do you see how talented he is?*

"Very talented," I agreed. "I think we should name him Star."

Delilah didn't voice disapproval, and as I watched Star

search beneath his mother for his first sip of milk, as the sun filled the wide sky all around me, I said to her, "Do you know, Delilah, that we are all made of stardust?"

All of us, in the whole wide world—me and her and the foal, Lily and her parents and brothers, my own mom and dad, Alice, Ronny, Will, even Andy and Gunner and that man in the alley—all of us made from stars.

The thing about life, I thought as Star drank his mother's warm milk, is that you have to choose it. And then you have to *keep* choosing it, again and again and again.

You can choose it by staring out at the vast horizon. By focusing on the smallest stone. By feeling humbled by the greatness of others. By claiming victory in a challenge. By judging. By loving. Through balance. Through knowledge. In wisdom. In grace.

I chose it by unlatching the door to Delilah's stall, by stepping inside and stretching out my hand to her foal.

His warm, wet muzzle touched my palm as gently and surely as a benediction, as sweetly as the breath of God.

ACKNOWLEDGMENTS

Writing a sequel, it turns out, is hard. Ideas that are explored in the first book must be considered more carefully, researched more deeply. I owe a debt of gratitude to several rabbis whose words and instruction guided me. First, Rabbi Steven Moskowitz of Temple Israel: our conversations were deeply illuminating and always sparked my imagination. Rabbi Abba Perelmuter, your Kabbalah class inspired several of my images, and your discussion of Abraham helped shape an early scene in the book. And Rabbi Geoffrey W. Dennis, author of *The Encyclopedia of Jewish Myth, Magic, and Mysticism*, your book and the email conversations we had were invaluable. Thank you all.

Heartfelt thanks to my agent, Rubin Pfeffer. See? I finished it! And thanks *again* for finding the perfect title. Every time we talk, I am blown away by my good fortune to be your client. Of course, I am also deeply grateful to Françoise Bui, my editor, who gently guided my writing away from the murkiest depths of purple prose. Thank you for believing in me, Françoise.

Once more I am indebted to my brilliant family of

readers—my siblings, father, and grandmother, all of whose support (of every kind) enabled this book to be born. And special thanks to you, Nana—it was in your library that I first discovered Agatha Christie, and some of my favorite memories are of curling up in a patch of sunlight, eating fruit, and thumbing through your paperbacks.

Finally, my own little family—Keith, Max, and Davis— what can I say to you? You are the beginning and end of my day, and my heart. I love you all.

ABOUT THE AUTHOR

ELANA K. ARNOLD thinks everyone has a story to tell. It took her a long time to find hers. She grew up in Southern California, where she was lucky enough to have her own horse, a gorgeous mare named Rainbow, and a family who let her read as many books as she wanted. She lives in Long Beach, California, with her husband, two kids, and a menagerie of pets, including her chicken, Ruby. *Splendor* is the sequel to *Sacred*. Visit Elana at elanakarnold.com.

FIND OUT HOW SCARLETT'S STORY BEGAN IN

Sacred

AVAILABLE NOW

After her brother dies, Scarlett shuts out everyone she cares about, and the only thing she enjoys anymore is riding her horse. One day, as Scarlett is racing around a bend, she meets Will—handsome, mysterious, and with a strange, growing desire to keep Scarlett safe. But as the two fall in love, Scarlett discovers that Will is keeping secrets that promise to hurt her all over again.

READ ON FOR A LOOK AT THE FIRST CHAPTER.

ONE
The End

*A*ll around me, the island prepared to die. August was ending, so summer had come, bloomed, and waned. The tall,
dry grass on the trail through the hills cracked under my mare's
hooves as we wound our way up toward the island's heart.

Summer sun had bleached the grass the same blond as my hair,
which was pulled into a rough ponytail at the nape of my neck.
The straw cowboy hat I always wore when I rode was worn out
too, beginning to split and fray along the seams.

The economy had done its part over the past few years to choke
the life out of the small island I called home—Catalina, a little
over twenty miles off the coast of Los Angeles. This summer, the
island had felt remarkably more comfortable, as the mainland's
tourists had largely stayed away. But even though it was nice to
have some breathing room for a change, it came at a price. Our
main town, Avalon, had seen the closure of two restaurants and a
hotel, and my parents' bed-and-breakfast had gone whole weeks
without any guests.

It was selfish that I enjoyed the solitude. Selfish and wrong, but undeniably true—solitude was a luxury, a rare commodity on a twenty-two-mile-long island that I shared with three-thousand-plus people, all of whom seemed to look at me differently lately, now that my brother was dead.

Yes, death was all around. The dry, hot air of August pressed down on me, my brother would not be coming home, and Avalon seemed to be folding in on itself under the weight of the recession, like a butterfly that's dried up, its papery wings faded.

As if she could sense my mood, my mare, Delilah, tossed her pretty head and pulled at her bit, yearning to run. Delilah was also a luxury, one my parents had been in the habit of reminding me we really couldn't afford—until Ronny died. Then, suddenly, they didn't say much to me at all.

I get it, your kids are supposed to outlive you, it's the natural order of things, but since Ronny had died, it was like I was dead too.

That was how I measured time now. There were the things that happened Before Ronny Died, and then there was Since Ronny Died. It was as sure a division of Before and After to our family as the birth of Jesus is to Christians.

Before Ronny Died, Mom smiled. Before Ronny Died, Daddy made plans for expanding our family B&B. Before Ronny Died, I was popular . . . as popular as you can be in a class of sixty-four students.

That was all different now. Since Ronny Died, my mother didn't seem to notice that a film of dust coated all the knick-knacks in the front room. My dad didn't weed the flower beds. More than a tanking economy was sinking our family business. We were bringing it down just as surely, our gloomy faces unable to animate into real smiles. We probably scared off the guests.

Ronny died last May in the middle of a soccer game. Cause of death: grade 6 cerebral aneurysm. He was just finishing up his freshman year at UCLA. We weren't with him. The distance between Catalina Island and the mainland seems a lot farther than twenty miles when your brother's body is waiting for you on the other side.

I blinked hard to clear these thoughts. They would stay with me anyway, I knew, but I let Delilah have her head, knowing from experience that while we were galloping, at least, my mind would feel empty.

My mare didn't let me down. Twitching her tail with excitement, Delilah broke into a gallop, her short Arabian's stride lengthening as she gathered speed, her head pushed out as if to smell the wind, her wide nostrils flaring. Her coat gleamed red in the afternoon sun.

Ronny used to joke that *Delilah* should have been named Scarlett, not me. Ronny was a literal kind of guy. And he liked to say that *I* should be called Delilah, because of my long hair. That was stupid, of course; in the Bible, Delilah wasn't the one with the long hair. It was her lover, Samson, whom she betrayed by chopping off his hair—the source of his strength—while he slept, damning him to death at the hands of the Philistines.

Ronny just shrugged when I explained all this to him. Sometimes he could be awfully dumb, for such a smart guy.

I wanted to cut off my hair after Ronny died. I stood in the kitchen the afternoon of the funeral, dressed in one of my mother's suits left over from her days as a lawyer, back before she and Daddy decided to move to the island to open a B&B. In my hands, I held a long serrated knife. There was a perfectly good reason for this: I couldn't find the scissors.

But when my mother came into the kitchen, fresh from burying her only son, and saw me standing in the kitchen with a knife in my hand, she freaked out. She started screaming, loud, piercing screams, as if I were an intruder, as if I planned to use that knife against her. Or maybe she thought I was planning to use it against myself, pressing the blade into flesh instead of hair. Then Daddy ran in and saw me there, and his eyes filled with tears, something I'd seen more times that week than I'd seen in the sixteen years of my life up till that point. He took the knife gently from my hand before leading my mother to bed.

Afterward, I couldn't seem to gather the strength to cut my hair. I had wanted to cut it because Ronny had loved it, though he'd never have admitted as much. He used to braid it while we watched TV. I wanted to cut it off and then burn it.

But my mother's expression had taken all the momentum out of my plans. So as I rode Delilah through the open meadow at the heart of the island, I felt the heavy slap of my ponytail against my back, hanging like a body from a noose in the elastic band that ensnared it.

Delilah tossed her mane and slowed to a trot, heading for a clump of grass at the base of a large tree. I thumped her neck with my palm.

"Good girl," I murmured as her trot became a slow, stretchy walk. I slid down her side and pulled the reins from her neck. She made a contented sound as she began pulling up bites of grass. I flopped down next to her in the tree's shade, her reins looped loosely over my wrist, and allowed my body to relax.

School would be starting soon. Junior year. This was supposed to be the best year of high school, even if the academic load would be tough: too soon to worry about college applications, and since I was no longer an underclassman, all the required PE classes were behind me. Still, I was dreading it. Just a few more days, and then I'd be yoked to school as surely as Delilah was yoked to me.

I tried to remind myself of the good things that went along with school in a halfhearted effort to cheer myself up. Lily would be back; that would be good.

My best friend, Lily Adams, was a member of the small wealthy class on Catalina Island. Her parents could have lived anywhere they chose. Independently wealthy as a result of some smart real-estate purchases in the early 1990s, they had come to Catalina because they thought it would be a safe place to raise their kids: Lily and her younger twin brothers, Jasper and Henry.

Catalina was safe, except for the occasional boating accident. The visitors bureau boasted that "violent crimes are virtually nonexistent on this island paradise." Well, the paradise part was dubious, but as far as I knew, it was true about the lack of crime here.

Because of their money, though, and because their livelihood wasn't dependent on the high season for tourism like almost everyone else's on the island, Lily's family got to travel during the summers. This year they were touring Italy. Her family had offered to bring me along; Jasper and Henry had a built-in friend (or enemy) by virtue of being twins, but Lily's parents thought it would be nice if I could come to keep Lily company.

That had been the plan, Before Ronny Died. Then, suddenly, my parents couldn't stomach the thought of my being so far away from them . . . though they hadn't seemed to notice me much this summer, and the three of us existed pretty much like strangers living under one roof all season long.

It made me angry that I had missed out on the trip. But I felt rotten that I could be mad at my parents for anything right now . . . and that I could be mad at Ronny, who was dead, for screwing up my summer plans. Lately I just wasn't a very good person.

Lily didn't seem to agree. She'd kept up a stream of communication all summer, through email, Facebook, and text messages, even though I rarely wrote back. She understood; she didn't hold my silence against me. I hoped things were going to get better now that she was coming home.

Friday afternoon. She would be in the air, on her way to Los Angeles from Rome. Then she and her family would come to Catalina by helicopter. They were the only people I knew who could afford to travel this way. Most everyone else took the ferry, and a few of the wealthier families kept their own boats for transportation to the mainland, but Lily's family coptered. Not bad.

I couldn't wait to see Lily again. The last time had been at our island's airport in early June, just a few weeks after Ronny's funeral. Her parents had embraced me effusively, Lily had been in tears at the thought of leaving me, and even the twins had given me shy, apologetic hugs.

"Two whole months!" Lily wailed. "How will I survive?"

I smiled grimly. "Fabulous food, handsome Italians, all the wine you can drink . . . I think you'll manage."

"But without you!" Lily moaned, shaking her short, dark curls. Lily had always been dramatic.

"You'll pull through," I promised. "And I'll be here waiting for you come September."

The helicopter had risen into the sky, Lily and her family growing smaller and smaller as they flew away, waving furiously until they were out of sight.

So, Lily's return. That was one good thing about school starting back up. And there was Andy, of course.

Before May, Andy had been my boyfriend. After May, it seemed silly and self-indulgent to have a boyfriend. With Ronny's death, it was like I had stepped over some invisible line into a world miles apart from the one I'd inhabited before the piercing phone call from UCLA Medical Center.

I didn't have much to say anymore. It had all been said. Lily understood and was waiting for me to reconcile my brother's death with the rest of life. Andy, on the other hand, wasn't quite as patient.

Andy was lots of things. He was handsome, for one. At just under six feet tall, with the well-muscled body of an athlete—which he was, the star of our school's baseball team, scouted even during his sophomore year by colleges—Andy was taller than most of the boys in our class. His cap of shining light hair looked nice in school dance pictures next to my long straw-colored ponytail. We were blond together.

He was whip-smart, too, taking all the advanced classes our little school offered and doing online classes with Long Beach State College. I had a theory that the teachers didn't even bother grading his papers anymore. I didn't know if Andy Turlington had ever gotten lower than an A in his life.

So we were well suited that way too, since grades were important to me. I was competitive, maybe because I'd grown up in Ronny's impressive shadow, maybe just because that's the way I was made. Andy and I enjoyed our unspoken competition, and though I couldn't keep up with him on the occasional runs we took together, I certainly held my own when it came to things academic.

All of this seemed dreadfully sophomoric after Ronny's death. Suddenly, I could barely force myself to breathe, let alone worry about setting the curve on the latest math test.

I don't know how much my parents noticed my disinterest in school, if they noticed anything at all. Mostly they were drowning in their own oceans of grief, and my teachers basically let me slide, passing me along with gift grades of As and A-minuses.

So there we were, my parents and I, three tiny islands on the greater island of Catalina, and it felt like the weight of the entire Pacific Ocean was pressing on my chest. Sometimes, when I noticed my mother clutching her hand to her heart, I knew she felt the same way.

There was no room on my private island for Andy, which he seemed to figure out soon after school closed for the summer. I failed to return his calls, failed to meet him and the other kids at the beach, failed to thrive.

Delilah was all the company I wanted. Andy had come to the

stable just once, at the end of June, determined, I guess, to get some response from me in person. He walked up to me while I stood at the wash racks, spraying the sweat from Delilah after a long run. When I saw him, it didn't register at first who he was. I remember wondering what this tourist was doing out here at the stable, and I called to him, "We don't rent horses to the public."

"Scarlett," he answered. "It's me—Andy. What the hell? Are you all right?"

Suddenly, the ever-present weight on my chest grew just a fraction heavier and I sank to my knees, the hose next to me spraying uselessly into the dry earth.

Andy rushed over, uncertain what to do with this much grief—with my tears, my wailing, my hands pulling my hair out of its braid. His hand hovered above my head for a while before he kneeled next to me, before he untangled my fingers from my hair and folded them in my lap.

"It's all right," he murmured, a terrible lie, but it was the best he could offer, and so I turned to him awash in grief, wiped my tears on the front of his blue-and-white Dodgers tee, and sobbed in his arms as he stroked my hair.

After a time, Andy kissed my forehead, then my cheeks, and then his lips found mine. I pressed my breasts into his chest, winding my arms around his neck, my teeth pushing hard into his lips as I took what comfort I could from his embrace.

He seemed surprised by my response, and I could feel him vacillating between pulling me closer and pushing me away. The part of him that was a sixteen-year-old boy won out, and he clutched me to him, his hands wandering up and down my back as he kissed me more deeply, his tongue exploring my mouth.

But it was as if his desire had flipped some switch inside me, and I was suddenly achingly cold. Andy realized that I was no longer returning his kiss, that I was sitting in his arms like a rag doll, and with some measure of self-control, he pulled away from me.

His arms were rigid, and his eyes, usually a bright blue, looked cloudy with a mixture of emotions I couldn't read. He stumbled to his feet, off balance, unusual for him, and cleared his throat.

"I don't know, Scarlett," he said. "Maybe you need some time."

Then he'd walked away, though over his shoulder he threw "Call me whenever" before climbing into his pickup and driving off.

Next to me, Delilah pawed the earth, her breath warm and moist in my hair. Sitting with Delilah under the tree, for the first time all summer I had the beginning of a desire to do just that—call him. It was like some part of me yearned to pick up my life where I'd left it. *Could I do that?* I wondered. Could I go back to being Scarlett Wenderoth, ace student, girlfriend, BFF? Or was that part of my life as dead as Ronny?

I sighed and stood, stretching my arms over my head. "All right, girl," I said, patting Delilah's neck. "Let's go home."

I chose a different route back to the stable. I was in no hurry to return to the B&B for dinner with my parents, so I opted to take the circuitous route through the valley toward the barn.

Delilah's barn was my second home—El Rancho Escondido, "the hidden ranch," a breeding facility begun by the Wrigley family way back in the 1930s. It was a private establishment, nestled in a valley twelve miles outside of Avalon. The only reason I could keep my mare there was that my mom was best friends with the manager of the ranch. I got my love of riding from my mom, Olivia, though she'd stopped riding when she got pregnant with Ronny. Her good friend Alice ran the ranch now, greeting the busloads of tourists that came by to see the horses and explaining the ranch's history.

My job was to stay out of the way when I was at the ranch, and not to brag too much around the island about my special privileges. It didn't hurt that my Delilah had been bred and born right here on Catalina, just like me. She and I were two of a kind—trapped on this island, at least for now.

Delilah didn't seem to notice this truth, much less mind it. For a fairly young mare—just five years old—she was remarkably calm. Before she had even been born, she'd been earmarked for me. My parents didn't have a lot of money, but they'd always been dedicated to giving their kids what they needed.

Ronny had needed lots of interaction with the outside world, so our parents had sent him away for part of each summer to stay with friends on the mainland. I needed a horse.

I didn't *want* a horse the way some girls ask for a pony; I *needed* a horse. All my drawings, all the little stories that I'd written as a kid, all my Christmas lists had been about one thing—horses.

And it had never been enough just to be around the Arabians at the stable. I'd felt a pressing need to have a horse of my own.

Delilah was a beautiful foal. I was there to see her birth. She was sired by a tall chestnut Arab named Nomad, and she was out of an unusually large mare named Rainbow. I watched as she emerged from her mother, slick and wet and beautiful, and I watched as she stood on shaky legs and searched under her mother for her first sip of milk.

I'd trained her. She had known me as long as she'd been alive, and she trusted me completely. So today, when I turned her off the main path and toward a rocky decline, her steps didn't falter.

I live in a beautiful place, I thought grudgingly. A fire had ravaged the island's interior just a few years ago, but the blackened landscape was recovering. Some species of plants were actually doing better now than before the fire; there had been too much growth, choking out light, and the plants had had to compete for ground and access to the sun. After the fire, with almost everything dead, there was room. Seeds still dormant under the soil might emerge this year, with the rain. But even dry and somewhat barren, Catalina was beautiful. Native sage and chaparral danced as the late-afternoon breeze picked up, and I took in a deep breath of the clean, salty ocean air. Delilah seemed invigorated by the breeze too, and she broke into an energetic trot even as we started downhill.

I leaned back in my saddle and pulled gently on the reins. "Easy, girl," I murmured, but Delilah tossed her head, eager to move forward.

I laughed, happy she was so spirited. After all this time, I barely noticed how strange the sound of my laughter seemed. "All right, then, if you insist," I said. "Giddyap."

I loosened the reins and dug my heels into Delilah's sides. With the grace that only a purebred Arabian can manage, Delilah loped down the hill, her neck long and loose, her haunches tucked tightly beneath her. As soon as she reached a flatter space on the trail she really let go. The pounding of her hooves on the hard soil became all I was aware of, da-da-*dum*, da-da-*dum*, and I leaned forward with the joy of the ride, my cowboy hat blown away and forgotten behind us, my heels pressed down in the stirrups, the waistband of my jeans pushing into my hips as I moved with the rhythm of her gallop. I felt my mouth pulled wide in a smile, and I felt *alive* and *free*, my heart full of something other than pain.

Then we rounded a corner defined by a wide oak tree, and my life irrevocably shifted.